FLOWER

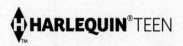

ELIZABETH CRAFT
AND SHEA OLSEN

FLOWER

www.HarlequinTEEN.com

ISBN-13: 978-0-373-21187-6

Flower

A Harlequin TEEN novel/January 2017

For Sarah Fain, your turn. —Elizabeth Craft

For Sky —Shea Olsen

"The only way to get rid of a temptation is to yield to it."

— Oscar Wilde

BEFORE

I WAS TWELVE YEARS OLD when I made the promise to myself.

It was the same year my mother died. She had always been reckless. Impulsive. Abandoning me and my sister, Mia, whenever a new boyfriend appeared in her life. I had watched my mother fall in love so often it was like she was desperate for it, like it was air and she was suffocating. She left us for one more breath, and in the end it killed her.

Love can undo you. It can take everything away.

And so I promised myself: no boys, no prom, no parties on Saturday nights. I would stay home, I would get straight As, I would go to college and make a different kind of future for myself. I wouldn't let anything stop me. I wouldn't let *anyone* stop me.

But that was before everything changed.

That was before him.

AFTER

HIS GAZE DROPS TO MY lips and lingers there, just before he places his mouth on mine. I kiss him back fiercely, my wrists bound by his fingers, his body pressed into mine.

I want more.

He breaks away to kiss along my jaw, my neck. His mouth is hot, his teeth nibbling on my skin. When he lifts his head to look at me, I see the dark need in his gaze. Our eyes remain locked as he kisses me. A simple kiss, a mere brush of lips against lips. Again.

And again.

Until our eyes close at the same time and our tongues meet, his hand gripping my hip. I reach for the zipper on his hoodie and undo it. He moans against my lips and a thrill shudders through me.

In this terrifying, wondrous, overwhelming moment, I would let him do anything.

Anything at all.

ONE

Two months earlier . . .

MY CELL DINGS IN MY purse, a high-pitched whistle that sounds like a faraway train. I dig through tubes of lip balm, receipts, and a Lone Bean napkin, finally extricating the phone.

It's a text from Carlos, my best friend since middle school. *What are you up to?*

Top secret, I reply, with two flower emojis for emphasis. Carlos *knows* I'm at work—I've worked at the Bloom Room, an upscale flower shop, every Monday after school for the last three years.

Don't you want to see ONE of Farrah's parties before we graduate? Carlos sends back.

Farrah Sullivan throws a party every time her dad leaves town, which is usually once a month. And even if it's a school night, most of the Pacific Heights student body shows up to get trashed. Farrah has a pool and a Ping-Pong table in her backyard. And her fridge is always stocked with free beer—or so I've heard. Carlos just doesn't want to go by himself because his crush will be there: Alan Gregory, the boy with two first names who goes to Worther Prep in Beverly Hills and who has been flirting with Carlos since they met at some indie concert in West Hollywood last month.

I sigh and lean my elbows on the front counter. *Sorry*, I type. *You'll do great without me, like always.* I miss out on all of the social functions: the parties, the clubs, the trips down to Venice Beach to watch the sunset while sipping rum from a flask. Sometimes I think it's a miracle our friendship has survived this long. But Carlos and I are soul mates, in the most platonic way. I am the predictable, dependable half, the one he calls whenever his latest relationship implodes, or when he gets sick and needs a mountain of gossip mags and a revolving selection of soup from his favorite restaurant in Santa Monica. And in return, he drags me to see bands I've never heard of in hole-in-the-wall basement venues on the rare night I'm not working or studying. He forces me to stay awake half the night talking to him on the phone and giggling until we fall asleep with our phones still connected. He makes me laugh. And I keep him from spiraling whenever he falls face-first in love with the wrong guy or panics that he'll never get accepted into a good college. We balance each other out. I can't imagine my life without him.

My phone chimes again: *I NEED MY CHARLOTTE.*

I laugh, blowing my choppy bangs away from my eyelashes.

Alas, your Charlotte told Holly she'd close tonight. Go have fun for both of us. You got this, I type.

This is my life: school; work four days a week at the flower shop; research internship at UCLA on Thursdays; then home to study at the tiny house I share with my grandmother, older sister, and baby nephew. Lather. Rinse. Repeat. It's not that I've set out to be the biggest social outcast in all of Los Angeles. But I have set out to be the first woman in my family to go to college, and I don't want to get derailed the way my mom and sister did—pregnant before they were twenty, and a trail of ex-boyfriends in their wake. Which is why, at eighteen, I've never kissed a boy, never held hands in the hallway between classes, never even been to a school dance.

Carlos texts a series of weeping emoji.

I reply with a kissy face.

Feeling like the loser friend who never gets to do anything fun, I open up the music app on my phone and hit START on a random playlist. An oldies song comes on—something my grandma would listen to—"My Girl" by the Temptations. I crank it up, surprisingly into it, and then turn my attention to decorating several bouquets for an eight-year-old's princess-themed birthday party. As the music crescendos, I twirl in circles, feeling a little silly, but determined to forget how structured and precise my life is. How it leaves zero room for anything spontaneous. I grab pink and white and yellow ribbon; I toss glitter onto the tulip petals and glue sequins to the vases; I sing along to the lyrics blaring through my phone. I dance like a total dork. I completely forget I'm at work.

I'm still lost in the moment when a shiver rises up along the base of my neck — someone's watching me.

I glance up from the mess on the table in front of me and catch my breath.

A boy is standing on the other side of the counter, hands in his pockets, looking at me. I didn't even hear the door chime when he came in. I flinch, straightening up from where I've been leaning over the bouquets, and realize that the wide neck of my tank top has sagged low over my chest, exposing the curve of my pink bra.

"Can I help you?" I ask, quickly silencing the music coming from my phone and sliding it into the back pocket of my jeans, swallowing down the embarrassment buzzing across my skin.

He studies me, his dark eyes lifting from my collarbone up to my face, as if he can't quite find the answer to my question. "I need flowers."

He's gorgeous, I realize: hard cheekbones and lips that meet in a firm line . . . lips that hold my gaze for a moment too long.

"Do you know what you're looking for?" I force my brain to cycle through its usual string of questions while my eyes continue to drift over him: torn jeans, close-cropped hair, and a thin T-shirt half tucked into his belt. The muscles of his arms are just visible beneath the cotton sleeves, and his chest is broad. He has the kind of body Carlos loves to point out on the streets of LA — guys leaving gyms and nightclubs or going for a jog down Sunset — tall, muscular, and lean.

Not that I should be noticing how he's built.

I blink and slide my gaze back to his face. There's something guarded there, as if he caught me assessing him and is waiting for the verdict. I can only hope my cheeks don't look as flushed as they suddenly feel.

"Not yet," he answers after a moment, his voice low.

"Follow me," I say automatically, stepping out from behind the counter. He keeps his distance behind me as we walk to the back of the shop, where a wall of roses and lilies and finished bouquets wait to be picked up by customers or loaded onto one of Holly's delivery trucks. I gesture toward the cooler, trying not to let my eyes settle too long on his face. There is a discipline to ignoring guys this attractive, and I pride myself on my mastery. But something about this boy is making me uncomfortable—too aware of my posture, my clumsy hands, my still-warm cheeks. "You can't go wrong with roses."

He looks from me to the flowers, his jaw clenching and unclenching. I know this routine, I see it all the time: Guy needs flowers for girlfriend's anniversary or to say sorry for something, but has no idea what color or how many or if they should be wrapped or in a vase, and then agonizes at the counter trying to decide what to write on the tiny square card that I will attach to the bouquet.

His eyes are on me now, and I can't help but steal another glance. Somewhere in the framework of his face, the structure of his perfect jawline, and the dark brilliance of his eyes, he looks vaguely familiar. Maybe he goes to my school—one of the tortured, brooding guys who smoke cigarettes between classes out by the parking lot.

"Do I know you?" I ask, instantly wishing I hadn't. If he does go to my school, I'd rather pretend I don't know him when I see him in the halls, avoid that awkward half smile and nod.

He shifts his weight, shoulders lifting with his hands still in his pockets, like he's waiting for me to answer my own question. Silence slips between us and the corner of his mouth twitches.

My phone whistles from my back pocket. I ignore it, but it chimes again.

"Popular," he says, one eyebrow raised.

"Hardly. I just have a persistent best friend." I slide the phone out quickly, turning the ringer to vibrate.

"You can answer it."

"No. He just wants me to go to some party."

"And you're not going?"

I shake my head. "I have to close up."

"And after that?" He tilts his head slightly, and I swear I know him—but there's something about him, something that tells me I should leave it alone.

"Homework," I answer simply.

"You can't take one night off to go out?"

I eye him, wondering why he even cares. "If I don't want to work at this flower shop for the rest of my life, then no."

A flicker registers in his eyes, the hint of a smirk, a shallow dimple on his left cheek.

"What's your favorite?" he asks, breaking the silence.

TWO

A KNOCK THUMPS ONCE AGAINST the classroom door and the whole class jerks in their seats.

Mr. Rennert, who has taught English at Pacific Heights High for longer than my grandmother has been alive, sighs and drops the dry-erase marker onto his desk. "Enter."

The door swings open, and Misty Shaffer, a junior with short, cropped hair and a constant grin that shows off her braces, steps into the room. I expect to see a note in her hand, something private to be delivered to one of the students. But instead she holds an enormous bouquet of roses.

Purple roses.

Lacy Hamilton and Jenna Sanchez gasp from their seats a row over, their faces ignited in hope, and chatter breaks out at the back of the room.

"Quiet down back there. You're still on my clock," Mr. Rennert warns in his usual dry tone. "Ms. Shaffer, you seem

"My favorite what?"

He angles his chin, nodding toward the displays all around us. "Your favorite flower."

"I don't really—"

"You must have one." The dimple flashes again, here and then gone. "You work in a flower shop. You're literally surrounded by them."

"I do . . ." I hedge. "But I don't think you'll want them."

His eyes narrow, as if he's intrigued. "That's not very good salesmanship."

I examine the buckets exploding with blooms—colorful orchids and fragrant lilies. Hydrangeas and peonies that are never in season but always popular. And the more unusual varieties—Astras, ranunculuses, dahlias, and camellias. "I like the purple roses," I tell him, and I think he's shifted a half step closer, close enough that I could reach out and touch him if I wanted.

"Why?" he asks.

"They signify fleeting love."

"You mean love that doesn't last?" he asks. "That's a little pessimistic, don't you think?"

"Not pessimistic, just realistic. Fleeting love is more common than the kind of love that lasts forever."

There is a beat of silence between us, and for a moment, I wonder what we're really talking about.

"So why would anyone buy the purple roses?" he asks.

"It's the only rose that isn't trying to be something it's not.

It's authentic and beautiful but people never choose it." I can feel his gaze on me and my skin warms—I've just told him far more than I intended. I turn back to the cooler, touching the handles as if checking to make sure it's closed.

"I guess I'll have to go for purple, then," he says.

It takes a second for my brain to wheel into action, to snap back into salesgirl mode. "Oh. Great . . . How many?"

"How many do you suggest?"

"A dozen?"

The smirk is back. "Now that's good salesmanship."

He follows me back to the counter, his scent lingering in the air: a cool, clean smell that I can't quite place.

I punch his order into the computer, feeling his eyes on me. "What's the name?" I ask, looking up from the screen.

"Excuse me?"

"Your name," I repeat. "I need your name for the order."

I'm still not sure he's heard me because his lips pull into a crooked half grin, like he has a secret he's not sharing.

"Tate," he answers at last.

I finish the order, then count out the bills he hands me and slide back his change. But instead of taking it from the counter, his hand reaches toward me, closing the space between us. His fingers graze my cheek just below my left eye. I suck in a breath. I start to ask him what he's doing, but then he pulls his hand away and holds it up in front of me. "Glitter," he says.

"What?" I squint at his fingers. The tip of his thumb and index finger are shimmering. *Glitter.* From the birthday party

decorations. "Thanks," I say, heat surging into my cheek like they've been pricked by a thousand tiny needles.

"It looked good on you." He's smiling fully now.

I shake my head, the embarrassment making my sk What is wrong with me tonight? "If you don't mind w I say, "I can make the bouquet for you now. Or you can pick them up tomorrow or we can deliver them to you?"

"Tomorrow," he says, taking the change from the c and shoving it into his pocket. "I'll pick them up."

"They'll be ready after ten a.m." I bite my lower li feeling awkward, half wishing he would just leave. "I hop girlfriend likes them," I add before I can stop myself.

His eyes soften. When he finally speaks, he rolls ov words slowly. "I don't have a girlfriend . . . Charlotte."

My breath slides down into my throat as he turns away the counter, walking toward the front of the store. He k my name. *How does he know my name?* Then my fingers the plastic name tag pinned to my tank top, where CHARLO stamped in white letters.

He pauses with a hand on the glass door and I stare, ho he won't turn around. Hoping he will. But he pushes out the evening light and I grip the edge of the counter, the so of my name on his lips repeating inside my head.

to be lost. Last time I checked I was teaching AP English, not Intro to Botany."

"Special orders from the front office, Mr. R," Misty says, unrepentant as she edges past him, all purple-and-green teeth. "The delivery guy said these couldn't wait."

Time seems to slow as she makes her way down the aisle. I think she's going to stop at Jenna's desk, and Jenna's posture says that she thinks so, too. But Misty stops in front of me, the bouquet nearly blocking her face. I blink up at her, the pencil in my hand stalled on the half-finished sketch of a winding vine I'd been drawing in the margins of my notebook.

"Charlotte," she says grandly. She holds the roses out to me—their purple petals nearly the same shade as her braces—and I can't seem to react, to lift my hands to take them from her.

It can't be.

Carlos jabs me in the side from his seat next to mine, prodding me to do something. The entire class is staring at me, including a clearly annoyed Mr. Rennert. I hurriedly yank the bouquet from her hands and set it on the desk. Misty stands for another moment in the aisle, her eyes wide, expectant, like she thinks I'm going to tell her who they're from.

"All right, Ms. Shaffer, you've done your job." Mr. Rennert eyes the flowers while I pretend I'm invisible. "Now perhaps you'll let me get back to doing mine?"

Misty spins around with one last grin, leaving as promptly as she arrived.

"Show's over, people. Let's focus," he adds, picking up the marker from his desk. But before he can say another word, the bell buzzes from the speaker over the door and everyone springs up from their seats. Mr. Rennert glares, first at the bouquet and then at me.

I rise slowly, as if the force of gravity is too strong. I can't even speak. It's all I can do to block out the whispers and lingering stares as people pass me on their way out the door. Jenna Sanchez throws me one last look over her shoulder, disbelief etched on her face. Probably the same expression is carved on mine.

"What are you not telling me?" Carlos asks, his tone almost accusing as the rush of the hall swallows us. We never keep secrets from each other—not that I've had any to keep. Backpacks and shoulders slam against me as I weave through the crowd, Carlos close behind. "Who sent you those?"

My fingers tremble as I pull out the card from the center of the bouquet, examining the envelope. It's definitely from our shop; I recognize the thin gold border around the edge. *Charlotte*, it reads in plain lettering on the front. The tiny card slips easily from the envelope, and glitter spills out with it, sticking to my fingers and raining down to the floor, dusting the tops of my navy-blue flats.

Because roses shouldn't try to be something they're not, the card reads.

"Um, explain?" Carlos asks, reading over my shoulder and brushing the dark shock of hair away from his forehead.

"My favorite what?"

He angles his chin, nodding toward the displays all around us. "Your favorite flower."

"I don't really—"

"You must have one." The dimple flashes again, here and then gone. "You work in a flower shop. You're literally surrounded by them."

"I do . . ." I hedge. "But I don't think you'll want them."

His eyes narrow, as if he's intrigued. "That's not very good salesmanship."

I examine the buckets exploding with blooms—colorful orchids and fragrant lilies. Hydrangeas and peonies that are never in season but always popular. And the more unusual varieties—Astras, ranunculuses, dahlias, and camellias. "I like the purple roses," I tell him, and I think he's shifted a half step closer, close enough that I could reach out and touch him if I wanted.

"Why?" he asks.

"They signify fleeting love."

"You mean love that doesn't last?" he asks. "That's a little pessimistic, don't you think?"

"Not pessimistic, just realistic. Fleeting love is more common than the kind of love that lasts forever."

There is a beat of silence between us, and for a moment, I wonder what we're really talking about.

"So why would anyone buy the purple roses?" he asks.

"It's the only rose that isn't trying to be something it's not.

It's authentic and beautiful but people never choose it." I can feel his gaze on me and my skin warms—I've just told him far more than I intended. I turn back to the cooler, touching the handles as if checking to make sure it's closed.

"I guess I'll have to go for purple, then," he says.

It takes a second for my brain to wheel into action, to snap back into salesgirl mode. "Oh. Great . . . How many?"

"How many do you suggest?"

"A dozen?"

The smirk is back. "Now that's good salesmanship."

He follows me back to the counter, his scent lingering in the air: a cool, clean smell that I can't quite place.

I punch his order into the computer, feeling his eyes on me. "What's the name?" I ask, looking up from the screen.

"Excuse me?"

"Your name," I repeat. "I need your name for the order."

I'm still not sure he's heard me because his lips pull into a crooked half grin, like he has a secret he's not sharing.

"Tate," he answers at last.

I finish the order, then count out the bills he hands me and slide back his change. But instead of taking it from the counter, his hand reaches toward me, closing the space between us. His fingers graze my cheek just below my left eye. I suck in a breath. I start to ask him what he's doing, but then he pulls his hand away and holds it up in front of me. "Glitter," he says.

"What?" I squint at his fingers. The tip of his thumb and index finger are shimmering. *Glitter.* From the birthday party decorations. "Thanks," I say, heat surging into my cheeks again like they've been pricked by a thousand tiny needles.

"It looked good on you." He's smiling fully now.

I shake my head, the embarrassment making my skin itch. What is wrong with me tonight? "If you don't mind waiting," I say, "I can make the bouquet for you now. Or you can either pick them up tomorrow or we can deliver them to you?"

"Tomorrow," he says, taking the change from the counter and shoving it into his pocket. "I'll pick them up."

"They'll be ready after ten a.m." I bite my lower lip, still feeling awkward, half wishing he would just leave. "I hope your girlfriend likes them," I add before I can stop myself.

His eyes soften. When he finally speaks, he rolls over the words slowly. "I don't have a girlfriend . . . Charlotte."

My breath slides down into my throat as he turns away from the counter, walking toward the front of the store. He knows my name. *How does he know my name?* Then my fingers touch the plastic name tag pinned to my tank top, where CHARLOTTE is stamped in white letters.

He pauses with a hand on the glass door and I stare, hoping he won't turn around. Hoping he will. But he pushes out into the evening light and I grip the edge of the counter, the sound of my name on his lips repeating inside my head.

TWO

A KNOCK THUMPS ONCE AGAINST the classroom door and the whole class jerks in their seats.

Mr. Rennert, who has taught English at Pacific Heights High for longer than my grandmother has been alive, sighs and drops the dry-erase marker onto his desk. "Enter."

The door swings open, and Misty Shaffer, a junior with short, cropped hair and a constant grin that shows off her braces, steps into the room. I expect to see a note in her hand, something private to be delivered to one of the students. But instead she holds an enormous bouquet of roses.

Purple roses.

Lacy Hamilton and Jenna Sanchez gasp from their seats a row over, their faces ignited in hope, and chatter breaks out at the back of the room.

"Quiet down back there. You're still on my clock," Mr. Rennert warns in his usual dry tone. "Ms. Shaffer, you seem to be lost. Last time I checked I was teaching AP English, not Intro to Botany."

"Special orders from the front office, Mr. R," Misty says, unrepentant as she edges past him, all purple-and-green teeth. "The delivery guy said these couldn't wait."

Time seems to slow as she makes her way down the aisle. I think she's going to stop at Jenna's desk, and Jenna's posture says that she thinks so, too. But Misty stops in front of me, the bouquet nearly blocking her face. I blink up at her, the pencil in my hand stalled on the half-finished sketch of a winding vine I'd been drawing in the margins of my notebook.

"Charlotte," she says grandly. She holds the roses out to me—their purple petals nearly the same shade as her braces— and I can't seem to react, to lift my hands to take them from her.

It can't be.

Carlos jabs me in the side from his seat next to mine, prodding me to do something. The entire class is staring at me, including a clearly annoyed Mr. Rennert. I hurriedly yank the bouquet from her hands and set it on the desk. Misty stands for another moment in the aisle, her eyes wide, expectant, like she thinks I'm going to tell her who they're from.

"All right, Ms. Shaffer, you've done your job." Mr. Rennert eyes the flowers while I pretend I'm invisible. "Now perhaps you'll let me get back to doing mine?"

Misty spins around with one last grin, leaving as promptly as she arrived.

"Show's over, people. Let's focus," he adds, picking up the marker from his desk. But before he can say another word, the bell buzzes from the speaker over the door and everyone springs up from their seats. Mr. Rennert glares, first at the bouquet and then at me.

I rise slowly, as if the force of gravity is too strong. I can't even speak. It's all I can do to block out the whispers and lingering stares as people pass me on their way out the door. Jenna Sanchez throws me one last look over her shoulder, disbelief etched on her face. Probably the same expression is carved on mine.

"What are you not telling me?" Carlos asks, his tone almost accusing as the rush of the hall swallows us. We never keep secrets from each other—not that I've had any to keep. Backpacks and shoulders slam against me as I weave through the crowd, Carlos close behind. "Who sent you those?"

My fingers tremble as I pull out the card from the center of the bouquet, examining the envelope. It's definitely from our shop; I recognize the thin gold border around the edge. *Charlotte*, it reads in plain lettering on the front. The tiny card slips easily from the envelope, and glitter spills out with it, sticking to my fingers and raining down to the floor, dusting the tops of my navy-blue flats.

Because roses shouldn't try to be something they're not, the card reads.

"Um, explain?" Carlos asks, reading over my shoulder and brushing the dark shock of hair away from his forehead.

Carlos is a good foot taller than me, and when he's standing up straight, the top of my head could actually fit beneath his chin. "And what's with all the glitter?"

I shove the card back into the envelope, my heart thumping inside my chest. *Tate.* He bought the flowers for me. What kind of insane person buys roses for a girl he doesn't know? And how did he find me here at school?

"Hello?" Carlos says beside me, waving a hand in front of my face. "Has my little Charlotte found herself an admirer at last?"

"Of course not." But my cheeks burn at the thought. "It's just some guy who came into the shop yesterday."

Carlos's mouth dips open, revealing the slight gap between his two front teeth. "You met him *yesterday* and he's already sending you flowers?" He touches one of the perfect buds, the vintage black ring he found at a garage sale two months ago glinting in sharp contrast to the purple petals. Carlos changes his style monthly: Today he's wearing a herringbone vest over a slouchy gray T-shirt and plaid loafers he took from his dad's closet.

"I don't even know how he found me," I say.

"Okay, back up. Start from the beginning. Was he cute or creepy?"

I frown at the memory of his perfect face, his dark eyes, and the easy way he leaned across the counter to wipe the glitter from my cheek.

"So he was cute," Carlos says with a grin, folding his arm over my shoulder. "It's okay, Char, you can think a boy is cute. Thinking won't ruin your life."

17

I scowl at him. "He was more than cute, if you must know, but—"

"How much more are we talking about?" His hand at my bicep tightens reflexively. "Handsome? Heartbreakingly gorgeous? Off-the-charts bangable?"

Leave it to Carlos. "—*but* it just seems arrogant," I continue, "to send me flowers when I don't even know him."

"Maybe he's *slightly* overconfident," Carlos agrees, spinning the combo of our shared locker—every year, after our lockers are assigned, Carlos and I choose whoever's is in the best location and the least beat-up, and that becomes our base of operations. This year, our locker has only two elbow-sized dents in the door, and the lock actually works sixty-percent of the time. Pacific Heights High is severely overcrowded, underfunded, and much less glamorous than its name suggests. There is no view of the Pacific Ocean—instead it's situated smack in the middle of Hollywood, surrounded by throngs of tourists and apartment buildings. All the wealthy, academically superior high schools are farther west, closer to the ocean. What I wouldn't give to have the opportunity to attend one of those schools. "But don't take it out on the flowers," Carlos adds.

I shove the massive bouquet into the locker, trying to seem indifferent, even though I'm careful not to let any of the stems bend or split. "Change of subject. Tell me about the party last night—did you see Alan Gregory?"

Carlos gives me a look, but accepts the shift in topic. "Last night was a total fail. Alan texted me that he had a physics test to study for so he couldn't make it to the party after all. I ditched out early and went home to watch old SNL reruns on my laptop."

I wrap my arm through his and squeeze. "I'm sorry. It's his loss. Maybe he'll call you for a date this weekend."

"Maybe." Carlos shrugs. "And maybe Mr. Gorgeous and Mysterious will send you another dozen roses tomorrow."

"Let's not get carried away." Today was mortifying enough.

"Hey, now." Carlos pauses at the end of the hall, forcing Sophie Zines to swerve around us. Sophie is pretty in that overly done, too much makeup, perfect hair and clothes kind of way. I've always felt plain and washed-out next to people like her, like a cardboard cutout, void of any color. My clothes are all from thrift stores or hand-me-downs from my sister. Thankfully I have Carlos to help direct my style choices, but I still can't compete with the Sophies of the world. "I like my sweet Charlotte just as she is," Carlos says, his tone serious. "The eternal virgin."

I wince, glancing ahead at Sophie, hoping she's out of earshot. Carlos may be comfortable talking about my sex life — or my lack thereof — in public, but me . . . not so much. "Not eternal," I correct softly. "I'm just waiting until after college — at least."

"So basically until the end of time?"

"Stop," I say, shaking my head even as I grin despite myself.

"You're some kind of saint, Charlotte Reed. And like I said, I love that about you, I do."

We push out into the daylight through the heavy double doors, the midday sun blinking down bright and hot.

"But someday," Carlos adds, lifting a hand to shield his eyes as we survey the front lawn, which is dotted with clusters of students sitting on the brown sunbaked grass or on the faded blue benches.

"Someday what?"

"You'll fall madly in love and I won't be able to tear you away from some primo male specimen with abs like a Spartan god."

"I think that's *your* dream guy," I shoot back, squeezing his arm. There is no dream guy fluttering around inside *my* head.

He winks down at me and pulls me across the lawn to our usual lunch spot. "You'll see, my pure, uncorrupted Charlotte. One day you'll meet someone who will turn your perfect world upside down."

THREE

OUR TINY, SINGLE-LEVEL HOUSE ON Harper sits tucked back from the street between two towering and slowly dying palm trees. A rusted Buick rests up on blocks in the neighbor's yard. A dog yips from behind a chain-link fence two houses up, and a siren screams down a side street. Yet a mere five blocks away, tourists converge on Sunset Boulevard; after snapping photos of gold stars sealed into the pavement, they ride tour buses to see the homes of rock stars and movie stars and reality stars up in the Hollywood Hills. So close, nearly tangible, yet a world away from the dilapidated, paint-peeling, sun-scorched neighborhood where I live.

The house is quiet when I step inside. I unwrap the bouquet of flowers over the kitchen sink, tearing away the clear cellophane and arranging them in a vase with lukewarm water. They're even prettier here at home, the soft petals like a breath of springtime against the dingy yellow walls.

"Who gave you those?" My sister's voice rises from the

archway separating the kitchen from the living room. The house is a claustrophobic rectangle of three narrow bedrooms, a combination kitchen/living room and one impossibly tiny bathroom. When I shave my legs in the morning before school, I'm forced to stick one leg out through the shower curtain and prop my foot up on the edge of the sink for balance.

"No one," I answer quickly, positioning the vase in the center of the kitchen table.

Baby Leo is balanced on Mia's hip and his little fingers clutch the fabric of her white shirt, stained from some sort of baby goo. She moves across the linoleum, and I tickle his chin. "They're nicer than the leftovers you usually bring home from the shop," Mia says.

"They were a special order that no one ever picked up." The lie slips out easily, surprising me. I never lie; I never have reason to. I wait for Mia to see through it, to grill me on why I'm bringing leftovers home before I've even gone to work for the day. But she's fussing with Leo's dandelion-fuzz hair, the roses already forgotten.

Mia lifts Leo away from her hip and his blue eyes turn to me, a gummy smile forming on his lips. I take him from her arms and watch as Mia runs her hands through her wavy hair, an exhausted motion, like she hasn't had a moment all day without Leo in her arms. Her sunken eyes betray a lack of sleep, and for a moment I feel like I'm looking at my own reflection. Mia is two years older than me, and even though we don't share the same father, we could almost be twins with our green eyes and caramel-colored hair.

"I don't know why you still wear that thing," she says, walking to the refrigerator.

"What?" I ask, bouncing Leo a little, smiling as he gives a gurgling laugh. Pressing my nose to his neck, I inhale his sweet baby scent—formula and talcum powder. At nearly eight months, he's more active and playful than he was just a few months back—his hands reaching out to snag a strand of my hair, legs wriggling in delight. He'll cry like a demon when he needs a nap, filling the house with his outraged wails; even Carlos has been known to preach the wisdom of abstinence whenever we babysit Leo. But even when I see how much having a baby has derailed my sister's life, I can't imagine our house without him. He is bright rosy cheeks and sticky fingers and giggles when he's seated in his high chair eating breakfast. I adore him more than I can say.

"Mom's ring." Popping the lid on a Diet Coke, Mia nods down at my left hand where the turquoise ring has slid slightly off-center. My father gave it to our mom when they first started dating, and she gave it to me once I was old enough not to lose it.

"It reminds me of her," I say, although that's not the whole story, and Mia knows it. It's a reminder of how she ended up—crashing into love again and again, the rest of her life burning in the rearview mirror—and how I want to be different.

"Hi, girls," Grandma says, stepping through the front door with two grocery sacks balanced in her arms. She kisses the top of Leo's head, earning a drooly grin. "There's my little man. Lovely flowers, Charlotte," she adds, stopping to breathe them in as she passes the table. I tense, braced for questions, but she's moved to the counter, unpacking the contents of the green-and-white reusable bags with her usual efficiency.

When we were younger, Carlos dubbed her "Grandma Garbo," after the stunning Greta Garbo, who was a cinema actress and Hollywood starlet during the twenties and thirties. Grandma has always loved that comparison. And watching her now, it's easy to see why. Grandma's dark auburn hair sweeps over her shoulders in gentle waves; her figure is still trim, her face free of wrinkles. Unlike other grandmothers, she's always seemed ageless. Beneath the crisp white collar of the maid's uniform she wears, I can just make out her favorite gold necklace—the one she got as a wedding gift from her mother-in-law when she walked down the aisle at seventeen. She was six and a half months pregnant when she said her vows and married my grandfather—because it was the right thing to do back then. You didn't have a baby if you weren't married to the boy who knocked you up. But they never had a honeymoon, never even saw their first wedding anniversary. Her husband left her shortly after the baby—my mother—was born.

And like some predetermined, screwed-up twist of fate, all the women in my family have made the same mistake. When my mom was seventeen, she got pregnant with Mia. And Leo was born before Mia even graduated high school. Already

I'm beating the odds just by having made it to my eighteenth birthday without a kid in tow.

Grandma places two new boxes of cereal in the cupboard, folds up the grocery bags, then goes to the refrigerator and pulls out a pitcher of water, slices of lemon bobbing at the surface. "There's chili in the fridge for dinner when you get hungry. I'll be gone until ten," she says, taking down a glass from the cupboard and filling it, a single lemon slice slipping into her glass at the last moment.

"You're working?" Mia asks. Grandma works long, often late hours cleaning offices downtown. She might be young for a grandmother, but at her age, she shouldn't be lugging heavy cleaning carts down hallways or bending over a vacuum for hours on end. Yet she refuses to let me help pay any household expenses with my Bloom Room paychecks; she says that everything I make should be for college. And whenever I protest her latest double shift, when it's obvious she's exhausted and her body aching, she waves me away. "How do you think I stay in such good shape?" she'll ask. "This job keeps me young."

"Amelia called in sick, so I'm covering for her," Grandma explains now. If she's unhappy at the prospect of another five hours on her feet, she doesn't show it.

"But I already made plans," Mia whines, and I wonder how she can even want to go out, given the shadows under her eyes. "My date's picking me up in an hour."

"I'm sorry, honey," Grandma says, her voice slightly strained. "I can watch him tomorrow," she offers placidly, setting the pitcher back in the refrigerator and reaching out to take a squirming Leo from me. Even though she disapproves of Mia's mistakes—mainly getting pregnant so young—she loves Leo every bit as much as I do. And she tries to be supportive of Mia whenever possible—including watching Leo so Mia can get out of the house when she grows restless. Which is more often than she probably should.

"We're going to see a band. They're not playing tomorrow." When Grandma sighs and shakes her head, Mia turns to me. "Charlotte," she pleads, drawing out my name. "Please? I really like this guy."

"I can't, Mi," I say. "I have to be at work in twenty minutes." I feel a pang of guilt. Maybe I should help my sister, call in sick. But it also might be better if Mia stays away from guys for a while. Isn't that how this all happened in the first place? A careless party hookup that resulted in pregnancy, the guy vanishing from her life just as quickly as he entered.

Mia turns on her heel, her mouth pinched shut in irritation, and marches back into her room, kicking the door closed behind her.

Grandma nuzzles Leo, who's busy trying to cram her necklace into his mouth, and shoots me a reassuring smile. "She's just upset," she whispers. "It's not easy with the baby."

"I know." Mia used to be my world, my best friend. We were the only two planets in each another's orbit. Queen Honeydew and Princess Poppyseed we called ourselves when we were little. We belonged to each other. But now Mia belongs to whichever boy will tell her that he loves her and give her extra money for diapers and new clothes. They don't realize it, but she uses them more than they use her.

I glance back at her bedroom door and wonder, not for the first time, how we could have ended up so different.

It's a slow night at the shop and I find myself staring out the front windows at the fading sunset, the sky dissolving into ribbons of pinks and orange. I check my watch: ten minutes past closing. Holly left thirty minutes ago and asked me to lock up. But not before we spent nearly the entire shift talking about my mystery admirer.

She'd gotten a call right after she'd opened the store this morning asking that the bouquet of purple roses be delivered to Charlotte Reed at Pacific Heights High, as soon as possible. And she'd spent the rest of the day about to burst, waiting for me to get to the shop so she could ask me nine hundred million questions about the boy who sent me flowers.

Holly knows I don't date. She knows I've never had a boyfriend. But she's a hopeless romantic and she wanted every detail—from what he was wearing, to *exactly* what he said, to how I felt when I saw the flowers arrive in my classroom. *Annoyed*, I told her, not that she believed me.

Now I push up from the stool, walk to the front window, and flip over the CLOSED sign.

I'm about to grab my purse and keys when the chime over the front door sounds behind me, signaling someone has

27

just stepped through the doorway. "Sorry, we're closed," I say, spinning around to politely usher whoever it is back outside. But my entire body freezes in place.

"I've always had bad timing." Tate stands with his hands in his pockets, lips quirked slightly to one side.

"What are you doing here?" I ask.

"I wanted to see you."

I exhale through my nose, my heart stuttering, then starting again. "You shouldn't have sent me those roses today."

"Why not?" The question hangs in the air between us, and his eyes pour over me like he could touch my skin with only his stare. He unnerves me. And I hate the part of me that likes the feeling. I've dealt with boys like this before at the shop — guys who act like I should swoon over them, who think they can make me crumble with just one look, but it's always had zero effect on me. Tate shouldn't be any different. He *isn't* any different. So why does it feel like I can't breathe when he's standing this close?

"You don't even know me," I manage to say.

"I know you like purple roses."

"That's only one detail." I glance back at the counter, wishing for a distraction, like my phone to magically start ringing. But no such luck. Taking a breath, I fight the urge to twine my hair around my finger.

"Most girls like a guy who notices the details." He raises an eyebrow and pushes his hands deeper into his pockets.

I grind my teeth in frustration. "I'm not most girls."

"No," he says, and the dimple is back for a moment. "I've noticed that."

"And you're here because . . ."

"Go out with me," he says out of nowhere.

It catches me off guard and I take a step back. "What?"

"You said I don't know you. Go on a date with me so I can." His voice is deep, provocative, and his eyes sway over me, through me, stripping me into pieces. He's dressed almost identically to how he was yesterday: faded jeans and a simple white T-shirt. But on his left wrist he wears a silver watch that I don't remember. It looks expensive.

"I—" My mouth hangs open, my mind unable to close around a thought. And something catches in my chest, a pressure I can't explain. I wish he would just leave.

But he doesn't. He steps closer to me and stops only a couple feet away, never taking his eyes off mine. My skin feels like glass, cracking and splintering just under the surface.

A car horn honks from the street, breaking the spell, and he glances over his shoulder just as a truck pulls away from the curb. His expression turns uneasy for a second before he relaxes once more into that thoughtless confidence. "I want to take you out," he says again.

I can't deny the tingle of excitement at the base of my neck. But I cross my arms, tightening my hands into fists, ordering my body to behave. "No," I say, and the word is hard against my throat. "I need to lock up, and I need to go home." I force my eyes to meet his, wanting him to see that I'm serious.

The dimple peeks out for a second, like he finds this funny. Or maybe he just enjoys a challenge. I imagine he probably doesn't hear the word *no* very often.

He glances at his watch, then at the door. "Good night, then . . . Charlotte," he says, his voice coiling over my name. And I suck in a breath, watching him slip out through the glass doors and vanish into the dark.

"He asked you out?" Carlos screeches.

I sink down in my chair, cringing. "Say it louder next time. I don't think they heard you in Orange County."

We're sitting in Mrs. Dixon's computer lab, where the Pacific Heights High newspaper club meets once a week after school on Wednesdays. This week Carlos is writing an article about the sycamore tree beside the west entrance that's slowly dying because everyone keeps carving their names into the soft bark of the trunk. During lunch, I used the school's ancient camera and took photos of the tree, documenting the hearts and names etched into the wood: *Weston luvs Cara. TM + AY*, which everyone knows is Toby McAlister and Alison Yarrow, their names eternally branded into the tree even though they only dated for two weeks and hate each other now.

"Sorry," Carlos says, not sounding sorry at all. "But my best friend just got asked on a date by Mr. Tall, Dark, and Delicious. I think I'm allowed to get caught up in the moment."

"I told him no," I remind him. I'm at one of the computers against the bank of windows overlooking the street outside,

30

sorting through the photos I took earlier, but the screen keeps freezing and I've already had to restart it twice. The computer lab is just another example of the school's dire lack of funds. But working on the *Banner* is good for my application to Stanford. At least, that's why I signed up, but I've actually started to enjoy it. Taking photos feels more anonymous than writing articles for the paper, and yet, sometimes it also feels more important, like a single photo can say more than four hundred double-spaced words.

"And you wonder why I worry. What else did he say?" Carlos prods from his computer next to mine.

"Nothing. I told him to leave."

"You did what?" Carlos looks at me like I'm insane.

"Well, I needed to close the shop." I hate that I feel defensive. I shouldn't second-guess myself for doing what I know was right. Better to quash any hope Tate had that I might go out with him—prevent him from coming back and trying again. So what if I was a little rude?

"I don't think you know *what* you need," Carlos mutters. I give him my best side-eye but he's unfazed. "And how fine did he look this time?"

I lift one shoulder and shake my head, ignoring the swift flood of warmth in my cheeks.

"Admit it," Carlos says, turning in his chair to face me. "You think he's totally hot."

"It doesn't matter," I say. "You know it doesn't. I've made it to senior year without getting distracted by a guy. I'm hardly going to let it happen now." It's not like I've never had a crush before. Edgar Hoyt, my lab partner in AP Chem class last year, used to make my breath catch whenever his hand accidentally brushed mine. Carlos thought I was insane to think Edgar was even remotely cute, but something about him—his square, dark-rimmed glasses; his sharp nose and toned arms that hinted he was more than just a brainiac—made my heart race. It didn't matter, of course. I don't date. I don't let a stupid crush take root inside me, where it can grow and unravel everything I've worked so hard for.

"But just to clarify, you do think he's knockout, drop-your-panties gorgeous?"

I sigh. He won't let it go until I've given him something. "I guess . . ." I clear my throat as an image of Tate—white T-shirt, dark eyes—flashes into my mind. "I guess I would say that's an accurate description."

Carlos snorts. "Coming from you, that's a declaration of love. Good. Now we don't have to pretend he's not hot when we talk about him again."

"We won't be talking about him again." I focus back on the computer screen.

"I'll remember you said that," Carlos says, and I can hear the smile in his voice.

There are several bouquets that have to be assembled tonight at work, and I lose myself in trimming the stems, tying perfect bows with organdy and grosgrain ribbon, and arranging them all into beautiful floral configurations. It's one of the best things about my job—creating something lovely that I know will brighten someone's day. I make a bouquet of sunflowers and hydrangeas for a fifty-year anniversary. Cheerful birds-of-paradise, lilies, and red hyperciums for a get-well-soon. A dozen roses in predictable red for someone named Emily. The card reads, *I may be an ass, but I'm your ass. Forgive me? Jim.* I have to laugh at that one. Boring taste in flowers aside, I find myself hoping he and Emily will figure things out.

That's the unexpected part of working in a flower shop. It creates a kind of intimacy you wouldn't expect. You can't help but wonder about the sick relative—will Aunt Ruth really get well soon? Or the milestone anniversary—I picture an elderly couple sitting on a bench overlooking the beach, watching the waves roll in at high tide, still holding hands after all these years. What would it be like to grow old with someone? To know that person inside and out, and love them anyway? Not just fall into the moment with some guy like Mom did, or Mia, only to fall right back out again.

When I finish the bouquets, I only have another hour until closing, so I work on my problem sets and study for my next calc test. I write out equations in my notebook, trying to keep images of Tate from surfacing—the slant of his eyes, the arch of his lips, the warmth of his fingers against my skin when they brushed away a fleck of glitter. I focus on derivatives and differentials. Not on thoughts of boys who stand too close and suck all the air from the room. Because *why* would I even think about him? I turned him down for all the right reasons, I remind myself—I've worked too hard to get this close to leaving this life behind. My crappy high school, our tiny house. There's more out there for me. I know there is.

When I hear the door chime again, I spin around too quickly and knock the scissors sitting on the counter beside me onto the floor, almost stabbing my right foot. "Shit," I mutter, bending down to pick them up.

"You all right?" a voice asks—a voice I recognize, because part of me has been secretly hoping I might hear it again.

I retrieve the scissors and stand slowly. "I'd be better if you'd stop sneaking up on me."

Tate is standing just inside the front door. In his hands he holds two cardboard trays with four carryout cups in each one. He gives me a brief once-over, lingering on the hand that still holds the scissors. "Will you drop the weapon if I tell you I brought you coffee?" He lifts one of the trays, extending it toward me like a peace offering.

"Eight cups?"

"I don't know you, remember? So I don't know what you like."

"Who says I like coffee at all?" I ask.

He glances down at the cups, then back up at me. "Do you like coffee?"

"I might," I tell him, though of course I do.

He moves to the front counter to set down the trays. The sweet scents of coffee and steamed milk and cinnamon fill the air.

"What are my options?" I know I shouldn't play along with his little game — I should just tell him to leave. But I ease toward the counter, drawn to the heady aromas despite myself.

"Black, no frills?" he asks, his gravelly voice making the question sound much more personal than it is.

I shake my head.

His eyes pass over the cups, then back to me. "Mocha, extra whipped cream?"

"Nope."

"Caramel latte with skim milk?"

I shake my head again. I'm actually starting to enjoy myself. Denying each option feels good, like I'm reminding us both that he doesn't have anything I want.

His eyes narrow, undeterred. Then he lifts one of the cups and holds it out to me. "Chai with steamed almond milk and a dash of cinnamon."

My head tilts to the side. Without answering, I take the cup from his hand, careful not to let our fingers brush. *Dammit.*

I detect the slightest self-satisfied smile tugging at the corners of his mouth.

"This doesn't mean I'm going on a date with you," I say.

"I'm not asking."

I take a sip of the chai and it instantly warms my tongue; it's exactly what I need to help me get through the rest of my homework tonight. "Thanks," I manage.

His eyes lower, focusing on my mouth, and I draw my bottom lip between my teeth as a sudden heat races through me. Then, because he never seems to do the expected, he grabs the two trays from the counter—still full, minus one cup—and turns for the door.

I open my mouth, about to say, *That's it? That's all you came here for?* When I remember myself and press my lips together.

He stops halfway to the door, says, "Enjoy the chai, Charlotte," and once again, he's gone. But this time, I can't help but hope he'll come back.

FOUR

THE NEXT DAY, IN ENGLISH, I don't tell Carlos about Tate.

At lunch, I don't tell Carlos about Tate.

After school, when I say good-bye before I head to UCLA for my internship, I don't tell Carlos about Tate.

I'm not sure what holds me back. Except maybe that talking about him will only make it worse. Because as much as I try not to . . . I can't stop thinking about Tate.

On Friday, it feels like my body is a charged electrical current, buzzing and snapping at the ends. I'm anxious to get to work—to see if Tate will come in again. I know I shouldn't hope for it; I know I shouldn't care either way. But no matter how many deep, calming breaths I take, the edginess remains.

The hours pass slowly, and any time the door opens, it's never him. When the last customer has left, I move to the front of the store, peeking out through the glass windows onto the sidewalk—looking for him. He isn't there. I tell myself it's better if he doesn't show up tonight—or ever again. But that doesn't ease the disappointment.

I remind myself again why I promised myself to stay away from guys—especially guys like Tate. My grandmother worked hard to give my mom a better life, and then Mom had us. Too young, not ready to support us. Our dads came and went, just like the rest of the boyfriends who demanded her attention, who took her money and time and happiness. I think about Mia and Leo, little Leo, who doesn't yet know what his mom could have been, that she's as smart as me, maybe smarter. But Mia won't be going off to college; her life is stalled now, stuck with all the potential in the world. There's no word worse than *potential*. It's the story of everything that will never be.

I carry my keys to the door, flip over the CLOSED sign, lock up, and turn off the overhead shop lights. I'm about to turn around, do my last sweep of the shop before I leave for the night, when I notice a sleek black car pull up directly in front of the store. The headlights send out beams of bluish light and the car makes almost no sound as it comes to a stop. It looks expensive. Really expensive.

The driver's side door swings open . . . and Tate steps out.

He turns toward the shop, the car making a swift beeping sound behind him. When he reaches the door and touches the handle, he realizes it's locked. He looks up and his eyes meet mine through the glass. My heart collides with my ribs.

He glances down at the metal door handle as if expecting me to let him in. But I lift the keys into the air and wave them briefly in front of him. *Sorry*, I mouth through the glass, smiling a little.

I catch a hint of disbelief on his face and it fills me with satisfaction. I may have waited around all evening for him, but that doesn't mean I'll jump at his sudden arrival.

I close out the register and watch him from the corner of my eye. Then I see him pull his phone from his pocket and press it to his ear.

A vibration buzzes from inside my purse. I dig out my cell to see a number I don't recognize. I glance out at Tate and he gestures for me to answer. I hesitate, but finally hit the green button. "Hello?"

"You locked me out." I try not to let the thrill of his voice wash through me.

"We're closed," I say into the phone.

"Hmm," he murmurs, as if weighing his options, what he might say to convince me to let him in.

"And how did you get my number anyway?"

"I've had it for days."

"That doesn't answer my question. And PS, it's more than a little creepy that you're calling me when I haven't even given you my number."

"I wouldn't have had to call if you'd unlocked the door," he says with irritating logic, and I look out at him standing on the other side of the glass. He tilts his head, staring up at the night sky, and then looks back at me. The night suits him somehow, the light from a streetlamp washing over him, illuminating the planes of that impossibly symmetrical face. For the briefest second I feel it again — that sense of familiarity that has nothing to do with the past few evenings at the Bloom Room. Then he shifts and the feeling fades.

"Still not answering my question," I counter, pointing to my phone. "How did you get my number?"

There goes the dimple. "Let's just say I have . . . resources at my disposal."

"What sort of resources?" I ask.

"People who figure things out for me." Another non-answer. But if he has *people*, he must have more money than I first thought.

"Don't you think that gives you an unfair advantage?" I ask.

"I think I need any advantage I can get." His gaze holds me captive through the glass windows and I can't seem to look away. "But now you have my phone number, too, so we're even."

"I didn't want your number," I tell him, glad that the darkness hides my telltale smile. I'm enjoying this too much.

"I think you did," he says. "Otherwise you would have hung up by now."

Several seconds pass and I can hear his breathing on the other end. It makes my stomach quiver and a warmth brush over my skin. "Is there a reason you stopped by tonight? I noticed you didn't come bearing coffee this time."

"You want coffee, it's yours," he says. "But this time you're drinking it with me."

"I—"

"It's Friday night, Charlotte. Go out with me."

There are countless reasons to say no. My mother's past. My sister's present. My future.

"One date," he continues, his voice low, almost hypnotic. "Say yes. What do you have to lose?"

Everything, I think.

But my chest flutters. My mind swims with delirious thoughts of being close to him again, breathing in his rich, heady scent—and maybe feeling his touch against my skin just one more time. That's all I need, just one more moment with him and then I can forget about him completely. I know I'm bargaining with myself. But I don't care. I can feel myself giving in. "If I go out with you once, will you stop coming here?"

"I swear," he answers, and I look to see that he's pressed his hand against the glass of the door as if to seal the pact. My skin burns as if he's touching me. I end the call, not trusting my voice to be steady.

I deliberately make him wait as I finish up in the shop, needing a moment to regain my composure. When I finally slip outside, he's leaning against the car, and my heart starts racing all over again. He smiles, and for a second, his face is more open than I've seen it before.

"Well?" I say, hoping it's too dark for him to see my flushed cheeks.

"You won't regret this, Charlotte."

* * *

We walk up Sunset Boulevard, on the fringes of Beverly Hills, where cafes dot the sidewalk, yellow and red umbrellas raised over round tables, white linens, and people sipping cocktails in the balmy evening air. It's a different universe from where I live in Hollywood, even though it's only ten minutes away.

Tate is quiet for several blocks and I like the silence. I'm afraid of what he might say if he speaks. Of what I might say in return.

"Are you hungry?" he asks finally, running a hand over his shaved head, only the short stubble indicating what color his hair might have once been: dark brown, I think.

"I guess," I answer, scratching at my wrist, rubbing over the lopsided triangle inked there, a self-made tattoo of blue ballpoint pen.

"There's a great place a few blocks up," he says. "Lola's."

I laugh, but then I see he's serious. One dinner at Lola's probably costs more than I make in a week. "Will they even let us in?"

"Why wouldn't they?"

"Because we're . . ." I pause, searching for the right way to explain, then spot a couple walking toward us, hand in hand. The guy is wearing a sharp gray suit, talking on his cell phone, ignoring the girl on his arm wearing studded high heels. "Because we're not them," I point out, nodding only slightly as they pass, all elegance and sophistication.

Tate glances at me sidelong, amused. "Good point," he says. "Then we'll sneak in through the back. I know a guy in the kitchen." One corner of his mouth is drawn up, and his eyes are wild with something mischievous. I shake my head.

But I don't stop walking; I don't tell him that I should probably go back to the flower shop, where my rusted powder-blue Volvo is waiting. That I should go home. I don't want to admit it, but I *like* this feeling: the stirring in my stomach, the flood of warmth across my neck and cheeks whenever he looks at me. *Just one date*, I remind myself. One date won't throw me off track. Just one date and he'll leave me alone.

I almost believe myself.

The windows of Lola's glow ahead of us, lit almost exclusively by candlelight. Carlos and I have strolled past slowly many times—Carlos hoping to spot any one of his many Hollywood crushes, me just along for the ride. But we've never been so lucky. It's nearly impossible to see the faces of anyone inside anyway, because it's so dark. Which I'm sure is the point.

As we get closer, Tate grabs my hand briefly and pulls me down into an alley. His palm is warm and strong, and I suck in a breath at the unexpected contact. He thumps his fist against a metal door once, then turns back to look at me. He doesn't smile, but his eyes seem ignited.

The door lurches open, grinding against the concrete floor before it swings wide. A man in a white coat and blue plaid chef's pants stands just inside, wiping his hands on a white dishrag.

"Tate," he says, his voice sounding more than a little surprised. He glances into the kitchen, then back at us, his eyes washing over me quickly. I have the feeling that we shouldn't be here—that this man isn't going to let us in.

But then the man's mouth lifts into a smile, he steps forward, and he and Tate embrace like old friends. "Hey, Ruben," Tate says.

"Good to see you, man," Ruben replies. "It's been a while."

"I know," Tate agrees, patting the man on the shoulder as they release. "Do you have an open table?"

The man nods, still smiling, obviously pleased to see Tate. "For you? Always. Follow me."

Tate takes my hand again, leading me through the kitchen, where all the prep cooks and servers stop to stare at us. Ruben pushes through a door out into the dining area and catches the attention of a hostess. Her gaze flashes over us, smoky eyes smudged with eye shadow; she's wearing a slim black dress that dips down between her cleavage. For a moment she seems paralyzed in place, like she's forgotten how to do her job, but then she smiles, revealing big, perfectly spaced movie-star teeth. "This way," she says sweetly, eyes flitting over Tate and then to me once more like she's gathering data, assessing my appearance—my clothes, my hair, my lack of makeup.

After a moment, she guides us along the back wall of the crowded restaurant. A quiet symphony of clinking glasses and silverware fills the air, the face of every patron aglow from the candles adorning each table. Even in the darkness of the room, I can tell this is the not the kind of place where a girl like me sits down across from a boy like Tate. Yet here we are, sliding into a booth in a relatively private corner of the restaurant.

Tate leans back, watching me like he expects me to speak first. As much as I hate to oblige him, I'm too curious about what we're doing here. "How often do you come here?"

"Often enough," he says easily.

I feel my eyebrows lift. "Apparently."

"This place has been around since the thirties," he says. "Humphrey Bogart used to drink here. It was just called the Club back then. He and the cast would come here after shooting *Casablanca*."

"I've never seen *Casablanca*," I tell him.

"What?" Tate sits forward.

"I know, it's terrible. I just . . . don't have that much time to watch movies," I reply, embarrassed.

"What do you do when you're not working?" he asks me. When I hesitate, he presses on: "You don't work at the shop every day, so what do you do on Thursdays after school?"

"You know my work schedule?"

"It's not hard to figure out."

"You realize that's what stalkers do . . . track their victims' schedules."

"You think I'm a stalker?" His eyebrows lift, his expression a little hurt.

"Let's just say I'm reserving judgment."

"I didn't mean to freak you out. I only know your schedule because I've been to your work a few times and noticed when you weren't there."

"And my phone number?"

"That was just a matter of convenience." Our eyes connect across the table; his mouth twitches, then breaks into a smile that looks a little too unrepentant.

I don't want to, but I smile back. I don't really think he's a stalker, but it's obvious he knows more about me than I know about him. "Fine," I relent. "I have an internship at UCLA on Thursdays."

"Doing what?"

"You'd think it was boring." I press my palms against the surface of the table, feeling the smooth white fabric tablecloth beneath my fingertips.

"How do you know?" he asks. "You don't know anything about me." It's the second time he's thrown my words from last week back at me. But the dimple flashes as he says it.

"I work in a lab at UCLA that studies how spores disperse from fungi in the environment. Specifically how wind affects the spores." I stare at him triumphantly, as if I've just won some battle, proving that maybe if he knew how epically boring my life was, he'd want nothing to do with me.

But he rolls right over my answer with another question. "Do you like it?"

"The research?"

He nods, his gaze intent. As if he actually wants to hear my answer.

"I guess."

"Wow, that's convincing," he says. "Why do you do it, then, if you don't love it?"

"I don't have to love it. It's just an internship and it's good for my college application." I glance away, hoping he'll get the hint that I don't really want to explain my choices to him. Thankfully, a waiter walks by and Tate signals to him with a quick wave of his hand. But instead of coming over to the table, the waiter nods back—a silent understanding—then hurries away.

Tate turns back to me, resuming his questioning. "So when you're not at school or working or at your internship, what do you do for fun?"

"You forgot to add the newspaper club after school on Wednesdays, and my French study group every other Tuesday," I say, half bragging, half embarrassed.

"I'm starting to worry you have no social life."

I smile and don't answer him, instead glancing across to the next booth over, where a handsome dark-haired man sits with an equally beautiful woman. I swear I recognize him: the face of someone famous perhaps. "Carlos would die if he knew I was here," I find myself saying.

"That's your best friend?"

I nod. "He's obsessed with celebrities."

"And you're not?"

"I don't have time to keep track of all the famous people in this city. However, if we see anyone even remotely famous, even a reality TV star, I might have to embarrass you and go get their autograph for Carlos." I keep my face serious. "I hope you don't mind."

"Not at all," he says, tilting his head and grinning. "I'll even help you get said autograph."

"Oh, really," I say, half laughing. "You'll have to let me know if you see someone, then, because I don't think I'd recognize Brad Pitt if he walked through the door."

"No?"

I shake my head, fingering the shiny silverware arranged on a white cloth napkin. "For a lifelong Los Angeleno, I'm tragically un-savvy in the celebrity identification department."

"Noted," he says, his lips curving again and setting me off-balance.

A man arrives at our table, wearing all black and holding a serving tray filled with plates. He arranges the dishes meticulously on the table and stands back. "The rest is on its way," he says, smiling politely at Tate. "Please enjoy."

"Thanks, Marco," Tate says as the waiter steps away.

"We didn't order anything," I whisper across the array of what appears to be appetizers.

"They know what I like," he says.

"Seriously, how often do you come here?"

Tate just smiles and I give in, lifting my fork to taste everything in front of me—delicately wrapped summer rolls and mandarin salad, a curry soup and an artful tower of grilled vegetables. Tate watches me, his gaze flashing across the table to see my reaction as I try each new dish. When the main courses arrive, wide flat noodles that make the air rich with the scents of ginger and spice, I'm unsure if I can eat anymore.

But it's so incredible that my taste buds demand just one more bite . . . followed by another, and another.

I sit back in the booth when I'm done, satisfied and full and really wishing Carlos was here to experience this. He would die if he could see me sitting in a booth at Lola's . . . across from a guy like Tate—any guy at all, in fact. If it wasn't rude, I would probably send him a text: *Guess where I am RIGHT now?* But I refrain.

The waiter never brings a check, but he exchanges another covert nod with Tate as the plates are cleared, which seems to be the only form of communication in this place. Tate sits back, too, eyeing me.

I think again how little I know about him, and how much he knows about me. Time to even the score. "Since I don't have the same *resources* at my disposal as you do," I say, repeating his earlier explanation for how he obtained my phone number, "I'll have to figure out who you are the old-fashioned way." He looks uneasy for a moment, even though my tone is light and teasing. His gaze narrows, like he's not sure what I'm getting at. So I ask, "How old are you?" Because it seems like the most basic first question to ask—and an important one.

He squints, folding his napkin carefully and placing it back on the table, then says, "I'm nineteen."

"So you've already graduated high school?"

"Sort of . . . but not from an actual school. I had tutors."

Trust-fund kid, I think but don't say out loud. Now it's all starting to make sense. "Interesting," I say instead, tapping a finger against my chin, as if I were a reporter piecing the story together.

"Oh, is it?" he replies with a smirk, eyes igniting on mine. He sees what I'm trying to do: extract whatever information I can out of him.

"How old are you?" he asks in return.

"Just turned eighteen." But I sense it's entirely possible he knew the answer to that question already. "Have you always lived in LA?"

"Not always. Only for the last few years." A woman at a nearby table squeals and Tate flinches briefly, sitting up straight and glancing across the restaurant. But the squeal turns to a drawn-out laugh and Tate settles back in his seat, turning his attention back to me.

"Where did you grow up?"

"Colorado, originally."

It's an answer I wasn't expecting. He seems so LA. So in his element here. I thought he'd say San Francisco or Orange County or even as far away as Seattle. But it's hard to picture him somewhere like Colorado, especially the way I imagine Colorado in my head—like one big ski commercial: white powdery slopes, small mountain towns, sipping hot cocoa in front of a giant stone fireplace. It's probably an exaggeration, but I like the idea of it. A wintery, idyllic life.

"I've never even seen snow," I tell him. "It must be strange to live here after that. I can't imagine."

"It is," he admits. "But I . . . sort of needed to come here for work."

He's never mentioned work before, and I tilt my head to examine him, like I'm seeing him again for the first time. He's wearing one of his basic cotton T-shirts, yet it's the kind of shirt that looks expensive. The type of thing you buy when you want to look like you don't care about your wardrobe, but you actually do. "You're a musician, aren't you?" I guess.

There's a beat of silence and his hands tense on the table. "Why do you think that?"

"It's just what I assumed after I first saw you." I shrug.

"So you thought about me after we met?" His face glows in the candlelight, accentuating the lines of his cheekbones and the straight slope of his nose. He makes it hard to look away.

"No," I lie. "You just . . . looked like a musician. You had that vibe, I guess." I don't exactly know how to explain it, but he has that laid-back, artistic, *don't bother me because I'm writing a song in my head* attitude.

"I have a vibe?" he asks, a smile returning to his eyes.

"So you *are* a musician."

His lips rise into a grin he can't contain. "Nice detective work."

"What can I say? Some of us don't need *people* to find things out for us. We just use our instincts," I tease.

He shifts his gaze away and looks uncomfortable for a moment, biting his bottom lip and tapping his fingers on the seat of the booth. I'm about to ask what kind of musician he is—if he plays in a band or if he's a solo artist, if he's a lead singer or a drummer—but he leans forward, elbows on the edge of the table, and speaks before I have the chance. "So you have good instincts—noted," he says, his eyes smiling. "Now it's my turn." He peers across the table at me like he's deciding what personal—and possibly embarrassing—question he's going to ask. I keep my lips pressed into a tight line, trying not to smile at the way he's eyeing me.

"I know you're a senior," he begins. "But what happens after high school?"

The question is not as cringeworthy as I had expected. "Stanford," I say, relieved, then add, "if I get accepted. And if I can afford it."

"What do you want to study?"

"Biology, I guess."

"What do you mean, you guess?"

I shrug. "Bio's a good major if you're premed, which is what I'm planning on. It has a lot of requirements in common with the premed reqs." This statement is the very same one I've given guidance counselors at school; I said it at the interview for my internship, and I've recited it in my head countless times like a mantra I won't forget. *This is the plan*, I tell myself. *This will give me the life I want.* But unlike the counselors and the internship coordinators, Tate looks like he doesn't believe me—like my well-rehearsed speech doesn't convince him that I know what I'm doing with my life.

"Okay," he says, lifting both eyebrows. "So after college . . . med school?"

"Yes," I say, more assured. "Probably." *Crap.* Why do I sound so hesitant—why, sitting here face-to-face with him, do I feel a nagging at the back of my mind that maybe I don't know what I'm talking about?

"And you've always wanted to be a doctor?" he asks, steering the conversation deeper into waters I'm suddenly not sure I can navigate.

"Not necessarily," I answer honestly, and this actually feels like the truth. "But I had to pick something early on, so I could, like . . . put myself on a track." It's not the most glamorous reason to pursue a doctorate. It's not like I grew up with a passion for medicine or science or wanting to cure some disease. But the one thing I have known my entire life is that I needed to map a course for my future—one that would keep me from repeating the mistakes of every other woman in my family. And becoming a doctor seemed like the most solid plan, the one that wouldn't allow room for any missteps or time for distractions.

"But is this what you actually want?" Tate asks, looking at me like he can sense the turmoil roiling around inside my head.

"It doesn't matter if it's what I want," I confess. "It's what I have to do."

He settles back in his seat, studying me, letting his eyes float over each individual feature of my face. And although normally this would cause heat to overtake my cheeks, right now, I actually feel safe under his gaze. "Well," he begins, "you're dedicated, and I admire that."

I don't respond. I don't know what to say. But I give him a soft smile in return, the rest of the restaurant slipping away into the background.

A second later, the moment is broken when a flash blinks from across the room.

Someone just snapped a picture. I glance toward the booth next to us, to the couple still sitting there, the man in his suit and tie. Maybe he really is someone famous. I start to lean out from the booth, to get a better look, when Tate abruptly stands.

"Ready?" he asks. I pause, thinking he might extend a hand as he did when we walked in. But he simply waits, his expression blank.

"Oh . . . sure." I get to my feet and he leads me back through the kitchen, past the cooks and the serving staff, who pause again to watch us leave. Ruben waves a good-bye at Tate, obviously busy prepping several plates of food, and we slip back out through the heavy metal door.

Outside, he doesn't steer us back to the street, but walks deeper down the alley until we pop out on the next street over.

"There's an ice cream place a few blocks up," he says. I glance over at him; whatever was troubling him when we left the booth is gone now, the gleam back in those dark eyes.

I know I should politely say no—tell him I've given him his date, and now our deal is done. Return to my car and let this night be only a brief memory; the night when I let myself pretend I was someone else for a little while—but for all the questions I already asked, there's something about him that makes me want to know more.

"Only if they have sherbet," I answer finally.

"Which flavor?"

"Lime."

"No," he says, his eyebrows lifting.

"No, they don't have it?" I ask, confused.

"No, you're joking, nobody likes lime sherbet," he says. But his voice is more incredulous than accusing.

"*I* like lime sherbet," I retort, defending my love for the sadly overlooked flavor. "And I don't care who knows it."

He smiles and shakes his head, as if in disbelief. "Then you might be the only *other* person on the planet who does."

I raise my eyebrows, unsure if he's teasing me again.

"I'm serious," he says, reading my expression. "It seems we were meant to meet."

"Clearly." I roll my eyes, but I can't help smiling. Enjoying these last few moments with him—before I need to say goodbye.

We cross an intersection, the streetlights flicking from red to green, the air warm and sanguine, people strolling down the sidewalk and stepping out of taxicabs at the curb, dressed for a night out. Then just ahead of us, a guy shouts something, his words muffled, followed by the shrill sound of breaking glass. Two men stagger out of a dimly lit bar right as we pass the door, their hands balled around each other's shirts, shoving and cursing. A girl screams.

I turn—and it all happens too quickly for me to react. One of the guys slams into my shoulder, propelling me backward. My feet skid beneath me, and I ram into something hard. Pain lances through me. I'm pressed against a car parked at the curb. The men haven't even noticed me; they're still wrestling, their bodies crushing me.

"Hey—" I try to shout, but it comes out as a wheeze. My hands push at them, trying to shove them off me, but their weight is too much. I can't even squeeze out from under them.

There are other voices now, a girl shouting from somewhere on the sidewalk, screaming for them to stop. And then a lower voice, familiar—Tate is yelling, too. All the voices mixing together, ringing in my ears. An elbow juts out, thrusting into my chin, and the pain is sudden and white-hot. I turn my head away, trying to block my face from another blow, when their shifting weight is suddenly gone.

I gulp in air, my fingers instinctively going to my chin, touching skin that already feels swollen and sore.

"Hey!" one of the guys howls in protest, and I blink. Tate is between them, driving the two guys apart, holding one of them by the bicep and the other by a handful of T-shirt.

More people emerge from the bar, gathering on the sidewalk to gawk. Tate's eyes cut over to me briefly, muscles flexing as he hauls the taller of the two men backward. A girl with straight black hair rushes over, her high heels clicking on the sidewalk as she runs to the guy Tate is still holding.

"Let him go!" she shrieks, as if this were all somehow Tate's fault.

Tate stares the guy down, hand still gripping his arm, before he finally releases him. "Asshole," Tate says.

The guy shakes his arm, scowling. His right eye is beginning to swell black and purple, a thin line of blood trickling down from his nose. The girl touches his face, trying to wipe away the blood, but he brushes her off.

"Who do you think you are—" the tall guy says to Tate.

Music thumps from inside the bar like a drum, shaking the warm night air. More people slip out from the haze of the doorway, holding bottles of beer and unlit cigarettes, probably still hoping to see a fight.

"Hey, you!" the guy shouts again, but Tate doesn't turn around. "I know you," the man adds.

Tate is elbowing his way toward me, reaching a hand out for mine, when the black-haired girl shouts, "Oh my God!"

"Are you okay?" he asks, touching my arm gently and scanning my face for injuries.

"Fine." Even though my chin already feels like it's the size of a tennis ball.

"Let's get out of here," he adds urgently, and I nod. A hand grabs at his shoulder and he yanks it away.

"It *is* you, man," says the guy with the bulging eye. The crowd is shuffling toward us, converging like insects, clustering and buzzing and thrumming with words I can't make out.

Tate's eyes are desperate now. "Charlotte," he says, only loud enough for me to hear.

"What's wrong?" I ask, disoriented, glancing at the faces closing in on us.

Someone screams: "It's him!"

Lights begin to pop around us, flashbulbs blurring my vision, making it hard to see. And then I hear it, clear as a bell ringing right beside my ear. "Tate Collins!"

Voices become pitched, frenzied. Bodies begin to throb against us, shoving us from all sides. Tate manages to grab my arm but I am limp, unable to move, to process what's happening.

"Tate Collins!" someone yells again.

"Charlotte," he repeats, but his voice is all but lost in the deluge of other voices. My ears throb, and the air feels suddenly thick and sticky, crowded by hands and eyes and pulsing lights.

Tate Collins. This boy, this way-too-hot boy who's haunted the flower shop and brought me eight kinds of coffee and tracked down my phone number and snuck me in through the kitchen of the most exclusive restaurant in town—of course he's no ordinary boy. He's *Tate Collins*.

My lips move, forming the name that feels sour on my tongue. "Tate?" I whisper, trying to shake away the images cycling through my mind, the stream of photos I've seen on TV; in Carlos's gossip mags and his Instagram feed; on the side of buses and taped to the inside of girls' lockers at school. Tate

Collins—pop star, heartthrob, chart-smashing music sensation, and arguably one of the most famous singers in the entire world—is standing right in front of me, dark eyes boring into mine, pleading.

I barely feel the pressure of bodies as I'm edged out from the crowd, pushed back in slow motion, away from Tate. But I don't resist. I watch as hands tear at his clothes, fingers graze his shaved head. His eyes slant down, away from the flashes that burst in an endless pattern of dizzying white.

I take a step backward, then another, the crowd filling the void where I last stood. I catch one final glimpse of Tate before I turn on the sidewalk and run.

FIVE

ON MONDAY, THE AIR IS warm as kids flee the school at the end of the day. It feels like spring even though it's almost winter—not that winter in LA really counts.

"The Lone Bean for coffee?" Carlos asks.

"Let's do it." I've been quiet today, and Carlos has definitely noticed. I don't know why I haven't told him about Tate, except that I'm embarrassed I let myself get carried away, and more embarrassed it was with *him*.

I'm not an idiot. I *know* who Tate Collins is. Everyone knows. Even if you avoid the tabloids like I do, even if you don't listen to his music or follow any celebrity gossip blogs, you know who Tate Collins is. Everyone knows about his string of model girlfriends; about his mega world tour where he was rumored to party with British royalty and nearly drowned when he fell off a yacht near the coast of France, totally wasted; how he got in a fight in a New York nightclub and was hauled off to jail. Everyone knows the ugly details.

I know Tate Collins, the legend. So how did I fail to recognize Tate Collins, the boy? The night he walked into the flower shop, I had a nagging sensation that he looked familiar—but I shook it off. Ignored it. Figured it was nothing. And here I'd been bragging to Tate about my stellar detective skills.

In my defense, he looked different, not how I remember him from the photos I've seen. The artfully styled star from the headlines bears no resemblance to the Tate I met. His signature perfect brown hair is gone, shaved down to stubble. And his eyes seem so much bleaker in person. Like he hasn't slept in far too long.

"What's up?" Carlos says, nudging me as we walk. "I can tell something's going on with you."

So much for fooling Carlos. I turn away so he won't see my eyes, won't see the hurt just beneath the surface. This morning, before leaving for school, I masterfully applied a layer of makeup to my chin to conceal the bruise that surfaced shortly after I was clocked by one of the guys fighting on the street Friday night. It's still faintly visible of course, and I shrugged it off as a flower shop mishap, telling Grandma and Mia, and Carlos before first period, that I opened one of the cooler doors too fast at the Bloom Room and it slammed into my chin. They all seemed to believe me. Even though I hated the lie.

"I didn't even see you at lunch," Carlos adds.

"I know." I shake my head. "I'm sorry." I sat in my car the entire lunch period until I heard the bell ring, replaying the events of Friday night: the dinner at Lola's, how I so stupidly said I had never seen a famous person in my life, while I sat directly across from one of the most famous rock stars in the *world*. No wonder he was able to track down my phone number—when he said he had resources, he wasn't kidding. Memories circle in my head, pieces I can't believe I didn't put together until now. Like that first night in the flower shop when I asked for his name and he paused, caught off guard, like he couldn't believe I didn't know who he was.

He must have thought I was so stupid. Everything I said, all the comments about how I had good instincts, how I just *knew* he was a musician. He was probably laughing to himself, thinking how oblivious I was. I cringe at the memory. It was all just some sort of game to him—see how long it takes for me to figure out the truth, and then watch the embarrassment register on my face. Thinking about it now makes me furious. What kind of an asshole does that?

I remember a time last year—a faint memory—when all the girls at school were abuzz with the latest Tate Collins gossip, when rumors circulated that he was quitting music: no more touring, no more albums released. He was done—but why? *No*, I scold myself. I don't care.

"Charlotte?" Carlos levels his gaze on me, his coffee-brown eyes kind and reassuring.

"I . . . I saw that guy Friday night."

"The one who sent you flowers—he came to see you at the shop?"

I flash back to standing in the Bloom Room, looking at Tate

through the glass, his phone at his ear and his expression calculating. Then I ruthlessly shake the image away. "He's come in every day I've worked."

Carlos blinks. "Seriously? And you didn't tell me?"

"I hoped he would go away. I didn't want to make a big deal out of nothing." This is only a partial lie. I did want him to go away, but every time he stepped through those doors I realized I also craved to see him. "He asked me to go out with him again on Friday." I pause, taking a breath. "And I said yes."

"You did what?" A car rolls by with its windows down. By some cruel coincidence, echoing from the speakers is one of Tate's songs. I don't know the name, but the lyrics are familiar—a ballad, a love song about falling for someone who's in love with someone else, and the cool tenor of his voice now strangely familiar, too—and it makes my stomach turn. How did I not hear it in his voice? Each time he spoke, the truth was right there.

"You went on a date? *Your first-ever date?* And I'm just now hearing about it?" Carlos's voice is rising—part excitement, part accusation.

I study the gray concrete, the flattened little circles of green and white gum pressed into the sidewalk. "We went to Lola's," I say.

"You went to *Lola's?* Why didn't you text me? I would have come by and stared at you through the window and been completely jealous."

For his sake I laugh a little. "Um, yeah, that's pretty much why I didn't text you." The laugh turns to a sigh. "But it doesn't matter. I'm never seeing him again." The crosswalk light turns green and I start ahead of Carlos.

"What—why?" Carlos calls after me, catching up midway across the intersection. "Is this about your crazy no-dating policy? Or did something happen?" He's focused more on me than on walking, and he nearly bumps into a blonde in a white skintight crop top toting a yoga mat.

"He's not who I thought he was." I shake my head, thumbing the strap of the book bag slung over my left shoulder. I don't want to admit to Carlos I went on a date with *the* Tate Collins—he'll never let me live it down. He'll want to hash out every detail; he'll bring it up every chance he gets. And what I need is to forget about the whole thing.

"Charlotte," Carlos snaps, and I blink up at him. "You all right?"

"I'm fine," I say, blowing out a breath of air.

A car rolls quietly to a stop at the curb beside us and I stare at it blankly for a moment, not really focusing. And then my heart leaps: It's Tate's car.

I squint, trying to see inside, but the windows are tinted. Maybe it's not him . . . but it must be. The car is too unique—shining black and near silent—to be a coincidence. Why is he following me? I just want him to disappear. I start walking again and Carlos falls in step. We're almost to the coffee shop. Just one more block.

We stop at the next intersection and Carlos turns so he can

look me squarely in the eye. "You don't seem fine," he says pointedly. "What exactly happened Friday night?"

I roll my tongue along my front teeth. "He was just using me, asking me out as a joke." I keep my eyes averted from the car that has moved back into traffic but is keeping pace with us, inching up Highland Avenue. "I'm just glad I figured it out now. It was a waste of time in the first place."

"I'm sorry, Char," Carlos says, and he hauls me into his long, lanky arms. I press my cheek against the soft flannel of his shirt and the familiar scent of him is soothing: minty and sweet like bubble gum. "But don't let this ruin you for all guys. There are still some good ones left."

"I think you're the last one," I say, lifting my head and drumming up my first genuine smile of the day. "And unfortunately I'm not your type."

"Sorry about that. If you were, I'd treat you like a goddess."

"You already do," I say, and he kisses the top of my head.

I pull away but Carlos keeps his arm wrapped over my shoulder, hugging me close to his side so we're forced to walk in step. We reach the Lone Bean, a small coffee shop decorated with old black-and-white photographs of Hollywood actors from the twenties and thirties hanging from the walls. As usual it's filled with people hunched over their laptops and a few kids from school who beat us here. We order our usual drinks plus a blueberry scone to split, then find an open table outside. Again, my thoughts stray back to Tate. I can't help but recall his surprise coffee delivery last week, the casual way he strolled through the door of the flower shop, balancing two trays of steaming drinks, and then left just as nonchalantly. As if it were routine, and I was just the latest girl to fall for it.

Carlos pulls out his American history homework and starts ranting about the test he had to take today, and how it was totally rigged because he doesn't remember them going over any of the material. I'm grateful he's changed the subject—distracting me from thoughts that keep cartwheeling back to Tate. But I'm also incapable of focusing on what he's saying. When he eventually stands up to use the restroom, I glance out to the street, and there at the curb is the car.

I lower my head and clench my jaw, allowing myself to stare at it for a moment. I know it's his car—who else's could it be? If he expects me to come talk to him, he's in for a surprise. He can just sit there all day if he wants to.

But then the driver's side door swings open and Tate steps out, looking irritatingly smoking hot in dark sunglasses and gray jeans. I swallow, stunned.

I realize I've never seen him in daylight before. He's even more striking, every feature illuminated: every plane of his face defined, along with the broad arch of his shoulders beneath his white shirt. I can even see a sliver of skin, of hard abs where the hem of his shirt has risen above the line of his belt, before it falls back into place. I gulp.

His gaze settles on me, eyes narrowed, and he strides toward me.

I don't want to talk to him. I don't want to do this. Why can't he leave me alone?

I firm my expression in place, watching him with such intensity that I hope he'll just turn around and go back to his car. But as he gets closer, my heart starts hammering in my chest. The divide between us shortens, until he's standing at my table, right in front of me, and I flash a side-glance to the other people seated nearby. A few are watching him, but it might just be because he practically demands to be stared at, admired. Even if they don't realize who he is yet, I know from Friday night that it's just a matter of minutes until he's recognized. It's a miracle we made it through most of our meal at Lola's undisturbed.

"Charlotte," he begins, his voice low.

But I lift a hand. "No—don't."

"Let me explain."

"You don't need to explain anything. I already understand."

"I don't think you do," he answers, taking a step even closer. But I shift back in my seat, putting another inch of distance between us. His eyes slide over me, like he's looking for something, then settle on my chin. "Did you get hurt on Friday?"

"It's just a bruise," I reply coldly. The swollen skin is nothing compared to the lingering sense of betrayal, but I'm not giving him the benefit of knowing he has the power to hurt me. "I'm fine."

He exhales deeply, realizing I'm not going to make this easy on him. I just want him to leave.

"Come for a ride with me," he asks. "Give me a chance to explain."

"I'm busy right now," I say, looking down at my textbook. My hands are clenched in my lap beneath the table, twisting together.

"Are you . . . here on a date?" he asks. Tate had been watching us walk here; he watched Carlos hug me, then kiss my head. And now I can see the tension in his eyes.

"Why would you care?" I ask. "It's not like you cared enough to tell me who you really are."

His shoulders tense. "I didn't mean to lie to you. But this isn't the place to have this conversation. Can I pick you up when you're done?" I sense the voices around us rising, the whispers becoming more certain. *Yes, people, it's true.* The *Tate Collins is standing in front of the Lone Bean, failing miserably at an apology.*

"I have work," I say shortly. "Besides, I'm not going anywhere with you." The anger feels swift and hot across my skin.

He glances to his left, to a table occupied by three girls, all staring directly at him. "Just tell me, does that guy mean something to you?"

I unclench my hands from under the table, sigh. "Yes, as a matter of fact. That's Carlos."

He looks relieved. But I don't want him to feel relieved . . . I want him to feel how I feel, betrayed and humiliated. I want him to know what a risk it was for me to go out with him in the first place, and then he lied to me, made me feel like I was just some stupid game. But all I manage to say, all that comes out, is, "I never want to see you again."

He scrubs a hand across the back of his neck. His lips part like he's searching for words that aren't there.

I steel myself against the alluring way he clenches his jaw, the framed outline of his body against the blue skyline behind him. There's just something about him—something captivating, seductive even—but I don't allow my thoughts to sink any deeper into examining what that *something* is. Because he's a liar. He tricked me. And I don't want anything to do with him.

Then, without another word, he turns away from me and moves back toward the street. I can feel his absence in the air, the space where he once stood now hollow.

Two of the girls at the next table rush to their feet and start after him. I hear them say his name. But he slips into his car without turning around to acknowledge them. They stand for a moment, disappointed, before they turn back.

Asshole, I think as he drives off. But some small part of me can't help but wonder what he would have said if I'd let him speak, if I had gone with him.

"What did I miss?" Carlos asks when he returns moments later.

"Not a thing," I say, flipping open my French textbook and looking down to hide my face. Carlos is too good at seeing through my lies. "Let's get some homework done before I have to head to work."

"Homework, it is." He plops down next me, grabbing a pen from his backpack.

Even as we study, I can feel the eyes of Tate's impromptu fan club, curiously watching. But I don't even look in their direction. I don't think about Tate—at least I try not to. But it's useless. I tell Carlos I'll be right back and head to the bathroom.

It's empty when I enter. But when I step out from the stall, a girl is standing at a sink—water gushing into the bowl—but instead of washing her hands she's just staring at herself in the mirror. At first I think she's one of the girls that followed Tate, but then I realize I haven't seen her before. Her eyes lift and she turns around to face me. She's wearing a black sweatshirt and black jeans—*very Goth*, I think—and her hair is dark and severe, cut in a harsh line just below her chin. She's pretty though, pale with a few freckles across her nose that make me wonder if she's a natural redhead, her hair only dyed black for effect.

Her eyes flicker just barely and I smile politely, moving past her to the sinks. But she follows my movement, her gaze fluttering over me like she knows me. The faucet automatically turns on when I stick my hands underneath it and the water is cool, streaming between my fingers.

"You should stay away from him," she mutters suddenly, her reflection staring at me through the mirror.

"Excuse me?"

Her lips turn down. "Consider this a friendly piece of advice."

My eyes flick to the door. Voices pass by outside but no one comes in. "What are you talking about?" I ask. But I have a sinking feeling I already know.

She takes a step toward me, as if she's trying to gauge something, size me up. I back against the bathroom counter, palms tightening around the edge.

"For your own good, stay away from Tate Collins," she whispers, eyes unblinking.

She looks as though she's going to say something else, but then the bathroom door swings open and the two Tate fangirls walk in, chatting loudly. The Goth girl flinches at the sight of them, her body stiffening. My mouth starts to open, to say something, when she darts for the exit, slipping out before the door swings shut.

What the hell was that? I gulp in a deep breath and sag back against the counter. One of the groupies glances over at me, looking like she wants to ask me something, but I've had enough of unsolicited bathroom chats. I head for the door and push it open a crack, peering out into the noisy coffee shop. The girl is gone.

Outside, Carlos is reclining in his chair, chin tilted to the sunlight streaming through the trees. "Fall in much?" he asks, peeling open one eye to stare up at me. Thankfully, he doesn't appear to have overheard any chatter from nearby tables about the recent Tate Collins sighting while I was gone. I sink back down into my chair.

I should tell him about Goth girl. But then I'd have to admit

I went out with Tate Collins, and I'm not ready to revisit the humiliation. And really, there's no problem with heeding her "friendly advice"—I plan on staying far, far away from Tate, regardless. I just want to put it all behind me.

I want to forget last week ever happened.

SIX

I CAN'T FIND A PARKING spot close to the flower shop, so I have to jog five blocks with my book bag thumping against my ribs. I know Holly won't be mad that I'm late—it almost never happens—but I still feel bad for making her wait nearly half an hour. I was already rattled from Goth girl, and then got stuck on a verb conjugation and lost track of time. After we walked back to school, my run-down old Volvo—a piece of crap I purchased last year for six hundred dollars with money I saved from working at the Bloom Room—wouldn't start. We were there for twenty minutes in the student parking lot, the engine wheezing each time I turned the key, until it finally groaned and chugged to life. Clearly, it hasn't been my day.

I grab the handle on the front door and swing it open, out of breath and sweating. "Sorry," I say quickly as I step inside, but then I stop abruptly, shocked by the scene before me.

"Can you believe it?" Holly asks. She's seated behind the counter, her heart-shaped face lit a soft blue by the computer screen, her dirty-blond hair pulled back into a ponytail. I don't respond—I can't. My eyes are scanning the store, the empty displays and racks where bouquets usually sit. Every flower, every bouquet and plant arrangement is gone. Completely gone. Only a few petals and broken leaves are left, scattered across the floor.

"Did we get robbed?" I ask, stunned.

"No, it's even weirder! He bought the entire store," she chirps. "Every last flower."

I let the door swing shut behind me, the bell dinging overhead.

"Who did?" I ask, although once again, I'm afraid I already know.

"Tate Collins—the singer," Holly answers, her voice thrilled, her blue eyes wide with amazement. "He called an hour ago, said he wanted to deliver them all to the children's hospital on Wilshire—the delivery trucks just left." Holly grins, lifts her hands in the air, then drops them against her thighs. "I don't understand it, but it certainly made our quota for the month. I was going to call you earlier, but it's been such a whirlwind—sorry. Anyway, there's nothing for us to sell. Hopefully, I can have more inventory shipped overnight, otherwise we might be closed tomorrow, too. Don't worry, you'll still get paid for the hours."

I nod numbly. I can't believe he did this. Does he think he can buy my forgiveness?

The door behind me chimes again as someone steps inside.

"Sorry to interrupt. You must be Holly, Charlotte's boss."

I swivel around and see Tate standing just inside the front door, hands in his pockets. He's wearing a dark gray button-up shirt, the sleeves rolled partially up his arms, and dark jeans. It's nicer than his attire from the coffee shop earlier, and he looks . . . good. Really good.

Holly stands abruptly, dropping a piece of paper onto the floor. Her total disbelief is clear on her face. "Yes," she says, her voice higher than usual. "I am. And you're—" She clears her throat. "You're Tate Collins."

"Thank you for delivering all those flowers on such short notice," he says smoothly. His eyes stray briefly to me and I shoot him a glare, not amused by what he's trying to do.

"Anytime." Holly's eyes widen, and she looks at me like she's trying to gauge my reaction, like maybe I don't realize who's standing in the shop with us.

"I was hoping I might be able to borrow Charlotte from you for the evening, if you don't need her to work?"

He probably thinks he's so clever, forcing me to take the night off by buying up the whole store. As if it's some grand romantic gesture. But it only makes my chest constrict tighter, the irritation swelling across my skin, making me want to scream. This is just another one of his games.

"She's all yours," Holly says.

"No," I interject sharply, turning to face him. "You cannot borrow me. I am not a *thing* to be borrowed."

The intensity of his gaze drives through me as he turns to

look at me straight on. "That's not what I meant, Charlotte. I just need to explain. I need you to know that I didn't lie to you."

"I don't care . . ." But my voice trails into a whisper. I glance at Holly for a second, but she's just staring, her jaw literally hanging open. "You need to leave."

A shadow passes over his face, his eyes intent on me. He's probably not used to anyone telling him no, but he pushes his hands into his jean pockets and backs away. "Okay," he finally says. "I'm sorry. I won't try to see you again." He studies me for another moment, then pivots around and pushes out into the fading light, the sun just barely lost over the city skyline.

I force myself to move, walk to the front counter, where Holly still stands paralyzed, her expression frozen. "Did I miss something?" she asks. "Did Tate Collins just ask you out?"

I shake my head. "It was more like a demand."

"And you told him no?" Now she sounds like Carlos.

"He's been coming here for over a week," I say, aware that that's not really an answer.

"Wait. Mystery boy. He was the one who sent you the roses?" I watch the awareness dawn in her eyes.

"The creepy stranger who stalked me and embarrassed me in class with a flower delivery? Yes, that's him."

Her posture relaxes. "Okay, so what happened to make you despise him so much?"

I avoid her eyes. "I went out with him Friday night, against my better judgment, but he lied to me. He didn't tell me who he was. He let me make a fool out of myself."

76

"Wait, wait." Holly holds up her hands; the stack of silver bangles studded with charms slides down her forearms. "Slow down. You went on a date with him and you didn't know he was Tate Collins?"

"I know, I know." I grimace. "I just . . . didn't recognize him."

"And let me get this clear. That's why you won't go out with him again, because he didn't tell you up front who he was, even though most of America—scratch that, most of the *world*—would have recognized him right away?"

"It sounds stupid when you say it like that." I grab the broom from the closet, start sweeping up some of the leaves that are scattered over the floor. I feel suddenly awful. There's a wrenching twist inside my gut.

Holly clucks her tongue. "Charlotte. He's probably so used to girls falling all over him, it was refreshing that you didn't."

"Maybe," I acknowledge, remembering when he stepped into the flower shop that first night. He had looked at me like he was waiting for something—probably for me to realize who he was. But I never did. And he kept coming back to see me; he kept finding reasons to walk through that door. Maybe Holly's right. "But it doesn't matter," I tell her. "It's over now." His words replaying in my mind: *I won't try to see you again.*

"Do you like him?"

I shift my jaw to the left, biting down on the truth, on how I really feel. "No. I mean, I don't know."

Holly leans forward against the counter. "He obviously really likes you. He bought out the store just to spend an evening with you, for God's sake. And I know you have your rules about boys, but you're a smart girl, Charlotte, and you've always been so responsible. Don't be afraid to live a little." The fine lines around her eyes pinch together as she smiles. "Just ask yourself . . . Did you tell him to go away because you're not interested in him, or because you're afraid you *are* interested in him?"

A feeling begins to swell inside me, expanding swiftly, as if all it needed was Holly's permission to take form. Not anger this time, much as I try to hold on to that. I can't deny the way I feel when I'm around him, the sensation of petals blooming in the core of my stomach. The way his eyes track over me, like he really sees me. The way he listens when I speak, like he can't wait to hear the next word from my lips. "Okay," I admit. "Maybe I'm interested."

"It's not too late," she says, nodding to the windows. "His car is still outside."

I turn and see headlights at the curb, the silhouette of his sleek black car outlined against the street. I hesitate.

"Go," Holly urges me. "Let him explain himself, and *then* decide if you want to see him again."

A smile breaks across my lips, and I walk around the counter, giving her a hug before I turn and run for the door.

"Call me if you need anything!" she shouts after me.

The car is still idling at the curb, its engine purring. Without thinking, I dart into the street in front of it. The headlights cast over me, a wash of whitish blue, and I can just make out the outline of Tate's body in the driver's seat through the tinted windows. I pause for a moment, remembering Goth girl and her strange warning. I consider what I'm about to do, then decide to put it out of my thoughts. Maybe I'm crazy, but I want to hear what he has to say.

I open the passenger door and swing into the seat. The car is low to the ground, and I glance around as I pull the door closed, not yet brave enough to look at him. The interior is black leather and pristinely clean: no fast-food wrappers or dirty sneakers, not even a water bottle out of place.

The breath stalls in my lungs. He waits for me to speak.

"Ask me again," I say after a few seconds have passed. I bring my gaze to his, and draw in a sharp breath at the look on his face.

"Ask you what?" His eyes cut through me, making it hard to think clearly.

"Ask me out again."

A glimmer of a smile reaches his lips. "Will you go out with me, Charlotte?"

"Yes." The word slips out easily now.

He reaches across my waist, grabbing my seat belt and buckling it into place. His fingers graze my arms and blood roars in my ears. I ignore it, staring straight ahead.

"I still want to know why you never told me the truth about who you are," I say. "So don't think I'm letting you off the hook yet. I need an explanation."

"You'll get one," he says, the corner of his mouth lifting as he revs the engine.

"Where are we going?" I ask.

"My house."

He pops the shifter into gear and releases the clutch. The car bolts away from the curb, zipping up Sunset and heading north. He drives aggressively, confidently, and even though I should be scared, I find myself smiling as we climb the Hollywood Hills. Then the car turns suddenly into a driveway and slows. I look ahead to see a gate blocking our way, but Tate hits a button on the dash of the car and the gate automatically swings open.

The driveway twists down a slope, and his house comes into view just beyond a tangle of broad trees. I lean forward, stifling a gasp. Stone and concrete and glass windows rise up three floors, and the roof swoops upward like it might touch the thin wisps of clouds in the darkness overhead.

Tate pulls the car around the circle drive in a swift loop, and stops beside two massive metal front doors. I glance over at him but he's already stepping out of the car and coming around to my side. He opens my door and takes my hand to help me out. The warmth of his touch sends a flood of nerves straight through me. It was only a few days ago when his fingers last threaded through mine, but for some reason it feels like a lifetime ago.

"Do you live here by yourself?" I ask.

He leads me up the white gravel walkway. "Yeah. There used to be other people . . . Now it's just Hank, but he lives in the guest house."

"Who's Hank?"

On cue, one of the impressive front doors swings wide, and standing just inside the house is a wide-shouldered hulk of a man. "What's up, T?" the man says, extending a hand and giving Tate a casual fist bump. Hank is tall and thick, with a shaved head and a neck as broad as a tree trunk. But his smile is easy and affable.

"Charlotte," Tate says. "This is Hank, my bodyguard."

"Except lately T's been leaving the house without me," Hank points out, looking over at me. "Said he wanted anonymity, and a bodyguard draws too much attention. I suspect it has something to do with you." He smiles, belying his harsh words, and reaches out for my hand, kissing the top of it. "So this is the Charlotte who's been torturing my boy," he adds. "I like that you haven't made it easy on him. He needs to be kept in check from time to time."

I smile up at Hank, trying not to dwell on the fact that I know someone who has his own bodyguard. "I do what I can."

"I don't think I like you two conspiring against me," Tate says, tugging on my hand.

"You done for the night, T?" Hank asks as we step into the foyer.

"I think so," Tate answers, and his eyes brush over me.

"I'll park the car in the garage, then. Let me know if you need it later."

"Thanks, Hank."

"And it was nice to meet you, Charlotte," Hank adds.

"You, too."

Hank closes the door behind him when he steps outside, and I'm startled by the expanse of the house before me. Dramatic concrete walls rise above us like a museum of modern art. Windows start at the floor, then sweep up to touch the ceiling. The whole place is lit by a soft golden light that seems to spring forth from every crevice and alcove, as if coming from the walls themselves.

We pass through the living room, where a large white piano sits in the corner, so shiny that it reflects the overhead light. Everything is clean and starched and perfect. Almost too perfect. There are no framed photographs of family and friends, no signs that this house is truly lived in.

Along one wall hangs a series of gold and platinum records—the titles of his hit songs and albums stamped below each one. It's surreal. It hits me again, all at once—I'm here.

I'm in Tate Collins's house.

SEVEN

THERE ARE MORE RECORDS THAN I can count, and I want to ask about them, but Tate keeps walking, brushing past them like they're not even there. The wall of windows overlooks a pool that seems to fall away on the far side, revealing a sudden drop-off and an expansive view.

"Are you hungry?" Tate asks. "I don't think I have much in the kitchen, but maybe some leftover pizza, or we could order something . . ."

"No, I'm fine." I don't have much of an appetite anyway. I'm still wary of him, still feeling guarded. Just his proximity makes my heart rate quicken. "Can we go outside?" I ask, drawn to the pale lights shimmering up from the pool. I don't know if I've ever been somewhere so beautiful.

He touches one of the doors and it begins to spread open like an accordion, the entire glass wall folding in on itself so that the living room is now completely open to the back lawn.

The air smells instantly of freshly mowed grass. The long,

rectangular pool stretches out before us, illuminated in a vibrant blue. Beyond the pool is a broad swath of lawn overlooking the horizon to the south, vast and wide and spectacular—the entire world suspended in the distance. Tate leads me to the edge of the grass and I sit cross-legged beside him, too awed to protest when he takes my hand. We sit staring out across the sloping hillside, which falls away, revealing the glittering, endless mass of lights that is Los Angeles far below. The city looks remarkable from up here, like a fairy-tale landscape stretching out to the dark ocean beyond.

"You get used to it after a while," he says, as if reading my mind.

"I don't think I would. It looks so different from up here."

"It's just an illusion." He extends his legs out in front of him. "From a distance, anything can look beautiful."

I shift my eyes away from the skyline, and allow myself to examine Tate's face. He always looks so guarded, his jaw locked in a tight line. I grow self-conscious about my hand in his, and pull it away, running my palms over the blades of grass.

"Why?" I ask then.

"Why what?"

I dig my fingers down between the blades, feeling the slightly damp earth below. "Why didn't you tell me who you were?"

His expression turns pensive, gazing out at the city lights for a long moment, and then he says, "I saw you, you know."

"Saw me?" I echo blankly.

"Outside the flower shop that first night. That's why I came in, because I noticed you through the window." He licks his lips. "You were singing, and you were practically covered in glitter, dancing to that song playing from your phone." His eyes flick down to my hands resting in the grass. "You were so happy and beautiful. It almost didn't seem real—like I was imagining you."

His words are like sparks, igniting the space between us. No one has ever said anything like this to me before, and though my rational mind knows he might say this to every girl he brings home, still, my whole body is a rivulet of electricity. Nerves dance along my skin.

"I didn't really need to buy flowers," he says. "I just wanted to talk to you. And when I realized you didn't know who I was, it caught me off guard." He frowns a little. "So I lied and said I wanted flowers. But they were always for you."

I brush my hands over my knees, trying to ignore my reaction to his words.

"After that, I knew I had to see you again," he continues. "You . . . intrigued me. I can't remember the last time I met someone who didn't know who I was." He actually looks a little self-conscious as he says it.

"So you only asked me out because I didn't recognize you?" I make my voice sharp, trying to cut the tension that's building between us.

"No. It wasn't just that." I can feel him looking at me now, but I refuse to turn and meet his gaze. I don't trust myself. "There was something about you—there still is . . ."

I'm not sure exactly what he means and I feel my forehead crease, but I still don't look at him. "You didn't need to lie," I say. The reminder of that night, with the paparazzi, and the crowd pressing in around us, triggers a knot inside my stomach. I felt so stupid. And, even though it had only been one date, completely betrayed.

"I didn't lie," he says, and I realize he's right. He didn't give me a false name or tell me things about himself that weren't true, but it still feels like a trick. "I wanted to see if you would go out with me, even if you didn't know who I was."

"So it was a test?"

"No—not a test." He shakes his head, and I feel his eyes slide over me: my cheekbones, my hair falling across my neck, my lips. "I'm curious about you."

"You shouldn't be," I tell him. "I'm not that interesting."

"I think you are," he says. "I want to know more about you. One date wasn't enough."

I don't answer. I can't. I can hardly keep my breath steady. He takes my hand again, brings my palm to his lips. I shiver as I watch the motion, the shape of his lips, then force my eyes away, back to the starry glimmer of city lights far below.

"Is that real?" he asks, his voice close to my ear.

"What?"

He touches the inside of my left wrist with a rough fingertip, outlines the dark blue triangle drawn there.

I snatch my hand away, and brush the triangle with my own

fingers. Recalling memories there. "It's just pen," I say. "I've always drawn it."

"Does it mean something?"

"Triangles are the strongest shape," I say. "They can withstand pressure on all sides." I turn my wrist away so he can't see it. "I think my mom used to tell me that, but I can't remember." Too bad it didn't work for her—she was never strong enough to say no to the men who pursued her. Just like Mia isn't strong enough either. But this symbol reminds me that I can be different.

"Do you need to be strong?"

"We all do . . . at some point," I answer. *Like right now*, I think. I need to remember my promise to myself. My future is already mapped out; I have a plan. And it doesn't involve Tate or the hundred butterflies quivering inside my stomach.

He exhales, loud enough that I can hear. "Do you draw other things, too?"

"Sometimes." *All the time.* I've always loved drawing and painting—when I was little I thought I'd be an artist when I grew up. But then I learned that most artists are not actually paid to be artists. Even Van Gogh and Monet weren't recognized in their time. So I came up with a more practical plan. Straight As, internship, Stanford, top med school, residency, job. But I don't tell Tate this.

"I wish I could do that: draw or paint, create something out of nothing," he says, leaning back on his elbows and tilting his head up to the sky.

"You make music," I say. "That's way more impressive than some doodles."

His fingers are only a few inches from mine, and I can't help but follow the line of his arm with my eyes, muscles taut up to his shoulder, to the broad slope of his neck, and the place behind his ear.

"I don't know if you can even call it music. It's all just sound design and tricks in a studio." He laughs bitterly, looking toward the sky, flooded with pinpricks of light—the stars so much brighter up here, not dulled by the glow of neon and streetlights. "I used to care about the music, it used to be mine . . . but not anymore. It's been stripped of anything authentic."

"Is that why you stopped performing?" I ask. I don't know much about the life and career of Tate Collins, but I've heard on the radio about how he hasn't done a single concert or released a new album in over a year. He basically fell off the map, right at the height of his career. No one seemed to know why. And I never actually cared . . . until now. Now that I'm sitting beside him, on his lawn, with his fingers, his shoulder, his body so dangerously close to mine.

He straightens. "There are other ugly things about the business." His gaze suddenly clouds over, like he's recalling things from another time. A memory I can't see. "I let it get out of hand, and I can't take it back."

"Take what back?"

But he doesn't answer. Doesn't even shake his head. His stare is caught in the distance—on something far away.

"But you still love to make music?" I ask softly, attempting to draw him back.

"It's been so long since I wrote anything, I'm not sure I remember how."

"I doubt it's something you forget," I offer, trying to sound encouraging.

He turns and looks at me for the first time since we started this conversation. He presses his lips together, his eyes softening again, like he's slowly coming back to the moment. "I hope you're right." And his mouth actually shifts into an easy smile, the dimple winking to life.

"Of all your songs, which is your favorite?" I ask, hoping I might help him remember what he used to love about his music, maybe even recall what had inspired him once.

"It's probably not one you've ever heard of."

I look away, slightly embarrassed. "To be honest, I don't really know many of your songs anyway." I bite the edge of my lip and give him a grimace that I hope passes for a smile.

He laughs—he actually laughs. "Even better." Then he jumps up from the grass, holding a palm open to me. "Come here," he says.

I let him pull me up, and before I know it, he places a hand on my lower back, pulling me close, then laces his other hand through my fingers, as we start to dance.

"What are you doing?" I ask, my heart battering against my ribs—my body pressed close to his.

"You wanted to know what my favorite song is," he says,

drawing me closer. "This is the best way to show you. It's a love song—it's meant to be slow-danced to." Before I can respond or protest or swallow the lump in my throat, he begins to hum. Softly at first, then whispering words to a song I faintly recognize—one of his songs. *"If you knew what this felt like, to be without you, you'd never have left me."* And in his voice, in the sweet, cool tenor of his words, I hear the sound of Tate Collins—the singer.

"Your eyes are like emeralds, your body like gold.

"If you could still love me.

"You don't know what you've done . . ."

He holds me gently, firmly, his voice a mere whisper, and I don't resist, letting my eyelids slip shut. A breeze stirs up from somewhere, unsettling the leaves of a nearby tree, and even though the air is warm, goose bumps rise up on my arms. His hand tightens on my back, his fingers pressing into my shirt as he leads me in a slow, lazy circle. I feel myself slipping further and deeper into this moment, letting it take hold of me.

I blink my eyes open and realize that he's watching me, his face unreadable. Without a word, he starts leading me toward the house. He turns to me just before we reach the door, his arms going around my waist as he presses me against one of the stone pillars that encircle his back patio. His eyes search mine. I can see his pulse pounding at the base of his neck and then he's leaning in close. Closer.

I take a deep breath, my chest brushing against his, and he closes his eyes. Tentatively, I settle my hands on his chest, drawing in a sharp breath at my own boldness. He's so warm. Beneath my palm I can feel the rapid beat of his heart.

Tate draws his finger across my cheekbone, just beneath my eye. His body is so close—only a thin layer of air and clothing separate his chest, his torso, his lips from mine. I tremble and close my eyes, my lips parting in anticipation. I can feel his breath, warm and soft, drift across my lips, and I know he's close. I know he's going to kiss me.

And I want him to.

His arms tighten around me as he pulls me firmly against him; not even an inch divides us. A whimper escapes me and before I can say, think, do anything else, he moves in, pressing his mouth to mine.

My senses overwhelm me. An explosion of nerve endings along the delicate surface of my lips. Unlike anything I've ever felt before. And everything I'd always imagined a first kiss should be. His lips move hungrily, gentle yet assured. I pray I won't mess this up, going on pure instinct as his mouth connects with mine again and again. He captures my lower lip with both of his, giving it a soft tug before releasing it. My knees threaten to buckle and I clutch at his shirt, gathering the fabric in my fists.

With every brush of his mouth on mine I feel like I'm soaring. He touches my face. My cheek, my jaw, my chin. His fingers drift down the length of my throat, my collarbone, lingering there. I suck in a shuddering breath, scared he'll dare to go further. Excited that he might go further . . .

My eyelids flutter open just as he breaks the kiss. Our breathing is harsh, our chests rising and falling in tandem, and he draws back for only a second, his dark eyes boring into mine. Asking a silent question that I answer with the tiniest nod.

And then he's kissing me again. More intensely this time, my lips parting beneath his, his warm tongue grazing my skin. I gasp against his insistent mouth and he takes advantage, deepening the kiss. My heart is racing when his finger traces down the center of my chest, between the twin curves of my bra, playing with the low neckline of my shirt.

Finally, my mind returns. Panic racing through me, I press against his chest so our lips break apart. I try to catch my breath, calm my crazed heart, but it's hard when he continues to toy with my shirt, his fingers brushing against my sensitive skin.

"God, Charlotte." He shakes his head. "I can't . . ." His voice drifts, like he can't quite figure me out.

Slowly, I look up at him, positive my cheeks are burning red. I should move away, but I stand paralyzed as he drifts his knuckles across my cheek, his touch making me shiver. I inhale sharply just as he moves in to kiss me yet again.

And then I blurt out, "I've never done this before."

"What?" He pulls back an inch.

"I just . . . I've never kissed anyone before." I close my eyes. Swallow hard, feeling like an idiot. *Why did I just tell him that?* Talk about a mood-ruiner. But I panicked; it was all happening so fast, it just came out.

Tate takes an almost imperceptible step back, but suddenly the night air feels cool all around me. "You've never kissed *anyone*?" He sounds incredulous.

I slowly shake my head. "I've never done—anything like this."

His gaze doesn't leave mine. "How is that possible?"

"It just . . . hasn't been a priority," I admit, glancing away from those penetrating eyes.

"But you've had boyfriends before, right?"

I feel my eyebrows furrow. "No, I haven't. I've been waiting," I try to explain. "But it doesn't mean I want to stop." I shake my head, humiliation rising through me. "I shouldn't have said anything. I don't know why I did. I'm sorry I ruined the moment."

"I'm the sorry one, Charlotte," he tells me, and I can hear a hint of regret in his voice. But I still don't expect what he says next. "Because I can't do this." His voice is flat, toneless, and yet the words are a sharp edge cutting straight through me.

He steps away, and the world rushes in: the night air, the sound of the wind through the trees, a car passing in the distance.

"You should probably go." His voice is soft but distant, and he's suddenly a million miles away. The void between us is cold, like his body never occupied that space, as if I imagined it all. "Hank will drive you home," he says, but I'm already having a hard time focusing on his words, my head starting to spin, unable to process what changed so suddenly between us.

I don't nod. I can't even speak. But I watch as he walks toward the house—feeling anchored, pressed against the stone pillar where he left me, reeling. He glances back once and a moment passes between us, but I can't read the expression on his face: maybe regret? Or is it embarrassment that he just made out with a girl so naïve that she had completely different expectations of the night than he clearly did? He must be wishing he had never brought me here. All he says is "I'm sorry, Charlotte," before he slips inside.

The next few minutes pass in a daze. Tate's bodyguard, Hank, ushers me out the front door where a black town car is waiting, idling in the driveway. He opens the back door and I stare, stunned, at the massive stone façade of the house. I expect to see Tate's face in one of the windows, curtains pulled back, watching me leave—but only the cold exterior stares back at me, leaving me completely and utterly alone.

EIGHT

IT'S WEDNESDAY NIGHT AND I'M sitting cross-legged on my bedroom floor, a textbook in one hand, Leo cradled in the other. Mia needed to take a shower and I offered to watch him. But I'm also cramming for a test tomorrow in AP History.

I tap my highlighter against the top of the textbook and look down at Leo, who is chewing happily on a teething ring that's shaped like a set of brightly colored car keys.

It's been over three weeks since that night. Three weeks since I let Tate humiliate me. Again.

And I still can't shake the memory.

School has been mind-numbing: a frenzy of papers and prep for exams. Work is a series of inconsequential days, each the same as the last, with no sign of Tate. I've buried myself in homework, put in extra hours at my internship—anything to keep me from thinking about him. I keep expecting to see him step through the door at work, or for another bouquet of flowers to arrive at school, but they never come. Holly, of course, was dying to know what happened after I left the shop that night with Tate. *I was right the first time*, I told her the next day when I came into work. *It was a mistake to give him another chance. He's a total jerk.* She pulled me into a hug and told me she was proud of me for taking the risk. And that I shouldn't let this one encounter with Tate ruin my perspective on love. But it's too late for that.

I tell myself I should be happy it's over. It's what I said I wanted. And yet, I can't stop thinking about him. And I hate it.

I hear the front door close and I know Grandma is home from work. She finds me in the bedroom, and as soon as Leo spots her, his pudgy arms lift in the air for her to pick him up. Sometimes I think she's his favorite. But just wait until he's older, when I can take him out for milk shakes and to the beach to make sand castles. Then I'll be the cool aunt, and Mia and Grandma won't be able to compete.

"How's the studying going?" Grandma asks, bending down to scoop up Leo. His cheeks pull into a smile as she lifts him high into the air, then rocks him in her arms.

"I think I've been staring at the same page for the last hour."

She gives a soft murmur of understanding. "You've seemed distracted these last few weeks."

"I know," I admit. "I don't know what's wrong with me." Even though I do—I know precisely what's wrong. My head will not let go of *him*.

"I can watch Leo, give you some time to focus," she offers,

walking back to the doorway, Leo clinging to her hip, the collar of her shirt already in his mouth.

"Thanks," I say, smiling up at her. But it's not Leo who's been distracting me. It's someone else. Someone I wish I could forget. But the more days that pass, the harder it is. Like my brain is revolting against me—and it's getting worse instead of better.

Grandma pauses in the door, rocking Leo in her arms, and turns around to face me. "You've worked so hard, Charlotte," she says unexpectedly, her face serious. "And I've never known you to let anything distract you from accomplishing your goals. I know how much is on your plate, with school and work, the internship and Stanford. I want you to know how proud I am of you for always keeping your future a priority. Whatever is occupying your mind these days . . ." She sighs. "Just remember, today's problems are temporary. Next year at this time, you'll be blazing your own path."

I nod. But after she's gone, I close my textbook and lean my head back against the end of my bed. I can't keep feeling like this. I can't pretend everything's fine.

I have to do something about it.

I'm driving too fast down Sunset, letting my foot press down on the gas pedal while my Volvo squeals with the increased speed.

Last night, sitting in my room, unable to study because my mind kept slipping back to memories of Tate, I realized I wouldn't be able to just forget. The night at his house keeps replaying over and over inside my head. And it isn't going to stop until I know what really happened—why he kicked me out of his house once he knew I had never been kissed. Why did it matter so much? Why did he push me away? I crisscross up the streets of West Hollywood. I should be home studying. Instead, I'm about to do something I might regret.

I turn the radio up louder and roll down the window all the way, trying to drown out my thoughts, numb the painful anger that beats inside my chest. My hair whips out the window, a flurry of strands twisting and knotting together. I grip the steering wheel and press down harder on the gas. The song on the radio ends and a new one comes on; the thumping beat shakes the car doors. My throat tightens at the sound of the voice rising through the speakers.

"If you could still love me (if you could still love me).

"If you could see what you've done.

"I can't sleep without you, the bed is too cold."

The memory blooms inside me before I can tamp it down; the way his lips felt against my ear, humming this same song, whispering the lyrics as we drifted beneath an endless canopy of stars.

"My dreams are like nightmares.

"Your hands are still on me . . ."

I slam my palm against the radio dial, shutting off the music in one swift motion. I make a quick right at the next intersection, turning away from home, away from the sane, rational girl who should be studying for exams tonight, finalizing my Stanford application, reading ahead in English. Instead, I follow the path we took that night, when the city lights spun and danced outside my tinted window, when Tate led us deep into the hills.

The route is easy to trace, as if my hands alone know the way, steering the car around sharp bends and up steep slopes until I reach the gate. But I don't have a clicker to let me in. I roll down my window and peer at the tiny blinking security light.

"Who is it?" Hank's voice comes suddenly from the speaker, surprising me, and I jump in my seat.

"Um . . . it's me. Charlotte. We . . . we met a few weeks ago." I have no idea why Hank would let me in. This was a stupid idea.

But then, after a pause, Hank surprises me: "Come on through."

My hands start to twitch on the steering wheel, tapping nervously. The gate opens and I accelerate, circling down into the driveway in front of Tate's house. I park and suck in a deep breath, finally walking up the steps. The massive front door swings open and Hank's hulking shadow takes up nearly the entire entryway.

"How can I help you, Charlotte?" he asks, looking past me to my dilapidated car.

"I need to see Tate." My voice comes out firm.

I hate the pity in his eyes when they return to mine. "Is he expecting you?"

I shift on the steps, looking past him into the house. The fireplace in the living room burns low, but I can't see anyone moving in the darkness.

"Is he here?" I ask.

Hank steps forward, his voice lowering. "I'm not supposed to say." His eyes cut back into the house for a moment, then to me. "But to be honest, he hasn't been himself these last few weeks. It might be good for him to see you." And then he pushes the door open wide behind him, stepping out of the way so I can walk past.

I blink up at him, shocked he's going to just let me inside, and I take several tentative steps into the hallway. I hear Hank leave and close the door behind him.

I'm alone in Tate's house.

Then, from the darkness, I hear footsteps. Tate emerges from the hallway to my right, wearing only a pair of jeans, his chest bare, illuminated in the flickering light. My breath catches at the sight of him. His skin seems darker in the glow from the fire, tanned by the sun.

I want to scream at him, tell him he's an asshole, that he had no right to treat me the way he did. I want to make him feel terrible, even though some traitorous part of me hopes there's an explanation, a reason for everything he said that night. But before I can form the words, he asks the first question. "What are you doing here?"

"I—" My hands shake, and I realize I'm nervous. I didn't come here with an exact plan. He squints at me, like he's trying to see me better in the dim light. Like maybe the reason is written in the lines of my face.

But then I find the words I know I need to ask. "Why did you make me leave that night?"

He turns away to face the fire, where the flames pop and spark.

"Is it because I've never been kissed before? You think I'm too innocent, too boring for you?" I press. I hate the way my voice sounds, but I have to know. "I just need to hear you say it."

"No," he says, flashing me a look across his shoulder.

"Then what?" I say, taking a step closer. "After everything you did to get me here, why did you push me away?"

He turns to face me fully. "I'm not right for you," he says, as if that explains anything.

I laugh—a cold hard laugh. "Excuse me? You obviously didn't think that three weeks ago, when you wouldn't leave me alone." I move closer to him, the heat from the fire intensifying. I want to understand.

"I'll just end up hurting you."

"What does that even mean?" I ask, my voice gaining volume, but his expression falls, his eyes sliding back to the fire. "You think I'm weak? Just because I've never been kissed? It's actually a lot harder not to do that kind of stuff than it is to do it, I'll have you—"

"That's not it," he cuts me off. His eyes seem suddenly tired as he faces me again.

"Because I'm not weak. And I can make my own decisions

about what's right for me," I say. I'm surprised by my own conviction. Especially because I'm not sure what I want. Did I come here to tell him off? Or to tell him he's making a mistake? I don't even know anymore.

He shakes his head, so slightly I almost can't tell. "It's better if you just go."

"*You* started all this, you sent me roses, you came to my work, you bought every last flower in the whole store. I wanted it to be over. After I figured out who you really were, I was done. But you came back, wanted to explain yourself. And I took a chance. And then you hurt me all over again. I didn't ask for any of it. But now . . . now I'm here. And I just want . . ." But I can't finish.

"What do you want?" he asks.

"I—" I shake my head. "I don't know."

He stares back at me, his lips parted, like he understands everything I'm thinking. "I didn't mean to hurt you," he says. "That's not what I wanted either."

"Then what do *you* want?" I ask, swallowing down the words almost as quickly as they leave my lips. I can't even trust my own thoughts anymore, my own voice. I'm saying things I normally would never say out loud—or think, for that matter.

"Charlotte—" he starts to say, moving toward me, but tentatively like he's afraid I'll run, bolt for the door, and never look back. But I'm locked in place. A million thoughts slamming against my skull, a tug-of-war, words colliding into one another in confusion. "I'm sorry for the other night," he

102

says, eyebrows slanted like he really is sorry, like it pains him to remember the events of that night. "I'm sorry for how I acted. I was just caught off guard. I didn't realize I was your first kiss. And there are things you don't know about me." He takes in a deep breath, focuses back on me. "But I've missed you." His mouth flattens. "I can't stop thinking about you. And I don't know why . . . but I haven't felt like this in a long time. And then you just show up here, and all I want to do is kiss you again, tell you not to leave. But I know that I shouldn't."

"Why not?" I ask.

"Because I might hurt you. Because our worlds are so different—and I don't want to mess up your life."

"Isn't that my decision, not yours? I'm smart enough to know what I can handle."

"I know you are," he agrees. "And that's part of what makes you so intriguing to me. You know what you want in life, you know exactly where you're going, and I envy that." I cringe a little at his description of me. As if I'm so responsible, so predictable. Maybe I don't want to be that anymore—at least not the predictable part. "I just don't want to ruin anything."

"You act like it's already destined to fail. Like there's no way we could be anything but a disaster." I can't believe my own words—I'm actually arguing with him about a relationship we're not even in.

"It's how my life has been lately."

"And so you're just never going to take a chance on anything ever again?" I sound like Holly, and *so* not like myself. I'm the queen of not taking chances, unless they're calculated. And now I'm asking him to take one. My logical brain has completely left this conversation—I'm now being driven by my heart.

He steps to within a foot of me, his bare chest reflecting the glow from the firelight. He studies my eyes, his breathing settling into a rhythm that I swear matches mine. "Is that what you want?" he asks. "To take a chance?"

I can't breathe. My lips part, I find words, then lose them just as quickly. I can't admit what I'm really feeling. To myself or to him.

But before I'm able to think of a way to deflect the question, he's suddenly moving toward me. He slides his hands up along my jawbone and draws my face forward, sinking his lips into mine. For half a second, I'm unable to react, my body rigid beneath his hands. But then the warmth of his mouth sinks through me and I give in—I kiss him back. I breathe him in, the air sliding from his lungs to mine. His lips are needy, searching. The tips of my fingers just barely touch his hard chest, and my stomach unleashes a flurry of wings.

My eyelids flutter and he draws back his lips for only a moment, testing the space between us, and then he kisses me again, gently this time. My heartbeat hitches wildly as his fingers shift across my cheek, tracing a line along my skin, down the curve of my neck.

He pulls his fingers away before going any lower and I'm afraid he's going to repeat what he did last time, wrench away from me and leave me all alone again. But this time he stays, drawing his fingers up through a section of my hair and tucking it behind my ear. "I'm sorry," he says, gently dropping his hand as if he's just broken some rule, invaded my personal space—lost control of himself for one brief moment—and now he needs to apologize. "I shouldn't have done that. But I had to."

"I'm not as breakable as you think," I tell him.

A smile warms his eyes. "I'm starting to realize that."

A moment passes and my heart climbs upward in my chest, craving his touch again. Wanting to feel his lips on mine. I glance at the floor, steadying myself. "What now?" I ask.

"Depends on your answer to my question," he says, his gaze locked firmly on mine. "Do you want to take a chance?"

I'm worried my voice won't be there when I speak, but it rises upward from my throat, a gasp of air. "Yes," I admit, surprising myself. "Do you?"

He shifts closer and I think he's going to kiss me again, but instead he says, "More than anything."

But then the light seems to leave his eyes and something else takes form there. "If we're going to do this," he begins, swallowing, "then we need to take it slow."

I feel my eyebrows pinch together, not entirely certain what he's getting at.

"I need to make sure you don't get hurt," he adds. I shake my head, *really* not understanding what he means. "There needs to be rules."

"What do you mean, rules?"

"Guidelines for us being together."

"You make it sound like it's a business deal," I say uneasily.

"It's the only way this will work. The only way I can protect you."

"You don't need to protect me," I say.

He winces slightly. "Yes, I do."

"This sounds more like control than protection. What exactly are you protecting me from?"

He sighs. "My life can be crazy sometimes. And things move pretty fast in my world. I don't want you to get caught up in it—I don't want you to do anything you don't want to do."

"Again, I'm pretty sure I'm capable of making my own decisions." I can feel the anger starting to burn my cheeks.

"I just mean that you might not be prepared for it—the chaos that comes with dating someone like me. You saw what happened that night outside the bar. The crazy fans, everyone wanting a piece of me. It can be overwhelming. And I want to protect you from it. That means we take it one step at a time, we don't rush into anything."

"What does that mean—you want to be the one who decides when we see each other, when we go on dates, how *far* we go?"

He runs a hand over his eyes, a weary gesture. "Look, I know it seems extreme, but you don't understand what it's like. That night after Lola's, that's the tip of the iceberg. Everything I do is amplified, it's scrutinized and studied and judged. I . . . I have to have control over everything I do."

"And you want control over me, too?"

"No. But dating me won't be like dating anyone else. It

comes with complications and I'm the one who knows how to navigate them. That means I need to set boundaries. For your protection and mine."

"Rules, you mean. And what if I want to see you, what if I want to kiss you? Am I allowed to do that?" My tone is short, and I realize I've crossed my arms, blocking him from getting any closer.

He blows out a breath of air. "Yes, of course. But there will be limits, at least at first. I need you to trust me."

I shake my head and look away from him, clenching and unclenching my teeth.

"It's just how it has to be, Charlotte." But his voice is not soothing or pleading. He knows I'm beyond comforting.

My mother's ring is suddenly heavy on my finger. I touch it with my thumb. "No," I say, a chill rising across my flesh. "This isn't what I want—not like this. I'm trying to understand, but all you want to do is set limits. That's not how it's supposed to be."

"It's the only way." Everything about him seems hard, suddenly.

My mouth goes dry. I can't believe what he's saying. I drop my arms and straighten my posture, looking him straight in the eye. "Then I guess we can't do this." I take a full step away from him, my eyes unable to blink, my hands shaking. My whole life has been about *me* having control: controlling my future, making all the right decisions. Blazing my own path, like my grandmother said. I've never let anyone control me, and I'm certainly not about to start now.

He doesn't even try to stop me, to convince me to stay, but I can feel him watching me as I turn and walk through the foyer.

I want him . . . but not like this.

I don't look back, rushing out through the front door, my feet slapping against the stone and my eyes stinging from the surge of tears.

The still night air sweeps over me as soon as I step outside and I gulp it in, imagining that it will cool my burning flesh, all the places where he touched me.

The places where I will never feel his touch again.

I throw back the blankets, the heat palpable, sweat rising in a sheen along the curves of my body. The window is open beside my bed, but no breeze rushes through. There's only the sound of insects ticking and humming, a world in motion.

I force my eyelids closed, my body now splayed out across the top of the sheet. But my brain won't stop cycling through memories of Tate. I can still taste his lips, his mouth on mine, the rush of his hands, the murmur of his voice as he sang his song against my ear.

Do you want to take a chance? he asked earlier tonight, standing in front of me right after we kissed. *I have to have control over everything. It's the only way this will work. The only way I can protect you.* His words keep replaying in my head. But why does he need control? What is he so afraid of? And why is he so certain I'm going to get hurt?

I roll over in bed, cramming my face against my pillow, trying to suffocate my own thoughts so I can get some sleep.

I need you to trust me, he said. And I want to—desperately, I want to trust him. But I'm not sure how. I've never been with anyone before—I have nothing to compare this to. Yet I'm certain no one Carlos has ever dated needed this much control over their relationship.

I know Tate's different. He's famous and wealthy and lives a life I probably can't even imagine. But Tate made it sound like he was actually worried something might happen to me—like dating him might somehow destroy my life.

I flip onto my back, eyes wide open, staring up at the white-spackled ceiling. I don't need his protection. Just like I told him tonight: I'm capable of making my own decisions.

And my own mistakes.

If this is what I want, then what am I so afraid of? If he needs control—fine. If he wants to decide how this relationship is going to work—who cares? If he wants to tell me how far is too far when it comes to being together—it's worth it.

This is *my* life. And if I want him, then I deserve to have him. I don't care about the stipulations. Or the fine print.

I roll over in bed and reach for my cell phone: 3:10 a.m. I cycle through my calls and find the number from the night at the flower shop, when he was waiting for me outside. It rings only once when he picks up, his voice deep.

"Charlotte?"

"Okay," I say into the phone. My body is still keyed up,

trembling from the sweat now cooling across my skin. "We'll try this your way."

I exhale as silence slips between us. I can hear his breathing on the other end, so clear that if I close my eyes, I could almost imagine him here in my room with me. "I've been thinking about you all night," he says finally. "I haven't been able to sleep." That explains why he answered on the first ring. "I'm glad you changed your mind." There is a smile in his voice, and that's when I know I've made the right choice.

I don't care anymore.

I don't care about limits or boundaries.

I don't care about sticking to my rules.

I just want him.

NINE

"**WHAT HAPPENED TO YOU?**" **CARLOS** asks, planting his elbow against the metal locker next to ours.

The memory of last night still hums inside my head: the 3 a.m. phone call to Tate, my skin ablaze from the humid night air. I suppress a smile so Carlos won't see. I'm not ready to tell him about Tate. Maybe a part of me is worried what he'll say—that even for all his teasing, he might actually be disappointed in me for going against my own no-dating policy. And then there's the fact that I'm dating Tate Collins. And I don't really want this information getting out—if I thought the spectacle of the flower delivery in the middle of class was embarrassing, I can only imagine the kind of attention I'd get if our relationship was public knowledge. So for now, for today, I'm not going to say anything. As much as I don't like keeping it from Carlos, I'm keeping Tate's words in mind and taking it slow.

"What do you mean?" I ask, dropping my backpack inside the locker.

"You're glowing."

"No, I'm not." But I touch my cheeks with my fingertips, as if I could wipe it away. I pull out my first-period history book — the brown paper cover filled from edge to edge with sketches of exotic flowers and dancing figures I've drawn during Mr. Trenton's more boring history lectures.

"You are," Carlos says, dropping his elbow and leaning in close. "I know you — you're glowing. Which is an improvement considering how mopey you've been for the last three weeks."

Amy Rogers shimmies in beside Carlos, trying to get to her locker, but Carlos doesn't budge, waiting for me to respond before he'll move.

I scowl at him. "I haven't been mopey." The words sound lame even to me. "I'm just glad it's Friday," I say, as if the approaching weekend explains my radiant complexion.

Carlos seems to believe me. "Well, *I'm* glad the old Charlotte is back. And I'm also in desperate need of a weekend. Mrs. Duncan clobbered us with homework in calc and I'm thinking of setting fire to my textbook in protest."

"I'm sure staging a demonstration will be a very effective solution," I answer, smiling up at him.

"Glad you agree. I've also decided to binge on Netflix tomorrow to forget all my woes."

I'm nodding along, but then my phone chimes from inside my purse, and I quickly rummage for it.

"I'll see you in English," Carlos says. "And, Charlotte . . .

welcome back." He turns and wends his way through the sea of students already headed to first period.

I pull out my phone, the screen still glowing from a text.

It's from Tate.

Can I see you?

My chest flutters, ignites, and I glance around the crowded hall, as if anyone walking by might somehow be able to figure out that I'm texting with Tate Collins. But everyone ignores me—as usual.

Yes. I type back.

Another text pops up on the screen. *Today?*

I'm about to respond when the four-tone bell blares from the hallway speaker above me: only five minutes until class starts. I slam the locker shut and weave into the crowd. As I walk, I type back, *Tell me where,* and hit SEND.

The day ticks by with excruciating slowness. We're reviewing more material for our exams, but I barely take it in, and there is a pop quiz in history that I hardly remember finishing.

Aside from a serious lack of sleep that's making it impossible to focus, I also keep checking my phone, waiting for a response from Tate that never comes.

At the end of the day, Carlos and I exit through the massive double doors, the sun streaming through the row of palm trees lining the street, and I lift a hand to shield my eyes. Carlos keeps talking, telling me how in PE today he accidentally nailed Amanda Coats in the face playing dodgeball.

"I felt terrible, obviously," he's saying. "But that girl wears too much makeup during PE and it's like the balls are drawn to her face—" If his story continues, I don't hear it. My gaze has drifted out to the street, past the mob of students fanning out away from the school.

There, at the curb, is Tate's car.

"I heard Mike Logan's having a party tonight." Carlos's voice slips back into my ears. "Maybe we should go. It might be entertaining."

"I can't," I say, turning my gaze from the car back to Carlos. He hasn't noticed it yet.

"What could you possibly be doing tonight? It's Friday, Char. Homework and studying can happen tomorrow. And you said Holly gave you the night off."

"I know—" I say, touching a strand of hair and tucking it behind my ear. "It's just . . . I should get a head start on studying for the next history exam. I think I bombed the quiz today."

"Doubt it. Charlotte Reed never bombs quizzes." He's right, except I haven't been as focused these last three weeks and even an A– would be a setback with Stanford looming on the horizon.

"I'll make it up to you next week. Coffee and reality TV at my house?"

Carlos exhales loudly. "Fine." But even annoyed with me, he kisses my cheek before heading away. "Call me tomorrow! I need your help with calc, don't forget!"

I wave him away, pretending to search for something in my backpack. When Carlos crosses the street and is out of sight,

I walk down the steps toward the car. It hasn't moved since I stepped outside. I start to doubt myself as I get closer; maybe I'm wrong—maybe it's not Tate.

But then the door swings open.

I pause, staring at the dark interior.

"You coming?" a voice speaks from the darkness—Tate's voice.

My heart leaps upward, and I do a quick sweep of the parking lot and front lawn. Only Jenna Sanchez, who I think is still upset that I got roses that day in English and she didn't, stares at me briefly from her circle of friends chatting on the sidewalk. But then she turns away.

I take off my backpack and slide into the passenger seat. Inside, Tate smiles at me. He looks almost shy. "Hey," he says.

"I didn't know you were picking me up."

"I wanted to surprise you."

"It worked." I try to keep a smile from breaking across my lips. I don't want him to know how happy I am to see him. It feels silly and girly and not like me.

"I know you probably still have doubts. But when you called last night, I . . . I couldn't wait to see you again."

I shift my eyes to his. He is curved lips and dark eyes and a million mysteries I haven't yet solved. And my heart starts to climb just by looking at him. Any exhaustion I felt earlier has quickly evaporated. Being here with Tate sets alight every nerve ending.

And then, in his hands, I notice a black strip of fabric. "What's that?" I ask.

"A blindfold." The dimple winks at me. "I want to take you somewhere and it's a surprise."

I hesitate, shifting uneasily in the seat. *A blindfold, seriously?* I should get out now. Head home and work on my Stanford essays, tackle my homework, give Mia a break with Leo, anything but this. But instead, I stay put.

"Charlotte," he says, his voice soft. "Do you trust me?" He said something similar last night. I know it's important to him and I want him to know that I'm trying. That I want to give this a shot with him.

So I nod. "I trust you."

I turn around in my seat, facing the window. My reflection stares back: wide eyes, hair drifting over my face. And then my reflection is gone. Tate wraps the black fabric across my eyes and I bite down on my lower lip.

"Is it too tight?" he whispers in my ear.

I shake my head. A heady warmth unspools in my stomach at the feeling of his breath, hot against my ear.

"No peeking," he adds.

The car begins to move, gliding out into traffic.

With my sight gone, the rest of my senses are heightened. I can hear the slow, easy breathing of Tate beside me. His scent is of clean, crisp cologne and something else, like the salty air of the beach. I imagine him moving closer, what it would feel like to have his hands on me, without my being able to see him.

There is silence between us for several blocks and then Tate finally speaks. "What are you thinking?"

"I'm not—" I begin, but catch myself. I can tell he wants a real answer, I can sense it in the tone of his voice—he wants the truth. But I can't bring myself to tell him I'm picturing his hands on my skin. "I'm thinking about the ocean," I say, partly honest.

"What about the ocean?"

"The air," I say. "It smells like salt and sun, and also slightly green. And—" I pause, but Tate doesn't speak. I can barely even hear his breathing now, like he's suspended, waiting for me to continue. "I'm thinking about the feel of the waves," I add, "when they rise up over your legs. When I was little, I always thought the sea was alive, trying to drag you out with it. It's so . . . desperate, like it tugs from the farthest part of the ocean floor. Sometimes I want to let it—let it take me out into the deep, where I could drift for thousands of miles. Until I wash ashore on some distant continent. I like the idea of that."

There's a long silence, and I wonder if he's looking at me. "I like the way you think about things," he says finally, and I hear him shift on the seat.

I lick my lips, then bite the bottom one. I hear Tate inhale. "Charlotte . . ." he says, his voice pleading.

"What?"

"Just . . . don't do that, okay?"

"Why not?" I say, and to my surprise, I'm comfortable again. I'm enjoying this. I take my lip back between my teeth, bite down gently. Knowing his eyes are on me makes me tingle all over. Like he's touching me, even though he's not. Like it's his teeth on my lip.

"Charlotte. I don't think I can handle it," he tells me, and I can hear the smile in his voice. "You'll make me crazy."

So he's not the only one with power here, no matter what he says. I lean back in my seat, smiling to myself.

The car comes to a slow stop and I realize the sounds of the city have dulled. We're not on a main street anymore.

I feel a sudden swirl of wind when the car door opens—it coils around me and sends chills rushing down my arms even though the air is warm and balmy. Tate's hands touch mine in a burst of electricity, and he guides me out of the car. A horn honks in the distance. I have no idea where we are.

We walk only a few steps before moving through a doorway into a building that smells faintly of dust and upholstery.

Then the toe of my shoe meets with something hard.

"Steps," Tate says beside me.

I lift my right foot, tentative at first, afraid I'm going to careen forward and land on my face. But Tate holds me firmly—one hand on the small of my back, the other laced through my fingers—as we move up a series of carpeted stairs.

"Where are we?" I ask when we reach the top, my free hand extending forward to feel for anything that might give away our location. But my fingertips feel only open air. And Tate doesn't answer. Instead, he leads me forward, then releases me completely. I feel unmoored, like I could fall at any second.

"Tate?" I whisper again, reaching my fingers up to touch the blindfold covering my eyes, but he is suddenly beside me, his hands trailing up my arms, slowly, slowly. I hold in a breath, feeling his fingers glide up my neck to the back of my head, where he finally loosens the blindfold and it falls away.

I have to blink to bring the dimmed expanse of the room into focus. It's a theater, grand and ornate, with gold rimming the arched ceiling and red curtains draped all the way to the floor. We are on a second-floor balcony, overlooking scores of empty seats below and a massive screen at the front. There are ladders against one wall and cans of paint and white cloths spread out across the floor. The theater is under construction.

"It's called the Lumiere," Tate says beside me. "Have you heard of it?"

I shake my head, looking at him for the first time since he untied the blindfold. He looks almost anxious, like he's hoping I'll like the surprise. "It's incredible," I tell him.

"It was one of the original theaters in Hollywood. It's been open off and on over the years, mostly showing second-rate films. But they're finally restoring it."

I walk toward the railing, touching the cool metal bar with my palms, and peer down at the first floor below. Some of the chairs are missing from the rows. "Are we supposed to be here?" I ask.

Tate's mouth softens into a smile. "I made arrangements."

I turn, noticing a small table set up beside two of the front-row chairs facing the railing. A fancy bottle of sparkling water, a massive bowl of popcorn, and little glass dishes with an assortment of colorful candies sit arranged on the white tablecloth.

He leads me to the two chairs and we sit. Almost immediately, the lights begin to dim, controlled from somewhere I can't see. All perfectly choreographed. I can't believe I'm sitting here with him—Tate Collins—in a theater that's not even open to the public. How does a person rent out a place like this? And how much did it cost him? But I wouldn't ask any of these things. Instead I say, "What are we watching?"

His left eyebrow lifts, a silent challenge. "You'll see."

As if on cue, the massive movie screen flickers ahead of us, the pale light playing across Tate's face. The black-and-white images take shape on the screen: a map of Africa, then it shifts to a grainy, distorted scene of a busy marketplace. The audio has that distant, echoed quality of an old movie. I smile, remembering our night at Lola's—he'd been so surprised when I told him I'd never seen *Casablanca*. And now we're about to watch it . . . together.

In the darkness of the theater, I can feel Tate's eyes on me. He seems so still, reclined back in his seat, his gaze palpable as he watches me during the first kissing scene between our hero, Humphrey Bogart, and his lost love, Ingrid Bergman, in a flashback in Paris—where they first fell in love. I wait for Tate to touch me, expect his hand to lift and cover mine where they're folded in my lap. Once, I even think he's going to brush my knee when he leans forward to pour me some water, but he never touches me, not once. He's keeping his distance. Only his eyes have managed to slip across my skin.

When the movie ends and the two lovers say their good-byes, the plane rising up into the dark horizon, the screen turns black and the lights against the theater walls illuminate once again. Tate turns in his seat. His eyes trail over my lips. "Did you like it?"

I touch a finger to the armrest separating us, a divide that cannot be crossed. "It was wonderful," I say, not sure how honest I should be when he's arranged this incredible surprise.

"But?" he asks. As usual, he hears what I'm not saying.

"It was just so tragic."

"Why do you think that?"

"They don't end up together. She leaves and then that's it. It's so sad."

"So you didn't like it?" he asks. But far from looking disappointed as I feared, he actually seems intrigued.

"No. I did. I loved it. It's just not how I thought it would end. It didn't seem right." I feel awkward admitting it, but his eyes are amused.

"It's a classic love story," he reminds me.

"But I want them to end up together. That's the point of a love story, isn't it? Two lovers sacrificing everything just to be together." I've never been a romantic, obviously, but even I loved *Romeo & Juliet*.

"They did make sacrifices." Tate pauses as if to choose his next words. "They gave each other up, even though they were in love. Sometimes life makes it impossible to be with the person you love."

I know this might be too bold, maybe I shouldn't ask, but I'm curious. There's so much I still don't know about him. And so much I want to know. "Have you ever been in love?"

He stands, his jeans hanging low over his waist. "No," he says briefly. "Have you?"

I snort. "Please. I told you I'd never even kissed anyone."

I think he's going to smile back, but instead his gaze is far away. I try to read something deeper in the cool darkness of his eyes, the subtle tightening of his jaw that makes the features of his face seem remote.

"You ready?" he finally asks.

I stand slowly, turning in a circle to absorb the massive theater one last time before we leave. "Thank you for this. I won't ever forget it."

He reaches for my hand, twining his fingers through mine, and we walk back down the red-carpeted stairs that I couldn't see earlier, to a metal door that Tate pushes open. The Tesla—I've learned Tate's sleek black car is called a Tesla—is waiting outside. And twilight has fallen while we were in the theater.

He opens the passenger door for me and I touch the roof of the car, about to slip inside, when I notice a group of girls sauntering down the alley, their short, glittery dresses shifting across their thighs, their heels dangerously tall. I glance down and I'm struck suddenly by the averageness of my own appearance: my plain jean shorts, my dirty navy-blue ballet flats and my brown hair pulled up into a ponytail.

I'm ordinary. I am not those girls. I'm not the Jenna Sanchezes or Sophie Zineses of the world, commanding attention wherever I go. And even though I am completely aware that sequined dresses and heels do not make these girls any better than me, something inside me feels envious seeing them: the kind of girl I imagine Tate *should* be with.

And I suddenly wish I had a wardrobe full of dresses, slinky black tops, and designer heels I could wear on dates like this. But I don't. And somehow Tate is with me anyway.

"Everything okay?" Tate asks beside me.

"Sure," I answer, sliding into the car. I was staring too long and Tate noticed.

There is silence as we drive—not an uneasy silence, but the kind that feels like we're both waiting for something. Once again, I can't believe I'm here. Not just because he's Tate Collins. I can't believe I'm on a date, that despite everything I've done to build a life that guys like Tate have no part of, I don't want today to end. It's like my insides are at war—wanting to stay away and urging me closer.

I tell Tate to park a block away from my house. I don't want Grandma or Mia to notice me stepping out of a car like this. The bouquet of flowers was one thing, but Tate Collins driving me home would be much harder to lie about.

Tate steps out onto the curb. I notice his gaze sweeping over the surrounding houses and apartment buildings: balconies cluttered with BBQs and plastic chairs and bicycles, my neighbor's Buick that hasn't moved in years, rusting where it sits. A boy is dribbling a basketball up the sidewalk, making occasional karate-type moves with his arms. He doesn't even notice us.

"How long have you lived here?" Tate asks. I wish there was a way to gloss over what he sees, tell him it's usually not this bad, or that we're only just living here temporarily. But that won't fix the truth—that this is my home.

"Most of my life," I say. "My sister and I moved in with my grandma when we were pretty young."

"Older sister or younger?"

"Older."

"Is she as smart as you?"

"Yes and no."

He smiles, sensing there's a longer story there.

"Thank you for the movie," I say again.

"I'm glad you liked it, but also hated it."

I smile up at him. "I didn't hate it," I argue. "It was just the ending I didn't agree with."

"You're a romantic, then?" he asks.

"Only recently," I say and feel myself blush.

We stand only a few inches apart, the air between us so still that I feel light-headed for a moment. Being this close reminds me of the way his mouth felt on mine last night, how he pressed his body against me, bare-chested, the heat from the fireplace making my skin thrum.

I take an unconscious step toward him, closing the distance between us to the merest inch. I want to feel him again, the taste of his mouth, hot and cold all at once. I stop breathing.

His fingers touch my waist, pressing into my hip bone. But he doesn't draw me nearer, just pushes gently against me, stopping me. He blinks, then refocuses.

"We're taking it slow, remember?" he says.

His eyes shift from my lips up to my eyes and I nearly laugh. I've spent my life avoiding guys—guys like Tate, especially. I thought they'd only want one thing from me and now here he is, telling *me* to slow down.

"Right," I say, forcing my body to straighten.

I should be glad that he wants to go slow. I shouldn't want anything more. And yet . . .

"Good night, Charlotte Reed," he says, releasing his fingers where they have lingered against my hip.

"Good night, Tate Collins," I answer, my voice much softer than his, and I take a step away, up the sidewalk.

I can hear the low hum of the Tesla idling behind me, but I don't look back. I refuse to be the girl who looks back. But I know his eyes watch me until I disappear around the corner.

And I can still feel his eyes on me long after I've buried myself between the cool sheets of my bed, pulling a pillow over my face and replaying the way his fingers swept deftly across my hip, keeping me from moving any closer, from touching him, from kissing him.

And I fall asleep dreaming about his hands.

TEN

MY PHONE IS VIBRATING ON the bedside table. I roll over just in time to see it fall from the edge onto the floor, still buzzing.

I reach down and pick it up.

I slept in. It's nearly ten a.m.

There's a missed call from Carlos, a voice mail, probably asking me what time I can meet up to study today. And there's a text from Tate.

Immediately, I open the text: *I want you to see what I see.*

I read it again, then twice more. I drop the phone onto the pale yellow comforter I've kicked off me and brush my hair back from my eyes. What does he mean? I think about responding with a question mark, but my phone vibrates again.

Tate: *I'm outside.*

I spring up from the bed.

There's no time to shower, so I shimmy out of my pajama shorts and tank top and dig through my narrow dresser for a clean bra and underwear, texting my excuses to Carlos in between pulling on each article of clothing. My bedroom window is open and the morning breeze is balmy. I dress in jean shorts—not the same pair from yesterday—and a pale pink shirt with a scoop neck that clings to the curves of my body. Every time I wear it Carlos whistles and says, "Damn, girl."

On Saturday mornings, Grandma goes to the senior center for Zumba. So the only person I have to contend with is Mia.

I find her in the kitchen, washing Leo's bottles, her sleeves rolled up and hair slipping out of a low bun.

"Where you going?" she asks, wiping her forearm across her forehead, water dripping down her temple.

"Out . . . to meet Carlos," I say.

"You usually do homework on Saturdays," she says absently, like she's not really interested in the answer.

I reach the front door, gripping the knob. I would prefer to tell as few lies as possible—so the sooner I leave the better. "Yeah. That's what we're doing. Working on calculus stuff." I wince—my voice sounds so false. But Mia doesn't seem to notice.

"I thought you could watch Leo for me tonight. I'm supposed to meet Greg at the Palapa. They're having live music."

"Greg?" I ask.

"Yeah, you know, Greg. The guy I had to cancel on a few weeks back because your extracurriculars are way more important than helping out your sister and spending time with your nephew?" Her words are harsh but her voice just sounds tired. "So, can you watch Leo tonight?"

I stare down at my hand on the knob. I want to help her—I really do. "Sure," I say. "If I'm back in time." I turn the doorknob quickly. I need to get out of here before she asks any more questions. "But no guarantees."

"Charlotte," she calls, but I'm already shutting the door behind me. I jog down the stairs before Mia can say anything else.

Tate is waiting for me a block away, the Tesla purring in place, around the corner where he dropped me off last night. My heart is thumping from the sprint and I take in a deep breath before opening the door.

"I was beginning to think you were standing me up," Tate says when I slide onto the passenger seat.

"You didn't give me much warning. I was still in bed."

His dimple flashes and his eyes flicker from some thought skating through his mind. I smile as he revs the engine and pulls away from the curb.

"I realized that I need to work harder to impress you," Tate says as we cross over into the polished neighborhoods of Beverly Hills, where the hedges are ten feet tall and gates guard the mansions inside. It's a funny thing about living in LA: A crappy house like ours is only a short drive from the biggest mansions in the world. A girl like me can meet a guy like Tate, like we exist in the same world. It's hard to imagine, and yet here we are.

"Impress me?" I ask, facing him. He watches the road as we glide past silver Mercedes and white Bentleys and steel-gray Ferraris, all with windows rolled down to let in the warm Pacific air.

"Renting out the famous Lumiere Theater to watch *Casablanca* apparently does not impress Charlotte Reed."

"Trust me, I was impressed."

"It's okay," he says, one eyebrow lifting, like he's not buying it. "I like a challenge."

He makes a sudden turn, pulling to a stop in front of a small valet stand.

"You don't need expensive things to be beautiful," Tate continues, his gaze seeming to take in each feature of my face. "But I want you to have them anyway."

"I don't understand," I say as he opens his door. "What are we doing?" But he's already walking around to my door, extending a hand to help me out. I step onto the sidewalk and look up at an impressive black awning, the words *Barneys New York* in white letters.

"Tate?" I ask, craning my head upward. I've seen Barneys from the outside, of course, but I've never stopped, never actually gotten out of the car. As if I knew they wouldn't even allow me to park my Volvo anywhere near here.

"Come on," Tate says, suddenly beside me, tossing his keys to a valet. He slips his fingers into mine and pulls me forward, but I stop at the doors before going inside, my stomach starting to flutter with nerves.

"I don't think—" I begin, unsure how to explain what I'm feeling.

"What's wrong?"

"You don't need to do this," I say, but he folds his arm around my waist and draws me to him. It's the most contact we've had since I showed up at his house the other night, and my body catches fire at the feeling of his arms around me.

"Charlotte, I saw the way you looked at those girls yesterday— after the movie? And I don't know how many times I can tell you how beautiful you are, but for some reason you don't see it. So I was thinking last night that maybe you need to *feel* beautiful, too. That maybe I can do that for you."

I smile, blushing again at the word *beautiful*. I know I'm pretty enough, mostly because Mia and I look so similar, but I've always downplayed my looks. They're not important to me, they never have been. But I can't help but glance toward the doors of Barneys, and wonder what's inside.

"You do," I tell him, meeting his dark eyes. "You already make me feel that way. But this . . . it's too much."

"It's not. And I told you, I like a challenge." He tilts his head down, his lips grazing my cheek.

A shudder races through me, and I draw in a shallow breath, biting the edge of my lower lip. "Okay," I acquiesce and he pulls me inside, his fingers strumming against mine: a rhythm, a beat tapping from his fingertips, as if music is inside him, wanting to be let out.

Inside the store, Tate speaks to a woman who seems to

have been expecting us, and before long I am being led by two salesgirls through what can only be deemed a fashionista's paradise. They pull short sequined dresses and silky tops and black leggings from the racks, swiftly carrying them away as soon as I've agreed to try them on. They lead me through floor after floor, a whirl of departments and brands and price tags far too expensive. And the entire time Tate is close by, sometimes looking distracted, like he's worried he might be seen by one of the other customers moving about the store, but whenever our eyes meet, he smiles—enjoying this maybe more than I am.

Eventually, the two salesgirls usher me back to the fitting rooms; they help zip zippers that I can't reach and smooth out wrinkles in the fabric when I stand before a massive full-length mirror. They swap out sizes and bring me shoes to try with different outfits. Soon I can't even keep track of what I've tried on and what I liked. But they seem to have a system.

Occasionally, I emerge from the dressing room to show Tate, but he rarely gives his opinion. "If *you* love it, then get it," he says, smiling. "And stop looking at prices. It doesn't matter," he adds when I try to put back a dress because it costs more than I make in an entire year.

My mind gets hazy somewhere around outfit number twelve, but before I know it, we're heading back out the doors, an enormous bag tucked under Tate's arm.

I'm not ready to think about how much he spent. Instead I smile down at the much smaller bag looped around my wrist. As embarrassed as I'd been when the salesgirls had brought me the pretty, pale blue push-up bra to try on under one of the dresses, the reflection in the mirror had been so . . . un-me, so strangely grown-up, that I knew it had to be mine, no matter the cost. It's the one item I wouldn't let Tate see or pay for. I considered it a personal victory when he moved away from the cash register with only a token amount of grumbling.

Outside, I look for the valet but Tate grabs my hand. "Time for the next surprise," he says, tugging me down Wilshire before I can protest.

The salon is tucked back off a side street. A discreet stucco building with a sign that reads simply Q. A man steps into the waiting area and introduces himself as Steven. His bleached blond hair stands up from his forehead like spikes on a fence, and when he smiles, it reveals a narrow gap between his two front teeth. Like Hank, he is tall and built like a weight lifter, with arms that flex beneath a skintight lavender shirt.

I look back at Tate once more, savoring his reassuring smile as the man leads me into a long rectangular room, to a seat among a row of empty chairs facing a stretch of mirrors.

Tate waits in the lobby. The entire place was cleared out just for us.

"How long have you had this hair?" Steven asks, pulling away the hair tie that held my ponytail in place, letting the coffee-brown strands hang loose over my shoulders.

I recognize Steven, I realize. I've seen him before, just snippets I think, on one of the reality TV shows Mia likes to watch. He's a hairdresser to the stars. Steven Salazar is his name, I recall. And *Q*, I remember now, is the name of his tiny white dog. His salon is named after his dog.

"Since about 1999," I answer dryly, then bite my lip, not wanting to offend the man who's about to take scissors to my hair.

He spins me around suddenly in the chair, pressing his palms into the armrests and staring directly into my eyes. "Close your eyes," he tells me.

"Close . . . my eyes?" I echo dumbly.

"Yes. I don't want you to *see* your hair, I want you to envision it." Steven Salazar's skin is like marble. He raises one perfectly arched eyebrow and the skin of his forehead doesn't even wrinkle.

I blink, then give in, shutting my eyes. "Now," Steven says in a hushed voice, as if whatever he's about to tell me is a secret. "Imagine you could have any hair you wanted. Imagine you could take any risk, and if you didn't like it, your old, boring hair would grow back tomorrow. What would you do?"

Boring? I open my eyes and squint, like I can picture something new. The word is right at the tip of my tongue but I hesitate to say it.

"Oh, do tell. I can see you have some scandalous thoughts swirling around in there."

"Blond. A little blond," I hedge.

Steven stands up straight and his eyebrows lift. "So the lovely brunette wants to go blond." He taps his finger against his temple and rolls his tongue against the inside of his cheek. "Hmmm," he says, pondering the word. Then he says definitively: "Highlights."

He whips me back around in the chair so I'm facing the mirrors.

"Hold on tight, girl, I'm about to give you the most exhilarating two hours of your life. Unless of course . . ." He winks and flicks his chin toward the waiting room, where I last saw Tate. I glance in the same direction, but I can't see him anymore. He's not sitting on any of the sleek wood waiting chairs. "Perhaps Mr. Tate Collins has already . . . enlightened you?" Steven adds, then pauses, bending low beside me and staring at me through the mirror.

"Not entirely," I hear myself say, and Steven flicks his head back in a laugh.

"Smart girl. Never kiss and tell. Not in this town."

Steven goes to work brushing a chalky purple liquid down separated strands of my hair, then folding each strand into its own foil. Then I wait, flipping through a gossip magazine. My heart trips when I spot a photo of Tate on one of the pages. He's standing in a crowd, one hand above his face, like he's trying to move unrecognized through the swarm of people. The caption reads, TATE COLLINS SPOTTED IN PUBLIC AFTER A YEAR IN HIDING. I realize it's a photo from the night we ate at Lola's, when he was mobbed outside the bar—the night I found out who he really was. Already that night feels like a hundred years ago.

Once the blond streaks have been seared into my dark hair, Steven wields a shiny pair of shears and begins trimming my hair one section at a time. I hold my breath, watching as pieces float down to the white tile floor.

When he's done cutting, the noise of the blow dryer fills the salon, and I actually close my eyes, not wanting to see the final result, afraid I'll hate it. Afraid I'll have regrets. But when he tells me to open my eyes, I can't help but blink at my reflection.

My hair drifts down to my shoulders in swooping layers that give the effect of a day spent at the beach: effortless and sun-kissed. The blond highlights magnify my green eyes — two emeralds that seem almost translucent against the platinum. I run my fingers through a section; streaks of my natural brown are still threaded among the beachy-blond. I lift it up and let it settle back against my shoulders.

I stand, leaning closer to the mirror. "I didn't know my hair could look like this."

"I am rather amazing," Steven says, winking. I smile and spin around to face him. "Now you look like the Charlotte you were born to be." I actually feel like I might cry, the emotion welling up behind my eyes. So much has happened today: Tate surprising me this morning, taking me on a whirlwind shopping trip, and now this. Without even thinking about it, I step forward and hug Steven. But he squeezes his arms around me like he's used to it. He smells like coconut and clove. "They all cry after their first time," he says, winking and laughing at his own implied joke.

"Thank you," I tell him, and I mean it.

"Oh, you're not done yet," he says. "This was only the

beginning." Again, he gives me a sly look. "Marielle will be doing your makeup next."

A woman emerges from a doorway to my left, her cheeks a rosy pink and her hair straight inky-black with severe bangs that almost touch her eyelashes. She takes my hand and Steven gives a little bow when I look back at him, just before I'm led around a corner and into another part of the salon.

I sit in a plush white chair, nervously tapping my foot against the metal rung beneath my feet. I've rarely worn makeup and I have no idea what to expect. The mascara wand feels like it's going to poke my eye out, and I'm pretty sure the eyelash curler is going to pull out every hair. But she artfully tilts my head this way and that like I'm her canvas and she is lost in the rhythm of each stroke of her hand.

"All done, Charlotte," she finally says, and I open my eyes. The reflection staring back at me belongs to someone else.

Seeing the new hair was like putting on a wig at Halloween— it looked cool, but somehow temporary—but seeing my face like this, so transformed, is like waking up from some strange dream.

"Do you like it?" Marielle asks. She drops her hands from her waist, still holding a makeup brush in her right fingertips.

I can't take my eyes off the mirror. My lips are glossy and somehow plumper, a pink that matches my cheekbones, like I've just finished a quick jog in cold weather. My eyes are lined with a sultry charcoal gray, and my entire face seems brushed in creamy porcelain. I look . . . incredible. And yet, I still look like me.

"I'll take that as a yes." She smiles and unclips a cape that had been draped around my neck. I look down and am reminded of the sad shorts and T-shirt I'm still wearing.

"I think there's something waiting for you in the bathroom," Marielle says. She takes me down a short hallway and opens a door on the left. Inside is a restroom with white chaise lounges and ornate mirrors painted gold with ribbons hanging along the edges.

And then I see it. Draped against a wall, hanging from a hook, is a long red dress. It's flowy, with a high neck and bare shoulders and one long slit up the leg. I had noticed it at Barneys but didn't try it on—I knew it would be too expensive, I could tell just by glancing at it. But here it is.

This feels like too much, more than I can accept. But when I run my hands down the soft fabric, I know I have to try it on.

I strip out of my old clothes and pull the dress over my head. It settles perfectly against my body—like liquid poured over skin, like it was constructed just for me. I touch my stomach, feeling the smooth fabric, then eye myself in the floor-to-ceiling mirror. I look . . . stunning. I can't say no to this dress. Just like I seem incapable of saying no to Tate.

Then I spot a pair of strappy black heels waiting on the floor—for me, I assume. I step into them, standing up and marveling at my height. *Will I even be able to walk in these?*

I fold up my old clothes, then stuff them into a plastic bag hanging from the back of the door, with *Q* printed on the front—clearly usually used to tote hair products.

Sucking in a deep breath, I leave the bathroom and walk out into the lobby.

Tate is standing beside the front door, staring out the window.

As if sensing me, he turns—and stops, frozen.

His expression is arrested, and for several breathless moments he's silent, his gaze washing over me. Then his eyes meet mine. "You," he says slowly, "are incredible."

The heat in his eyes unsettles me and I have to force myself to exhale, to breathe, to not crumble in the wake of his gaze. "Thank you for the dress," I say, touching the fabric along my waist. "It's beautiful."

"You're beautiful," he says, and he takes the plastic bag from me. Already it feels like a lifetime ago that I wore the clothes inside—a different Charlotte, in a different reality.

But I'm getting used to this one.

Il Cielo is not a restaurant—it is another world. Enchanted and magical and dripping in vines that crawl up the redbrick walls and chandeliers that hang from a sea of lights that turn everything a smoldering golden-white.

I feel like I'm in a fairy tale: some lost scene from *A Midsummer Night's Dream*. A world imagined by Shakespeare, where fairies and unrequited lovers dance and make love and confess their obsessions for one another.

Tate sits across from me in the outdoor garden, nestled into a far corner. Our waitress is a tiny, bouncy thing with a pixie haircut and rosy cheeks, which only further inspires the feeling that we've been transported to some romantic otherworld.

Tate watches me as we eat and it sends threads of heat across my skin. I wonder again how just a look can make me forget everything I promised myself, forget my mom's mistakes, and Mia's.

"Tell me about your family," Tate says, almost as if he's reading my mind.

I sigh. "Well, my mom had me when she was really young, and she died when I was twelve. I never knew my dad. I have an older sister, too, and she has a son named Leo. He's almost nine months old. And we all live with my grandmother. There's not that much else to tell."

He levels a look at me, like he knows there's more. "I'm sorry about your mom," he says. "You must miss her."

The memory of the night she died seeps into my mind, even though I try to keep it at bay. Mom and her boyfriend at the time, Ray, drove their brown Chevy straight into a concrete barrier on I-5 just south of San Clemente. They had been drinking, and were so pumped full of drugs that the police said if the car crash hadn't killed them, they might have OD'd later that night anyway. Which is not exactly a comforting thing for a twelve-year-old to hear. But I had been eavesdropping from my bedroom doorway when the two policemen stood in my grandmother's living room, telling her the news. Mia and I had been living with Grandma for three years at that point, only seeing my mom sporadically every couple months when she'd show up, needing a place to crash for the night.

"I do," I say. "But it's sort of complicated. My mom left us when we were pretty young, so I don't know . . ." I shrug. "I've spent most of my life trying not to be like her, to be honest. That's why I didn't want to go out with you in the first place. She couldn't tell a good guy from a bad one, and . . ." I trail off.

"You thought I was a bad guy?" Tate asks, his expression bemused. "Do you still think so?"

I examine him, as if I'll be able to tell more the harder I look. "Well, going by your very well-documented history in *People* and *Us Weekly*, I'd have good reason for thinking that." He starts to defend himself but I go on. "But my own empirical research is leading me to a different conclusion."

His scowl becomes a laugh, and I find myself savoring the sound. It's the first time I've heard him laugh like that—easy and unrestrained. "Empirical research, huh?"

"I'm very scientific," I remind him with a smile.

We are still laughing when we step back onto the sidewalk, and the flash of a camera explodes across my vision.

"Tate," a man shouts. And he snaps another photo.

Tate reacts immediately, pulling me against his side and putting his hand in front of my face to block the next series of bursts, the staccato of camera flashes.

"Tate!" the man shouts again, clearly trying to get Tate to face him. "Who's your date? Why have you been in hiding?

Tell us her name!" He uses the word *us*, as if there were more of them—other paparazzi—but he's the only one. Either he was tipped off, or camped out in hopes of spotting someone famous leaving the restaurant.

Tate pulls me away from the man, up the sidewalk. The camera keeps flashing and I shield my eyes with my palm.

I see the Tesla ahead. Tate rips open the side door and pushes me inside. He dives into the driver's seat and peels away. Flashes from the man's camera continue to explode against the blackened car windows until we weave into traffic.

Tate pulls up to my corner, puts the car in park, and leans back against the seat. The easy mood from dinner is a distant memory; he is stiff, his jaw set.

"At least there was only one of them," I offer, tentatively reaching out to touch his arm.

"I'm sorry," he says. "I should be more careful with you. I should never have taken you there."

"I'm fine," I say. It all happened too fast to process. And Tate seems more shaken up than I am. They're just photos— it's not like we were doing anything scandalous, anything worthy of a headline, at least I don't think so. I can't imagine the photographer will be able to sell them or use them for anything.

But Tate doesn't look at me, his expression still rigid. "I don't want you to be photographed. I don't want your life to change just because I'm in it."

"I know. But it's already changed. Not just because of the things you did today—the clothes, the salon, or the movie yesterday. You're changing me just by . . . by being with me. And it's what I want. I told you before that I'm willing to do this with you—I'm all in. You don't have to feel like you need to protect me."

His hands loosen around the steering wheel, falling into his lap. He turns to face me. "How do you do that?"

"What?"

"Say exactly what I need to hear, at exactly the right moment?"

I stare at him in the bluish glow from the dashboard, his features lit on one side, a sharp contrast. "You're the one who usually says exactly the right thing," I tell him, thinking of all the moments when his words undid me, convinced me to go on a date with him, go for a ride in his car, then when I agreed to be with him on his terms. He has a way of making me forget about everything else. Except him.

He smiles, his eyes falling to my lips.

I meet his gaze, then say what I'm thinking, damn the consequences: "Can we go back to your house for a while, before I have to go home?"

He doesn't answer right away. "I can't take you to my place," he says finally, looking away out the front windshield. "I'm not sure I'll be able to control myself."

"What do you mean?"

"The way you look tonight . . . I can't keep my thoughts

focused." He swallows. "I don't trust myself. I don't trust myself with you."

I feel my heart rise swiftly in my chest. Desire suddenly sings through my veins. This day has made me someone different, bold, and I'm not afraid to touch him this time. I lift my fingers and reach across the car, stroking the side of his neck, letting them drift upward, finding his jaw and then his lips. The tips of my fingers graze his bottom lip, pressing against them, feeling their warmth, and my insides shudder.

He turns to face me, my fingers still against his mouth.

"Charlotte." The word is throaty and deep.

He touches my hand with his, pulling it away. "If I kiss you now, I won't be able to stop. I won't stop until . . ." He squeezes my hand, then rests it back in my lap. I see his eyes trail over my legs hidden beneath the dress, then back up to my neck and then my lips.

I open my mouth to speak, but he stops me. "Not yet," he says.

I exhale and every ignited cell of my body turns to ash, extinguished by his words. My heart thuds down into my stomach.

I never imagined I could feel this way, that I would be the one pressing him for more, wanting a kiss that he won't give me. But he has boundaries I don't understand. Rules that make no sense to me.

My brain switches into practical mode, rescuing me from my drowning thoughts. I glance down at my dress. I can't go inside like this.

"I need to change," I say.

Tate looks at me, hesitates, then nods, understanding. He ushers me out the passenger door and into the backseat, where the bag that holds my old clothes is waiting alongside the other shopping bags from today. He slips in the door after me so he won't be seen by any unsuspecting neighbors, but then color rises in his cheeks as if he realizes suddenly how close we are back here.

"I won't look," he says, turning his head away as if to punctuate his words.

I realize he expects me to change right here, in the car. The windows are tinted nearly black, so there's no risk of anyone outside seeing me, but still, Tate is right beside me, a breath away.

But I don't really have another option.

I unstrap the black heels and slip my feet out one at a time. The soles of my feet had begun to ache, and I rub my heels briefly. I attempt to unzip the back of my dress, but in this awkward position I can't reach the clasp or the top of the zipper. "Could you . . ." I wave a hand to indicate what I mean, the words somehow too intimate to say aloud.

He turns and his eyes seem darker, steady and unblinking.

I shift on the seat so my back is to him, and for a moment he doesn't touch me. But I can hear his breathing, hear the hesitation in every exhale.

Then his hands are against the base of my neck, lingering a moment too long, before finally finding the clasp and then sliding the zipper all the way down to my waist. I feel his breath

144

faintly against my exposed back and I press the front of the dress to my chest, then peer around to look at him.

His face looks almost pained, like it's taking every ounce of effort for him to not reach out and touch me again—to keep from tearing the dress the rest of the way off of me. Then, noticing my gaze on him, he quickly turns to face the other window, giving me a sliver of privacy.

I arch my back, sliding the dress down my legs to my ankles. It sits like a mound of red silk on the carpeted floor of the car, still shimmering even in the dimness of the backseat. The air is mild, but I feel a tingle across my bare skin. I fold the dress quickly, then place it in the salon bag, pulling out my old clothes and dressing as fast as I can. The entire time, Tate never twitches, never turns to catch a glimpse of my partially naked body.

When I'm done, I feel like Cinderella after midnight, returned once again to normal in my everyday Charlotte clothes.

"Okay," I say softly, so he knows I'm done.

He starts to open his door, then stops, turning back to face me. For a moment he still looks uncomfortable, like the idea of me half naked sitting right beside him is still playing through his mind. "I want to see you again," he says, searching my face. "This week."

I feel my eyebrows pinch together. I want to see him again, too—I don't even want to say good-bye. But a reminder of all the things I have to do this week slams through me at once:

an upcoming calc test, an AP English paper that's due. "It's a crazy week at school. Plus I told Holly I'd pick up an extra shift."

"Maybe you shouldn't work at the flower shop anymore," he says.

I tilt my head, thinking maybe I misheard him. "What—why?"

"So I can see you more. You already have so much going on."

"I need the job and the money," I say, wiping away a wispy tendril of hair when it drifts into my face.

"I could buy the flower shop from your boss, then hire someone else to work there for you."

"Tate," I say, frowning, shocked to hear him talking like this. Is it his control thing again? "I like working there. And just because you have a lot of money doesn't mean I'm looking for a free ride."

I'm half expecting an argument, but instead a smile creeps onto his lips, punctuated by his dimple. "I like it when you do that."

"What?" I ask, still feeling a little defensive.

"Make that face. When you're unhappy about something, your nose scrunches up. I like it."

"Tate." Annoyed he isn't taking me seriously, I open the door on my side and step out onto the sidewalk. I try to keep my face somber, to be clear that he can't push me around, but when I glance back, his mouth lifts fully into one of his rare grins, and I can't help but smile back.

He climbs out of the car after me, touches my arm, holding it by the wrist, then brings it up to his lips. He kisses the triangle ink mark on the inside of my left wrist, his eyes trained on mine the entire time.

"Fine. Keep your job, but I still want to see you, and if that means I have to buy out the Bloom Room's entire inventory of flowers every week and send them to various hospitals, then that's what I'll do."

I shake my head. "Good night, Tate. Thank you for another amazing day."

"Good night, Charlotte. I'm glad you enjoyed it."

I walk backward for several steps, Tate watching me, then I turn and hurry the rest of the way up the sidewalk.

When I reach the front door, I hide the bags behind a large empty flowerpot, then sneak inside to make sure the coast is clear. I find Mia in the living room, half dozing, half watching TV with Leo in her lap, asleep. Grandma's bedroom door is shut, the light just peeking through the crack at the bottom. Seizing my opportunity, I sneak the bags into my room, avoiding Mia's eyes. She's probably not happy with me, since I didn't come home in time to watch Leo so she could go on her date with Greg. But I had a date of my own to worry about, and Leo, much as I adore him, is not my responsibility.

I take one final look in the mirror over my dresser, seeing the glamorous stranger reflected there. Then I wipe my face with a Kleenex, watching the beautiful makeup turn to a smear of creams and grays on the tissue. I stuff the shopping bags into the back of my tiny closet, afraid to hang the clothes on hangers in case anyone sees.

Just before bed, Grandma pushes open my partially closed door to say good night and stops at the sight of my hair. I lie—another lie. I tell her Carlos took me to get it cut and colored, that it was a belated birthday present, that he wanted me to have a brand-new style for the holidays.

She's standing in her white cotton pajamas, the ones she's had for years, the ones she irons each night before bed. Her auburn hair is in a braid down her back. She looks tired and there's also something else: worry, concern, mistrust maybe, playing on the features of her face.

"It looks beautiful," she finally tells me. And I try to ignore the surge of guilt. In all the years I've lived with my grandmother, I've never had to lie to her until now—until Tate.

After she has gone to bed, I slip between the sheets and call Carlos. I apologize for skipping out on our study date, but I don't say anything about the day with Tate—I'm not ready to dissect every detail, to share every moment we've spent together. A part of me likes having a secret, something that's mine, and mine alone.

He's the only thing in my boring, responsible life that belongs just to me.

ELEVEN

MIA BURSTS INTO MY ROOM, the glow of her cell phone hovering over my face as I blink awake.

"What the hell is this?" she demands.

I rub my eyes, trying to focus, my gaze moving to the clock on the bedside table—it's not quite six a.m. And just as my eyes adjust to the glare of her cell phone, the picture on the screen suddenly registers in my brain. I jolt out of bed, grabbing the phone from her hand.

I stare down at the image—at the photo of Tate. And walking beside him is *me*. It's from our dinner two nights ago. The photos I didn't think anyone would be interested in seeing.

"Wanna tell me what's going on?" Mia asks. But I don't answer her. I swipe through a series of four more images on the gossip site. But it's not as bad as I feared: Tate's hand is blocking most of my face. "I know you think I'm an idiot, Charlotte," Mia continues to say, "but you have to realize that I know my own sister when I see her. And you're wearing Mom's ring. I can see it in that one." She points a finger at the image on the screen, and there, on my left hand, lifted in the air to block the camera flash, is Mom's turquoise ring. There's no mistaking it.

Crap. I swallow down the sickening feeling that rises up inside my gut. *The ring.* I won't be able to talk my way out of this one. "You're right," I admit, exhaling deeply. "It's me. I was with him on Saturday."

Her sharp green irises seem to swell and expand, like she's seeing me for the first time. "What the hell were you doing with *Tate Collins?*"

I hand her back the phone and cross my arms. "I'm . . . seeing him." It's actually a relief to say—a sequence of words I've never said before in my entire life. Admitting it feels like stepping off a cliff, taking a leap, but once you've done it, you realize you can fly, and the weightlessness is incredible.

"Like, you're dating him? You're dating Tate Collins?" It occurs to me how many people refer to Tate by his full name—like he's a larger-than-life entity, not a living, breathing person, flaws and all. Maybe that's why he hung around me in the beginning; to me, he was just Tate, and that was a novelty.

Mia's temples twitch and her brow wrinkles. I can't tell if she's mad I didn't tell her sooner, or if she's jealous. I've never had anything for her to be jealous of before, at least not in the boy department. Sure, sometimes I think she wishes she still had her freedom—wishes she could go out on a Saturday night without needing a babysitter. But I never had my freedom either. Not really. I was bound by a promise I made, a predetermined life that didn't involve boys. Didn't involve Tate. But now I find myself tumbling faster and faster into a different life. And I don't want to turn back.

"Yes," I answer plainly. "I'm dating him."

She slips her cell phone into her sweatshirt pocket. "I should've known the new hair wasn't really a gift from Carlos. Are you going to tell me how you met a world-famous pop star in the first place? And how he asked you out?"

I sigh. "He came into the flower shop one night. And then . . . it all just happened. I didn't plan any of it."

"Grandma is going to be furious. This will destroy her."

I step quickly toward her. "You can't say anything, promise me. Grandma can't know."

Mia slides her jaw side to side, then clamps it back in place. "And why should I keep your secret?"

"Because I've covered for you plenty of times," I say. I can't believe how difficult she's being. I guess she liked it better when I was the boring sister who didn't have a life. "I watched Leo for you last month so you could go meet up with some guy after you told Grandma you were going to a job interview. And remember the night you came into my room at one a.m. and asked me to sleep in your bed next to Leo's crib so you could sneak out to see that guy you met—the married guy? I didn't get any sleep that night and I had a final the next day. And—"

"Fine," she snaps, cutting me off before I can continue listing all the times I've saved her ass. Not that I ever did it for her, exactly. I did it for Leo. "But when Grandma does find out," she adds, "I'll deny ever knowing anything. I won't have her pissed at me, too."

I brush my fingers back through my hair. "Okay," I say, cringing at the idea of Grandma ever finding out about Tate.

Mia moves absently to my dresser, touching the assortment of books and lip balm and pens scattered across the top. "I can't believe Perfect Charlotte has finally broken one of her own rules," she says, and I can't tell if it's concern or satisfaction in her voice, or some complicated mixture of both. "And with Tate Collins, no less." Her mouth tugs to one side. "Have you slept with him yet?"

"No," I retort. "Of course not. Not that it's actually any of your business."

"You're right. It's your life, Charlotte," she says, and now she just sounds weary. "You can mess it up if you want to."

"I'm not messing anything up, Mi. I'm just . . . living."

"I've said that very same thing before," she says, walking to the doorway. I can hear Grandma out in the kitchen, starting a pot of coffee. "Just be careful."

Once she's gone, I grab my cell phone from the bedside table. *There are photos of us online,* I type to Tate, then hit SEND.

An hour later, I'm standing in front of my closet, trying to decide what to wear to school, my mind stuck cycling through the paparazzi images of Tate and me. *Will anyone else figure out it's me? Will Grandma somehow see the photos?*

I pull out the large shopping bag of brand-new clothes tucked in the back of my closet. I really want to wear one of my new outfits—I want to feel even an ounce as confident as I did on Saturday. But I also don't want to draw any more attention to myself.

Then my phone dings from the bed and I grab it quickly, hoping it's from Tate. And it is. *Saw the photos,* it reads, in reply to my earlier text. *Are you okay?*

Fine. My sis figured out it's me. But so far that's it. Are you okay?

I'm only worried about you.

I really want to talk to him, hear his voice, but I can't risk Grandma overhearing.

Another text chimes through. *My publicist says the media doesn't know who you are. They're just calling you the Mystery Girl. My team is working to keep it that way.*

Thanks, I reply. His team. He has a team, the "people" he'd spoken of early on. Yet another reminder of the vast differences between us. I shake my head and check the time on my phone. I have to get dressed or I'm going to be late. *Heading to school. Can we talk later?*

Of course. And then: *Going crazy without you already.*

I opt for basic jeans and a T-shirt. I'm not yet sure what I'm going to face at school; better to blend in, act like nothing's changed.

But as I weave through the hall, the weight of Monday morning is evident on everyone's faces. Nobody knows, I tell myself. How could they? Sure, there are photos of Tate Collins and some mystery girl now circulating every online forum and blog and social website, but the face of the girl was obscured, a blurry wash of makeup and dirty-blond hair. Only my sister would make the connection.

But then a tall figure eases in beside me, blocking my slanted view of the hallway from my locker. "Hiding won't help anything."

I lift my head and Carlos is staring down at me, his eyebrows forming a perfect arc across his forehead. But he's not looking at me with sympathetic eyes. He's mad at me. *He knows.*

"Carlos," I begin. But he lifts his right palm in front of my face—long, elegant fingers, the swooping lines across his palm that tell his fortune: three kids, loads of money, and a life that will stretch to at least ninety years old. We once had our palms read in Venice by a woman who smelled like onions. She said my fate line split in two—not necessarily a good thing—and that I had two possible choices, two life paths I could take. I had forgotten about that moment until now, with Carlos's palm hovering in front of my face.

"Should I ask the obvious question, or do you want to just go ahead and spill everything?" he asks, dropping his palm and shoving both hands into the pockets of his gray slacks. His button-up shirt is navy blue with the eggshell buttons fastened all the way to the top so the collar presses tightly against his throat.

"I didn't want to keep this from you," I start.

"But you did."

"I know. I just didn't want anyone to know . . . not yet."

"I'm not anyone, I'm your best friend."

"I'm so sorry." Looking up into Carlos's eyes, my heart feels like it's being crushed and all the life squeezed out of it. "I was going to tell you."

"When? If those photos hadn't been taken, if I hadn't noticed a strikingly unique turquoise ring on the left hand of the mysterious blond-haired girl walking beside Tate Collins, and then found you looking suddenly very blond this morning, when exactly would you have told me?"

I swallow—he's obviously really, *really* mad. "Soon," I tell him, trying to sound convincing. "I was just . . . waiting for the right moment."

He blows out a breath through his nostrils, not buying it. "And Tate Collins?" His finger taps against the open locker door. "Mind explaining how that happened?"

"He came into the flower shop," I say, echoing what I told Mia this morning. "Then he sent me those roses."

"Tate Collins is Mr. Gorgeous and Mysterious?" His mouth falls open, eyes equally as shocked.

"Yeah." It really starts to sink in how long I've been keeping this from him—since the beginning. And I can see it registering in Carlos's face as well. I've been a terrible friend. "I turned him down several times. I tried to make him go away," I say, as if this explains my lack of honesty with him. *If Tate had just vanished*

after that first night, there would be nothing to tell—nothing to hide.
"But he just kept coming back. Finally I went on a date with him, and that's when I realized who he was."

"You didn't know he was Tate Collins?"

"You know I'm not good at that sort of thing."

"But he's . . . Tate Collins!"

"Trust me, I already feel like a colossal loser for not realizing it sooner."

"And how exactly did you end up leaving Il Cielo wearing a stunning red dress and your hair looking like that on Saturday night?" His eyes sweep dramatically over my new hair color.

"Tate took me shopping. And to Q, the hair salon in Beverly Hills," I admit.

"He took you to see *Steven Salazar*?!"

I nod and watch as a smile breaks across Carlos's unwilling lips. Of course he knows where all the famous people go to get their hair done. He probably even watches Steven's reality TV show.

"I think I might be more hurt that you didn't text me immediately and ask me to come join you at Steven's salon than I am about you keeping Tate Collins a secret."

"It was stupid not to tell you," I say, hoping my voice sounds as regretful as I feel. "It just all happened so fast, I barely had time to take a breath."

"Your shopping and beautifying day happened fast, or your romance with Tate?"

"Both."

Carlos's expression softens and he drops his hand from the locker door. "I love you, and I can't stay mad at you." Then his eyebrows lift. "But you better not keep a single detail from me from now on. I want to know *everything*. Spare nothing."

"Deal," I say, risking a smile.

Then, without warning, he wraps his arms around my waist, scooping me up and spinning me around before he plops me back against our locker. Everyone near us glances in our direction, before resuming their conversations or sipping their coffees or swapping out books from their lockers. "You're dating Tate Collins!" he proclaims in a hush, like he wants to be sure I realize the gravity of the situation. "The fact that you're dating at all is astounding. But gorgeous, uber-famous Tate Collins, whose music *I* have been obsessed with for three years but you couldn't care less about . . . *that* Tate Collins!" Carlos sucks in a deep breath, like he's about to pass out.

I draw in my top lip to keep from laughing. "Yeah," I answer softly. "I guess that would be him."

"When Charlotte Reed decides to date, she doesn't waste time with average high school boys, she goes big—mega pop star big. And I've never been prouder of you."

His comment forces me to think about how *not* proud my grandma will be if she finds out. "You don't think I'm weak?" I ask, my voice suddenly small. "You know my rule about dating, and I've just completely broken it."

"You're not weak," he says, leaning in close. "You've just finally realized what you've been missing. It's not like anything else has changed—you haven't given up any of your goals, you haven't dropped out of high school. You're just going to have a more exciting love life to go with it." He winks and we both smile. And just hearing that Carlos isn't disappointed in me makes me feel better.

The bell rings, and suddenly everyone in the hallway starts to scatter.

Carlos reaches past me into the locker and grabs his calculus textbook. "See you in English," he says. "I'll be daydreaming about you and Tate Collins until then."

I roll my eyes playfully and close our locker door, then head in the opposite direction to AP History.

Whatever I was expecting when I got to school this morning, it's not what I get. No one so much as glances in my direction the rest of the day. I know others have seen the photos—Jenna Sanchez and Lacy Hamilton whisper about them while Mr. Rennert lectures on symbolism in *The Catcher in the Rye*. But they're focused more on the girl in the photo's "sick" red dress than on the girl herself—and then suddenly they're talking about Tate's body and Carlos grins and elbows me and I force myself to pay attention to Holden Caulfield.

But that's when I realize I'm in the clear. Because Tate's new mystery girlfriend could *never* be nerdy, bookworm-slash-good-girl Charlotte Reed. A girl like Charlotte Reed does not attract the attention of Tate Collins, worldwide music sensation. And by the end of the day, I'm grinning to myself. They're all wrong about me.

Incredibly wrong.

My life starts to feel more and more normal. I finish my college applications, go to work, study for tests, do everything just the way I've always done it. Except for one thing: Tate. Only Mia and Carlos know about my Friday and Saturday dates with Tate Collins, the rendezvous at his house or at intimate little restaurants where Tate reserves the whole place for just us. He tells me about his music and that he hasn't wanted to write anything new in a long time.

We're more careful about the paparazzi, steering clear of any major hot spots. Tate gets asked to do interviews and talk show appearances, *Rolling Stone* even wants to do a feature article about his sudden reappearance after a year, and to tell the world who his new mystery girl is. But he turns them all down. He doesn't want to talk about us, about the last year. He just wants privacy, and to be with me.

So instead, he takes me on long drives down to Laguna Beach. Once we go as far as La Jolla, where we sit on the patio of a small, hole-in-the-wall ice cream shop overlooking the ocean, sharing a dish of lime sherbet.

Carlos is my alibi during these late nights and weekends. I tell Grandma we're spending all our free time studying at the library or at Carlos's house—that it's too hard to focus at home with Mia and Leo always there.

When really I'm with Tate.

But even when we're parked in his car overlooking the Pacific, or we're curled up on his couch watching whatever movie I choose, we still don't kiss. *Not yet*, he tells me whenever I draw close. *Not yet*.

The first night of winter break, I sleep fitfully. Images of Tate crisscross through my mind, melting into my dreams. We are in my bedroom, alone, but it feels normal, like he's supposed to be here. I can barely make out the features of his face in the dark, but I know his eyes are pouring over me, I can feel it. And then he reaches out and pulls me against him, kissing me. His hands move quickly and I feel dizzy even in the dream. My heartbeat quickens and his fingers are suddenly beneath my shirt, tearing it over my head and I am pulling him to my bed. And then his voice is there, clear and smooth against my ear, *Charlotte. Charlotte.*

But then the voice is too sharp, too loud. "Charlotte!"

My eyes flinch open.

"Charlotte."

I sit upright. It's Mia, standing in my bedroom doorway.

"Are you awake?" she asks.

"I am now."

"Look out your window. You have to see this."

"What?" I pull the blankets up to my chest. It's morning, but it's insanely early, the light outside still a dim bluish gray, the sun not yet up over the horizon.

"I noticed it when I got up with Leo. You have to see."

"See what?" I ask, not wanting to leave the warmth of my bed.

Mia walks into my room, yanking open the curtain. "Look," she demands.

I throw back the blankets and follow her to the window.

At first I can't see; it's brighter outside than I thought and I press my palms to my eyes—it reminds me of the night with Tate, when the photographer's flash blinded us as we left Il Cielo. And then I realize why it seems so bright. Everything is white.

Snowy white.

The yard below my window is blanketed in fluffy, crystalized snow. It hangs over the limbs of the palm trees; a smooth, frosting-like layer. All the way out to the sidewalk, it coats our yard like a Christmas scene from a classic movie.

"How?" I ask aloud.

Mia shrugs, rocking Leo from side to side. He makes a little sucking noise, his lips puckered. "I have no idea. I don't think it's ever snowed in LA."

"And it's too warm," I say, sliding open my window and sticking a hand out into the mild air.

Then our green eyes meet and we both know.

"Tate," I murmur, closing the window. I grab my phone from the bedside table and see I missed a call from him five minutes earlier, since my phone was set to silent. Quickly, I go to the closet, grab a sweater, and pull it over my pajama shorts and tank top. But I stop short before going out the door. Mia is still standing beside the window, watching me. She could tell Grandma, she could go wake her up if she wanted to.

But then she shrugs, and gives me a little nod. "Go on."

I smile at her, then hurry into the hall and out the front door.

It's like stepping into a winter wonderland.

I've never seen real snow before, but it looks just as beautiful as I'd always imagined. Suddenly, I wish I had a professional camera with me so I could take pictures—the light, with the sun just about to rise, is pinkish and gorgeous, refracting across the crystalline layer.

Everything is quiet. A stillness that seems amplified by the snow. No one has walked through it yet, there are no other footprints—I am the first one. It feels powdery and icy and slightly crumbly all at once, sending shivers up through my feet, barely protected by my flimsy slippers.

How did he do this? And why?

At the side of the yard stands a picture-perfect snowman, catching some shade under one of the palm trees. A bright red scarf has been tied around its neck and two black stones sit in its snow-packed skull for eyes. And tucked in one of the twigs that form the snowman's arms and hands is an envelope.

I carefully pull out the card inside.

The stationery is solid white, a hint of glitter sifting off the top. Written in cramped block letters, it reads: *Look in the backyard.*

Normally our backyard is just a sad square that backs up against a chain-link fence dividing our house from the neighbors'. But in the snow, it's transformed. And there, sitting on the old rickety bench where Mia and I used to play pirate ship and capture-the-castle, is Tate.

His dimple flickers as I run to him.

"Why?" I breathe.

"You said you'd never seen snow."

I'm smiling so big it almost hurts. "This is definitely a first."

He taps my nose, gently. "But not the last. I want you to come home with me, to Colorado. For Christmas. A snowy Christmas."

I can't help it—I lean in and kiss him. And finally he doesn't stop me, just pulls me onto the bench, which he's covered with pillows and blankets that are soft against my bare legs as I curl up beside him.

"Are you warm enough?" he asks, his mouth close to my ear.

"Almost." A shiver races through me and I shudder.

His arms tighten around me. "Better?" I feel his lips brush against my earlobe and I can only nod in reply. I'm over-whelmed with him actually being here, at my house, in my backyard, holding me. Inviting me to go home with him, meet his family. It's all so perfect.

My heart light, I start to pull away, but he draws me back toward him, his mouth landing on mine once again. He cups the side of my face, his fingers gentle despite his searching mouth. His other hand moves to my waist, his fingers gathering my sweater up, up, until I feel the warmth of his fingers against my skin.

I can't wait to go home with him—see where he grew up,

better understand who he is and why he's so guarded. And then a thought skitters through my mind: If he wants me to meet his family, then I want him to meet mine. I've spent so much time keeping him a secret, denying even to myself how I'm starting to feel about him. But if he's serious enough about *me* to bring me home with him, then I need to show him that I'm serious about him, too.

"Come inside, Tate," I tell him. "I want you to meet my family."

TWELVE

"THIS IS A BAD IDEA, Charlotte." Grandma stands in the doorway as I sit on my suitcase to zip it up.

"You can't change my mind," I tell her, trying to keep my voice gentle.

"After everything you've worked so hard for, you're just going to fly to Colorado with some boy you hardly know? Some *celebrity* who lives in a completely different world from you? What about your promise not to date, to focus on your future—you're just giving all that up now?"

"I'm not giving up anything." I grab my phone from the bed and shove it into my back pocket. "Nothing's changed, except there's someone in my life who I care about, and he cares about me—obviously enough that he wants me to meet his parents. I thought you'd be more understanding."

Grandma met Tate the other morning, after he surprised me with the snowy invite to Colorado. Mia had stood in the kitchen doorway holding Leo, tongue-tied for once in her life as she eyed Tate like he was some foreign species she'd never seen before. I thought she was going to start snapping photos of him right there. And even though Grandma was polite and shook his hand, offered him coffee and breakfast, and smiled sweetly, as soon as he left, she began grilling me with questions, telling me I had completely lost my mind. She scoured various gossip sites, studying up on his history of bad behavior. "He's not like that," I told her, but I can tell she doesn't believe me. She thinks his every documented mistake is the whole of who he is. But of course she can't see what I do.

"How do you expect me to understand you throwing your life away?" she says now.

"I'm not throwing it away." I sigh. "And if you choose not to support me, it's won't change anything. I'm doing this whether you like it or not."

"I didn't want it to come to this, but you're not leaving me a choice. My house, my rules." It's the first time she's ever spoken to me this way—her voice laced with a combination of frustration and futility I'd thought was reserved for Mia and, when we were younger, our mother. "I won't let you make the same mistakes the rest of this family did. You're not going with him to Colorado, and we're done discussing it."

I lift my suitcase from the bed and meet her gaze. "I'm eighteen, so you can't stop me from doing anything." I regret the statement almost as quickly as I've said it when I see the look on her face. But I don't allow myself to back down. This may be her house, but it's my life. "Please just trust me, okay?"

I add more softly, hoping she'll see how important this is to me. "I'm smart, remember? Trust me enough to make my own decisions."

"You can be brilliant and still be stupid at love," she says. "The women in this family always are." It's nothing I haven't thought myself over the years, but hearing her say it now is like a physical blow. The choices my family made in the past might not have led to happily ever after, but Mia and I wouldn't be here if those choices had been different. Neither would Leo. It's tough not to feel in this moment like my grandmother resents our very existence. I wheel the suitcase around her, then down the hallway. She doesn't reach out for me, doesn't physically try to stop me—maybe because she knows there's nothing she can do.

I try one more time when I reach the front door. "I know you're worried, Grandma. I love that you care so much about me. But you taught me to have a good head on my shoulders, and I know what I'm doing."

Her shoulders sag, and where before there was anger on her face, now there's only weariness. "I'm not so certain you do."

I feel a pang of guilt as I open the door and step outside with my suitcase. She doesn't hug me good-bye, doesn't offer any other parting words. I'm going, and there's nothing she can do about it. *This is my life*, I remind myself. And I close the door behind me.

Tate sent a limousine to pick me up and bring me to the airport, and the sleek, shining car stands out starkly in our dingy street. Kids point and stare as I quickly dart toward the limo and get inside. These same kids made snow forts and snow angels in our yard before everything melted. We're definitely the most popular house on the block these days.

But once we start driving, my worries fall away. The day is mild and warm and I roll down the window, letting my hand make swooping waves in the air as we drive.

I think the driver is taking me to LAX, but instead we go north, eventually pulling into an airport I didn't even know existed. VAN NUYS AIRPORT, the gate reads as we drive through. The limousine drives right out onto the tarmac, where a white jet sits with the stairs already down and the door open.

My heart begins to thud as I climb the steps, glancing back at the limo and the driver as he hands my suitcase to another man, who carries it toward the plane—a private jet, I realize.

When I step inside the first thing I see is Tate, sitting in the far back on a cream-colored couch that stretches the entire length of one side of the plane. He's wearing a plain gray T-shirt and jeans, effortlessly handsome. He stands as soon as he notices me.

"Hi," I say almost shyly. I haven't seen him in a few days, and I can't take my eyes off him. He looks like *the* Tate Collins right now, the bad boy, the rock star every girl at my school would die to be able to utter a single word to. And I am standing across from him in his private jet.

"Hi," he says back, dimple pulling inward. "I've missed you."

"It's only been a few days," I say, trying not to seem too

pleased. "I had to do Christmas early with Grandma and Mia and Leo."

He walks across the space separating us and runs a hand down my hair. "I'm glad I got to meet them. But I'm even gladder to have you all to myself for the moment."

It's strange how desire can sneak up on you. I never knew what it was to feel this way, but when I'm with him, my body craves things my brain knows I shouldn't. And with Tate's breath so close to my lips, all I want to feel is his mouth on mine, for him to kiss me. But he shakes his head, as if shaking away the temptation, and drops his hand.

A woman steps out from a little room near the front of the plane. "I can take your coat and purse, if you want," she offers with a gleaming smile. Her hair is fastened like a pinwheel at the back of her head, with a fake green-and-blue orchid clipped on the side. She's pretty and tan and I wonder how many exotic locations she's flown to in the last week.

"Thank you," I say, handing her the coat draped over my arm—the winter coat I just bought, never needing one until this trip. Carlos helped me pick it out, dragging me to nearly every thrift store in town until we found a coat that looked hardly worn and was within my budget. *Promise you'll text me every day,* he had insisted. And I agreed.

The flight attendant busies herself at the front of the plane, and Tate watches me as I look around.

The sofa is long and modern, and from a glass vase I assume is glued to the end table, purple roses bloom. I finger one of the tender petals, then smile up at him. Tate doesn't miss a trick.

"So?" he asks, arching a brow.

It's nothing like the planes I've seen in movies. And I've never flown anywhere before. I sink down on the leather couch and make a mental note not to eat or drink anything— knowing me, I'll spill all over the place. "This is more than I was expecting," I tell him.

Tate sits beside me, resting a foot on his opposite knee, totally at ease.

"It's grotesquely large," he admits. "You can say it."

"Do you always fly like this?"

"Not always. But it's easier. Less hassle."

"Fewer fans and paparazzi, you mean."

His expression turns rueful. "Yeah. That, too."

"Are you excited to see your family?" I ask.

He leans forward, dropping his leg and resting his elbows on his knees. "It's good I'm going home. It's been a while."

I notice that doesn't exactly answer my question. He has a habit of avoiding topics that make him uncomfortable. "How long?" I ask him.

His shoulders lift. "A few years."

"Are you serious? You haven't seen your parents in *years?*"

"They haven't exactly agreed with my lifestyle. With everything that's happened. They don't really understand."

"But they must be proud of you—of everything you've accomplished."

He nods. "They are. But when things . . . got to be too much for me last year, I don't know. It was easier for me to stay away than to face that they were right."

"So why now? Why are you going home after all this time?"

He lifts his head to look at me. "Because of you."

"Me?" I don't understand.

"I want them to meet you. And I want you to meet them. You're important to me and having you there will make it easier."

I touch his forearm and lean forward, resting my chin against his shoulder. "I'm glad you're taking me home," I whisper beside his ear, and I see him close his eyes.

The flight attendant brings us a fruit plate and sparkling water with lemon wedges and croissants. He tells me to ask for whatever I want. If I'm craving pancakes or crème brûlée or toasted hazelnuts, the flight attendant will somehow magically prepare it. The plane is fully stocked, he tells me.

But I just want to curl up beside Tate, settle my head on his chest, and stare out at the world below. Miniature houses and patchwork farms and mountains that rise up snowy and white—I can't resist taking pictures, even though it's just with my phone. Maybe I can Photoshop them later, at school, work on them until they look more like the landscape that's unfolding below me.

Finally, I put my phone down, and close my eyes. "Sleep if you want," Tate whispers against my temple, folding his arm around me. He begins to hum against my ear, his breath warm on my neck. It's a melody I don't recognize—not one of his songs—but even muted, his voice is effortless and beautiful. And I listen for a while before I tilt my head up to him and ask, "What song is that?"

"Nothing special. Just a tune I've had stuck in my head."

"For a new song?" I ask tentatively.

"I don't know," he answers softly. "Maybe."

I close my eyes, feeling the vibration of his lips murmuring against my ear. Sometimes the fullness of his mouth brushes across my earlobe or along my hairline and I stifle a shiver.

I let myself drift in and out of sleep, listening to Tate Collins hum for me, my own private melody.

If our yard had resembled a winter wonderland, Telluride, Colorado, is the set of a Christmas movie. Several feet of freshly fallen snow have already piled up on the tarmac and more is drifting down from the dark sky. A black SUV is waiting for us when we land, and we hurry from the plane to the car, the sharp, cold air slipping through our coats.

"You're shivering." Tate reaches out to take my hand from my lap. "And your fingers are freezing."

"All part of the winter experience," I say, still marveling as we drive through town. It's just after sunset, and the storefronts are lined in silver and white holiday lights, displays of paper cutout snowflakes and elves in green pointy hats set behind the glass windows. It's a fairy tale. "I like it here. It feels like a place you're supposed to come back to."

He presses my palm to his lips, holding it there for several seconds, his mouth warm.

"Good," he says.

We pull up to a house on a street that winds along a low hillside. All the homes are cloaked in snow, powdery drifts that have collected on the roofs and cover the lawns. They look like gingerbread houses, twinkling with Christmas lights. Some even have blown-up snowmen in their yards and plastic Santas with reindeer on their rooftops. People put these up in LA, too, but here they look natural instead of gaudy.

"I can't believe you used to live here," I say, stepping out from the SUV and standing in the driveway of his parents' house, a two-story chalet-style home with a mailbox decorated with blinking red lights. Compared to our house, it's a palace, but it's nowhere near the size of Tate's fortress in LA.

"Me neither," Tate says, sucking in a deep breath and taking my hand again. "Ready?"

"I think I'm more ready than you are," I say.

Tate looks stiff and uncomfortable, like he's preparing for battle. His grip on my hand tightens as we walk up the icy steps to the front door, his thumb tapping against my forefinger.

But when we ring the doorbell and a lovely middle-aged woman with Tate's eyes opens the door, we're both immediately enveloped in a rush of hugs and the scent of cinnamon and pumpkin and wood burning from a fireplace. It's hard for me to understand what could possibly make Tate nervous about coming back here.

We shuffle into the entryway, Tate's mom, Helen, clutching Tate while his dad, Bill, shakes my hand. Bill has speckled gray hair and the same chiseled chin and jawline as Tate. He's wearing a festive red sweater with a Christmas tree stitched onto the front that looks like it might have fit him ten years ago, but now is being stretched along every seam. Helen probably forced him to wear it—an effort to seem in the holiday spirit.

Then something barrels past me, a flash of brown fur, almost knocking me over. The dog is enormous—a big, fluffy, auburn-colored thing with white around his eyes and muzzle.

"Rocco!" Tate says, burying his hands into the dog's fur. Soon they are a tangle on the floor, Rocco licking Tate's face over and over again. I can't help but smile, seeing him like this—where he grew up, in his old house, with a dog he obviously loves. It reveals a side of him I haven't yet seen. Even though he was nervous coming here, it hasn't taken long for him to open up. And I feel lucky that I get to experience this with him, see who he used to be before all the fame.

"Charlotte," Helen says, leading me away from the doggy reunion and into the cozy living room, gesturing for me to sit on the gigantic red plaid couch. She plops down beside me. "You're even more beautiful than Tate described," she says. Her cheekbones are high and her short brown hair slides across her shoulders like a curtain. She's pretty, with delicate features and tiny hands.

"He described me?" I ask stupidly. I shouldn't be surprised, considering he had to warn them he was bringing someone home for the holidays, but every reminder that I'm on Tate's mind brings its own fresh thrill.

"Of course. When he told me he was coming home and he was bringing his girlfriend, I wanted to know every detail."

Girlfriend. My mind reels at the word. We've yet to discuss any labels, both of us content just to live in the moment. I glance down at Tate, who is still on his knees, wrestling with his old pal.

"We got Rocco when Tate was nine," his mother tells me. "That dog practically raised him."

"And Tate hasn't been back to see him in years," his dad says, his voice edged with accusation. A second of uneasy stillness overtakes the room.

Tate's eyes flash to his dad, then to me—his jaw a hard line.

Helen rushes to say, "It's so nice to have you both here now. I've made up the guest room," she adds. "I hope you'll be comfortable, Charlotte."

"I don't need much," I assure her, smiling at her and then at Tate, who is finally pushing himself up from the floor, his hands still scratching the dog's ears.

"Our kind of girl," Bill says. And I sense he implies more than just the obvious. I think about what Tate said on the plane: how his parents didn't agree with his lifestyle. The money and the big house and the private jets—they don't understand any of it. They are ordinary people and they appreciate ordinary things. In which case, we're going to get along perfectly.

After a pause that Tate makes no effort to fill, Helen stands from the couch. "Well, I guess I'll show Charlotte to her room." Her mouth is curved in an uneasy smile. "Tate, honey, your room is just how you left it last time you were here. You can put your things in there."

"Your mom keeps it like a museum," Tate's dad says. "Like she's waiting for you to move back in." I can't tell if it's meant to be a joke—nobody laughs.

Tate and his dad bring in our suitcases while his mom leads me down a hallway on the first floor to the room where I'll be staying—not with Tate. Obviously not with Tate. I'm not sure what I was thinking.

"Coming, Charlotte?" Tate's mom calls from in front of me.

I shake my head, bringing myself back to the moment. "Be right there."

The next day, we drive to a massive lot that has been converted into SANTA'S TREE WORKSHOP—as the wooden sign hanging from a fence announces when we pull in. Apparently, picking out a huge, beautiful tree on Christmas Eve is a Collins family tradition. I can't help sighing with envy.

At our house, Grandma pulls out a deteriorating plastic Christmas tree she's had since the nineties. We position it in the corner of the living room beside the TV, and hang a single strand of lights and the dozen or so ornaments she's had for equally as long. We've never had a real live tree.

"Divide and conquer?" Tate's dad says as we stand in line

for cups of hot chocolate. The girl working the stand is dressed like an elf—complete with stick-on pointed ears.

"Works for me," Tate says, not meeting his dad's gaze.

"Each couple brings back a tree; whichever is the best goes home with us."

"Deal," Tate agrees, and shoots me a look—he clearly intends for us to win. But my mind is stuck on the word *couple*. Is that really what we are—Tate and I?

Before we separate, I steal a last look at Tate's mom. Her eyes are bright and dewy from the cold. She seems happy to finally have her son home, even if there is still obvious tension between Tate and his dad. Her family is back together. And that's a start.

Santa's Tree Workshop is gigantic, far larger than any of the corner lot tree stands we have in LA. There's a small outpost called Santa Land where kids line up to sit with a jolly-looking Santa. There are booths where you can buy festive knit hats, toy trains, even a small fenced area where you can pet a reindeer. This is more than tree shopping; this is a holiday emporium of everything tinsel-laced and candy-cane coated.

I pull Tate over to the reindeer. The majestic creature stands behind the fence, munching a pile of hay, and I lean against the fence and gently extend my fingers to feel his woolly coat. He blows hot air across my hand and licks me with his long tongue.

"Hey," Tate says beside me, stroking the reindeer's mane. "This girl's taken."

I smile and pull my hand away. The reindeer drops his head back to the hay.

"He's cute." I lean against Tate, pressing my forehead into his chest. Breathing him in, feeling his heartbeat rise beneath his coat, makes my body flood with a warmth that the cold cannot reach. Tate seems so different here—he's not worried about the paparazzi trailing him wherever he goes, and so far, no fans have recognized him. Maybe because no one expects Tate Collins to be strolling through a Christmas fantasyland in Telluride, Colorado. But it also feels like more than that. Like there are burdens that weigh on him in LA, but he's managed to leave them behind.

"Shall we start our search for the perfect tree?" Tate asks into my hair.

I nod and pull away. But he keeps his hand laced in mine.

"This contest is rigged, you know," Tate murmurs, still not looking at me. Some of the hurt and vulnerability from yesterday returns to his face. "My father thinks he knows what's best—no exceptions."

"Then let's just have fun," I suggest, and duck around the side of the reindeer's pen, our bodies hidden by the wood siding of a shed.

"I can work with that." Tate surprises me by pinning me tightly against the wooden wall. His body against mine, his hands around my wrists, his breath hot against my neck make me feel bold. I smile up at him, silently daring him to kiss me.

His gaze drops to my lips and lingers there, just before he

places his mouth on mine. I kiss him back fiercely, my wrists bound by his fingers, his body caging me in.

I want more.

He breaks away to kiss along my jaw, my neck. His mouth is hot, his teeth nibbling on my skin. When he lifts his head to look at me, I see the dark need in his gaze. Our eyes remain locked as he kisses me. A simple kiss, a mere brush of lips on lips. Again.

And again.

Until our eyes close at the same time and our tongues meet, his hand gripping my hips. I reach for the zipper on his coat and undo it. He moans against my lips and a thrill goes through me.

In this terrifying, wondrous, overwhelming moment, I would let him do anything.

Anything at all.

He moans again, then breaks the kiss. "What are you doing to me?" he asks, sounding tortured. His face is stark and serious, his lips swollen and damp from our kisses.

"I think you've got it backward," I whisper, breathing deeply. I can't believe the way Tate makes me feel—like I'm being drawn to him by some invisible thread. I've always pictured myself trudging up a steep hill, forcing myself forward under the weight of school and work and my own impossible expectations. With Tate, I feel light. I feel free.

He doesn't say anything more, just shakes his head, then pulls me deep into the rows of trees, an endless sea of choices. We drag out several, examining them more closely.

"Why did you ever leave Colorado?" I ask, finally breaking the silence as he wedges himself back between a cluster of trees, certain he sees the perfect one tucked in the back.

"I always knew I would. I wanted to be a musician since I was young."

"But you left without your parents?"

"Sort of. I won a singing competition in Denver when I was fifteen. They flew me out to LA so I could perform in front of a record exec. He signed me on the spot."

"And?" I prompt.

"And . . . everything changed. I went on tour, I made two records that both went platinum within a year. It happened so fast I didn't really have time to think about what was happening."

"And your parents didn't move with you to LA?"

"They did at first. Traveling back and forth between here and there. But as things got crazy, as I got more . . . well-known, they started trying to tell me how to live my life. Maybe they were right, but I didn't want to listen."

"I'm sorry," I say.

Tate steps out from the crush of tree limbs, bringing with him the thick scent of fresh pine needles. "I did things I wish I could take back," he says more seriously now. "But I'm not that person anymore, Charlotte. I want you to know that."

I'm not entirely certain what he means—it feels like there are still things he isn't telling me, important things, but his face has turned guarded. I decide not to ask, not right now.

Instead, I move in to give him a chaste kiss. "Charlotte," he whispers against my lips, then kisses me again. His lips are warm and our breath comes out as vapor in the cold air. I don't want him to let go. I want his mouth to press against mine until winter evaporates into spring. I want to stay here, hidden among the Christmas trees until the night shifts over the sky and everyone has gone home. But Tate lifts his mouth from mine, both of us a cloud of warmth in the frosty snow. And then I feel the flakes, floating down from the muted gray sky. It's snowing. Soft crystals land in my hair and on Tate's shoulders.

And in that moment, in his arms, I have everything I could possibly want.

Tate and I agree on a skinny, floppy-looking tree. Nothing like what I pictured we'd choose. It sags a little on one side and bows oddly near the top, but somehow, it's perfect. Tate carries it over one shoulder back to the entrance, where the holiday music continues to blare from the overhead speakers, now mixing with the falling snow.

Much to my surprise, Tate's parents selected an equally homely-looking tree. Tate's dad studies ours, running his hands over the limbs with a serious look on his face, then turns to Tate and says, "Looks like we both know how to recognize a good thing when we see it." And he actually smiles, clapping Tate on the shoulder. Helen laughs and brings a hand to her mouth, like she might cry seeing the tension between them lift.

It takes Tate a second to absorb the compliment, to realize his dad is trying to make an effort, but when he does, I can see his face lighten. His eyes find me, his dimple flickering to life.

We decide to purchase both trees. But when Tate reaches for his wallet, his dad waves it away. "You might be Mr. Moneybags, but I'm still your father."

His mom snaps a photo of us standing beside our chosen tree, one of Tate's arms around my waist, the other holding up the lopsided tree. The snow drifts down around us in slow motion, and the twinkle of Christmas lights feels like a holiday dream.

I never want to wake up.

THIRTEEN

WE EAT DINNER BESIDE THE fire, baby potatoes and green beans and a cauliflower soup that tastes so amazing I keep closing my eyes with every bite, just to savor it. Until Tate points out my repeated eye-closing and everyone laughs.

We move into the living room and I steal a moment to send a text to Carlos, attaching the photo of Tate and me beside our tree, the snow like a halo around us. After a brief debate with myself, I send it to Grandma, too. Maybe it's rubbing salt in a wound, given how we left things yesterday, but maybe she'll see how happy we look and stop worrying quite so much.

Helen and Bill drink wine, and tell a few stories about what Tate was like as a child. Tate looks on, face stony, but I'm too amused to make them stop. This feels just like the perfect family life I always imagined. Christmas with my grandma and sister has always been a quiet affair, with Mia often preferring to spend the day with her friends or her boyfriend du jour. And when my mom was alive, holidays usually involved spending Christmas Eve sleeping on the couch of whatever guy she was dating at the time. The thought sobers me, and as the conversation drifts off, I stare into the fire, wondering if I'm somehow making the same mistakes that she did. *But this is different*, I tell myself. Tate isn't like other guys.

"Well, Bill," Helen says finally, setting her half-full glass of wine on the coffee table and standing up, "Tate and Charlotte might be used to waiting up for Santa, but we are not. Shall we call it a night?"

Bill swallows down the rest of his wine, patting Tate once on the shoulder before he rises and follows his wife into the kitchen, where they put things away and flick off the lights.

Once they've gone upstairs, Tate walks me to my room, touching a strand of my hair and circling it once around his finger before dropping his hand.

"I liked this day," I tell him. "With you."

His mouth edges into a smile. "I hope you get everything you want for Christmas tomorrow."

"I'm pretty sure I already have," I say.

I see the momentary struggle in his eyes. I want to touch him, pull him into my room with me. And his gaze says he might not be able to say no.

But then he clears his throat, resolve tightening the features of his face. "Good night, Charlotte."

"Good night," I respond, my voice barely above a whisper.

He leaves me in the doorway and moves down the hall. I

watch until he slips into his bedroom and quietly shuts the door.

I should stay in my room.

I should go to sleep.

The house has fallen still, but my brain won't turn off.

He's all I can think about. The day has been too perfect, the heated kisses against the wall of that shed, and then his gentle kiss between the rows of trees, his touch telling me what he seems unable to say with words.

I cross the room twice, pacing, touching the window, leaving icy fingerprints against the glass. The snow continues to fall, making half moons on the sills of the window outside.

The rational, disciplined side of my brain tells me that just being here with him, in his house, is enough. *We need to take it slow.* His words ring in my ears. But why doesn't it feel like enough—why is his touch never enough? My heart thumps against my rib cage, battling my mind.

I want him. I don't care if it's reckless, if it goes against everything he's said, everything my grandma and sister warned me about. I need him in this moment.

I flip open the top of my suitcase and dig through the clothes inside. I find what I'm looking for: a short, lacy white dress. Tate bought it for me that day at Barneys and I've never worn it, and certainly never thought I'd have reason to on this trip. But I packed it anyway—I packed nearly everything in my closet, worried I'd be unprepared.

I undress, leaving my clothes on the floor, and slip carefully into the delicate dress. The fabric is pure silk and drapes over my skin like something made of air.

I pull on the black robe I brought as well—another gift from Tate—and tie the silky band around my waist.

I'm really doing this.

I leave the bedroom and tiptoe across the hardwood floor, my heart battering chaotically in my chest, unable to find a steady rhythm.

Then something moves ahead of me in the dark.

I freeze, holding the robe against my chest—afraid it's one of his parents, up to grab a glass of water or late-night snack. But then the movement comes into focus, padding down the hall toward me: Rocco. When he reaches me, he lifts his head and sniffs my leg. I run a hand over his furry head, rubbing one of his ears, and his tail wags, thumping once against the wall. Then he turns, satisfied that I'm not an intruder, and ambles back to rest beside the living room fire.

It's cold tonight, and goose bumps begin to rise up on my bare legs.

I stop outside of Tate's door, my heart now a drum in my chest. There is sound on the other side—a guitar, I realize, playing faintly from inside. I lift my fist, resting it against the grain of the wood. I knock, once, then twice, but only gently. The guitar doesn't stop playing and Tate doesn't come to the door. My mouth trembles as my fingers grip the doorknob, pushing the door open.

Inside, there is a lamp switched on against one corner, a chair resting beside it. On the walls I can faintly make out posters: Led Zeppelin, Jimi Hendrix, and Michael Jackson. Several skateboards are lined up beneath the large bay window and on the dresser against the opposite wall are stacks of vinyl albums next to an old record player. Everything is organized and tidy—preserved by his mom after all these years.

And sitting at the end of the bed is Tate, a guitar held to his chest, bulky headphones over his ears, and a notebook spread open beside him. He's humming, staring out the window at the snow swirling against the glass, and strumming his guitar so effortlessly it's like the notes just stream from his fingers. I recognize the melody: It's the same one he hummed in my ear on the plane.

And then he stops, his palm pressed against the strings to make the sound abruptly end. He turns and catches me standing in his doorway.

"Charlotte? Are you all right?" He sets his headphones on the bed.

"You were writing music," I say foolishly, stepping farther into his room. "You haven't done that in a while."

He looks at the guitar, then the window, then back at me. The glow from the lamp sends lazy shadows across the walls of his room, bleeding out of the darkness.

"I was feeling inspired." His eyes are on me now, the familiar look of wanting etched in his gaze, the iron control that always seems so close to cracking. "Did I wake you up?" he asks, standing from the bed. "Was I too loud?"

"No." I shake my head, steeling myself. Electricity dances and pops across my skin. "I wanted to see you."

His eyes settle, lowered on some part of me, but my focus has blurred slightly, the whole room swimming.

"I've waited long enough," I hear myself say. I take another step closer. He is within arm's reach, but I don't touch him. Instead, my fingers unravel the silky band around my robe, letting it slip open to reveal the white dress underneath. I'm not shaking anymore—I'm in control now.

He won't stop me this time. He wants me, too—I know he does, I can see it in his eyes, dipping low to follow the thin fabric of the dress clinging to the form of my body. He exhales, like he's trying to steady his thoughts. I touch one shoulder of the robe, letting it glide down my arms onto the floor. Tate's mouth opens like he's going to speak, but nothing comes out.

My vision razors, everything suddenly sharp and in focus.

My heart is steady and I slide my hands against his chest, feeling the fabric and the hard shape of his muscles underneath. His scent is on my lips; he still smells like the ocean, even though we're a thousand miles away.

"Charlotte."

My fingers find the thin strap of the dress, pausing there before tugging it downward. There is nothing underneath this thin veil of fabric. Excitement writhes inside my belly. The strap moves easily from my shoulder, trailing down my arm.

His hand lifts, touching the strap on my other shoulder, sliding his fingers beneath it. His touch is like fire and his eyes trace my lips. I silently plead for him to kiss me, lifting up onto my tiptoes.

He swallows, a heavy movement, like his mind is battling the rest of his body. "I told you, Charlotte," he murmurs, eyes focused intently on the strap he holds between his fingers. But then: "I told you how it had to be." Tate's fingers move swiftly, sliding out from beneath the strap—leaving it where it is—then touching my other arm, dragging the other strap back up to my shoulder.

No, my mind shouts. My gaze snaps to his face, but his eyes are blank, the heat I swore I'd seen moments before gone as if it had never been.

"It's too soon," he says, and I want to scream, I want to cower and hide. "I'm sorry—"

"Don't," I interrupt, humiliation swelling big and hot beneath my skin, threatening to burn me from the inside out. "Don't bother."

Those dark eyes seem to darken even more, cast over with some blackness I can't see through.

My head throbs, little pulses shooting through my temples. I bend down and yank the robe from the floor and leave him standing in his bedroom. I can feel his gaze on me as I leave, but I don't look back. My eyes are already burning.

Once inside my room, I bury myself beneath the sheets, still in the dress. The weight of my mother's ring feels like an anchor on my finger.

For an hour, I toss and turn. Just as I begin to drift, I hear a soft knock at the door. Eagerly, pathetically, I race to the door, certain it's Tate. Certain he's here to apologize, to tell me the truth about what's happened to him, why he keeps pushing me away.

It is Tate. But he's not here to make up. One look at him—the set mouth, the eyes that won't quite meet mine—and I know what he's going to say.

"You're sending me home." Because I crossed a line—I dared to breach the invisible barrier that Tate has built between us, the one he's told me is for my own good. But studying the distant look on his face, I realize it was never about my protection. It was always about his. Keeping me at a distance, preventing me from getting too close. And when he doesn't deny that he's sending me home, I say, "So that's it? We're just done?"

His shoulders seem to tense at my words. "Charlotte—"

"It's fine. It's for the best, actually." I can't believe how steady my voice is, how calm. "What time am I flying out?"

The question stretches between us. He could apologize. He could tell me that I'm wrong, that he's sorry and that he doesn't want me to leave. But he doesn't say any of those things. He lets the silence bury me, suffocate me. In that moment, I think I might hate him.

His eyes close briefly, and he almost looks pained, before opening them again to fix on something just over my shoulder. "A car will be here at seven."

I want to scream at him. I want to pound my fists against his chest and tell him how much he hurt me, how much he's still hurting me. But instead I choke down every bitter thought, and turn away, closing the door on Tate. Closing the door on us.

FOURTEEN

A STORM IS PRESSING DOWN on the town, a wall of dark gray in the distance. We're almost to the airport when the snow begins swirling around the car that carries me away from Telluride. It's Christmas day, and I'm heading back to LA alone. The car skids a little, drifting toward a snowbank before the driver corrects our course, but for some reason I'm not scared. I feel an odd sense of numbness. Like I'm drifting through a dream again—but a different sort of dream.

I board the same jet we had taken here, and the same flight attendant greets me. The green-and-blue orchid is in place in her hair, but today it looks droopy and somehow bereft.

"Coffee?" she asks when I sit down on one of the reclining chairs. I make a point not to sit where Tate and I sat on our way here. I don't want to remember how differently I felt on that flight, how hopeful.

"Thank you," I tell her gratefully.

Once we're in the air, I stare out the window at a world of white as we fly through layers of endless clouds. There is no blue sky, no land far below. Just white.

"He seemed happy," the flight attendant says midway through the trip. She is pouring me a fresh glass of water.

"Excuse me?" I say.

She touches her hand to the roof of the plane as we move through a stretch of turbulence, the cabin jerking from side to side before leveling out. Ordinarily, this would terrify me, but it's like I'm blank inside.

"Tate," she clarifies. "I haven't seen him that happy in a long time."

I let out a rush of air, and spin my mother's ring around my finger.

When I realize that she isn't going away, I ask, "Do you fly with him often?"

"I work most of his private flights. He likes to use the same crew." She smiles. "His regular pilots were back in LA today, which is why you've got two new pilots—these guys are local, out of Denver." She nods up to the cockpit, where the closed door blocks the pilots from view. "I stayed in Telluride. Figured I'd just wait, enjoy the snow for Christmas until you both were ready to head home. I don't have much of a family anyway. My boyfriend and I split a couple months back."

"Sorry," I murmur. How many people have changed their plans, their lives, for Tate Collins? Everything in his world revolves around him. He decides what he wants, who he wants, and when. He's so afraid of losing control that he ended up losing me.

She shrugs. "But Tate, he's a tricky one. He's been so different the last year. We used to fly him to Vegas every other weekend; him and a dozen friends, supermodels, and pop stars like him. He'd take impulsive trips down to Mexico or Miami. But in the last year, he's hardly left LA. And then, the other day, he got on the plane with you, just you. I thought maybe you were the one."

"The one?"

She smiles gently. "Well, he needs a dose of normal in his life."

I should smile politely and go back to staring out the window. Wrap the numbness around myself like a shroud. Instead I turn to give her my full attention. "Do you know what happened to him a year ago—what made him change, leave the music world?"

The shrug is one-shouldered this time, as if the story annoys her. "Not sure. There were rumors of course, that he got a girl pregnant and he was trying to keep it secret; that he was involved with drugs. People talk. But none of it sounded like Tate. Something else made him quit music, something bigger than all that gossip."

The plane begins to lurch as we enter more rough air and she grabs onto the back of a seat to keep from falling over. "Better buckle in."

The jolting turbulence doesn't bother me. I stare blindly

out the window as we start to descend. LA reveals itself, silvery and blue. The ocean expands out to meet the sky and I feel a sudden sense of relief—I'm home.

The sun is high when we land at the same private airport. Tate's town car is waiting on the tarmac, Hank standing beside the back door. Seeing him makes my throat swell, tears threatening to break free again. Someone else who's given up his Christmas for Tate.

"Your chariot awaits, milady," Hank says in a falsely cheerful tone as I slide into the back of the town car, and I wait while he loads my luggage into the trunk.

When he climbs in the driver's seat, I can feel his eyes on me in the rearview mirror. I shrink back in my seat, praying he's not going to mention Tate's name, or try to tell me what a good guy he is at heart. As if reading my mind, he lets out a quiet sigh. "Let's get you home, Charlotte."

I roll down the window, wanting to feel the mild California air against my face. I lift my fingers through the window as we pull away from the tarmac, feeling the breeze. We pause at the gate, waiting for it to slide open.

But when it does, I hear the sudden rush of voices, the *click, click, click* I remember all too vividly. Men with cameras have gathered just outside the gate and now they are surrounding the car, clamoring next to the window, practically spilling inside. I don't have time to block my face from view; it's too late, they already have my picture.

"Charlotte!" they yell. And I realize: They know who I am.

How? And how did they know I'd be here, getting off a plane on Christmas Day, when my plans didn't change until the middle of last night?

As Hank curses, my thoughts tumble backward, to the crew, the new pilots the flight attendant had mentioned. Did they somehow tip off the media, give them my name, tell them I was the mystery girl Tate has been keeping a secret?

Either way, it doesn't matter now. It's done. Yet I can't help but panic as my fingers fumble for the window button, trying frantically to roll it up as Hank inches the car forward through the small mob that has gathered. He pounds the horn and shouts dire warnings, all of which go unheeded.

"Charlotte, *Charlotte!*" they continue to call. "What's it like dating the sexiest singer alive? Did you meet his parents? Is there a ring?"

They know who I am, but they don't know what happened—they don't know that I returned early because Tate ended it between us. Somehow, that makes it even worse.

"Hang in there, honey," Hank says, gunning the engine to show he means business. "Time to ditch the vultures."

The window finally slides upward, sealing shut the outside world. With a squeal of tires, Hank pulls out onto the street, speeding away from the flash of cameras.

My grandmother is not easy on me—not at first.

"What did you think would happen?" she asks while I sit

at the kitchen table, slumped and defeated, my suitcase still propped up by the door.

"It was a mistake," I tell her, staring down at my hands in my lap. "I shouldn't have gone."

I think about the mob at the airport, the flashes of cameras. Mia popped her head into the kitchen when I first got home, her voice uncharacteristically gentle as she told me that the photos were already online, then disappeared back into her bedroom—I think she realized Grandma wanted to talk to me alone. Moments like this, I'm glad I don't have Twitter or Instagram or Snapchat, where I'd be forced to see the same GIF of myself trying to roll up the backseat window over and over again.

Grandma refolds a stack of towels and straightens the row of spice jars on the counter. She's upset. When she's upset, she paces, she fidgets, she tries to keep her hands busy.

"I'm sorry," I tell her. "You were right. You were completely right about him."

She turns to look at me and I'm surprised to see there are tears in her eyes.

"Grandma," I breathe. "I'm so sorry."

She takes a deep breath. She wraps her arms around me.

"It'll be okay," she tells me. "It's good that you found out now, before things went any further."

But there, circled in her arms, I can't help but feel like it did go too far. I went too far. I felt too much. And now I don't know how to feel anything else.

FIFTEEN

IT'S A RELIEF TO BE back at school, to have something to do with my days. For the last week of winter break, I spent most of my time at home, avoiding anything that could remind me of Tate. I took a few extra shifts at the Bloom Room, but it wasn't enough to distract me.

Carlos folds his arm over my shoulder, forcing me to fall in step with him as we walk to English. "I never liked his music anyway," he's saying, his chin held high as we move through the sea of people, all staring directly at me.

Everyone knows by now. Everyone knows that I, Charlotte Reed, had some sort of fling with Tate Collins. And now they all stare. They look at me like they're trying to see something they've missed for the last four years—some part of me they just didn't notice. But I'm still the same Charlotte, at least on the outside. Just maybe a little blonder.

"Nice try," I say to Carlos. "You're obsessed with his music."

He grunts and flips his hair back from his eyes. "Not anymore. I deleted all his songs from my playlists, even the *Love Is a Verb, Live Tour* album." He pauses, as if expecting me to be impressed, but then rushes on. "I have stripped my life clean of him."

"I wish a simple 'delete' would rid him from my life."

"There should be an app for that."

"Yeah, I'd pay at *least* ninety-nine cents for that one." I smile.

Carlos winks and pokes my ribs. "See? You still have your sense of humor. You'll be fine."

I'm not so sure. But the days and weeks find a way of tumbling past, even when memories of Tate rise up inside me: the way his hands felt that first night when we danced on the grass and he sang into my ear, the way his lips fit perfectly against mine, like we were made for each other. I try to pretend that none of it ever happened. I throw myself into school, into work. I stuff all the clothes he bought me from Barneys back into their bags — I plan on giving them to Mia or donating them to a thrift store. But I just can't bring myself to do it, so I cram them into the very back of my closet — out of sight. To Mia's unending joy, I babysit for Leo in the evenings after my shifts are over, barely letting myself have a moment alone.

I give in and go to parties with Carlos when he promises it'll help. I drink beer (well, I drink *a* beer, but it's gross so that's about as far as I get). I try to be social. I show up at beach bonfires, chat with classmates I've only really known in passing until now. Sometimes, when something epically funny happens, like Andy Strauss losing his trunks after diving into the rough midnight surf, we laugh and in the warm glow of the fire I forget for an instant about everything before.

But then I find myself staring blankly into the flames, and I can't help but think about him.

Him.

Him.

One of those nights brings me to Alison Yarrow's birthday party. Her parents actually leave town so she can invite all her friends over and throw, basically, Pacific Heights High's biggest bash of the year. Even bigger than prom, some say.

I've never been invited before. I've never wanted to go.

But this year, Alison stops me in the hall before calculus and personally invites me. "I really hope you'll be there," she says, like she's truly counting on me coming, like my presence at her eighteenth birthday party will somehow solidify her most-popular-girl-at-school status. Everyone still thinks I'm with Tate, no matter how many times I deny it, or maybe the fact that I *was* with him is enough to catapult me to a different social stratosphere.

I pick up Carlos and we drive to Alison's house at the base of the Hollywood Hills. Alison isn't exactly rich, but she has a pool and her backyard is lush and manicured by an actual gardener that comes once a week.

Alison spots me as soon as we walk through the sliding glass doors onto the back patio, and she runs up and gives me a hug.

"You came!" she screeches, holding me out at arm's length. As if she and I have been besties since kindergarten.

"Beer, margaritas, and fiesta snacks are all over there," she adds with a nonchalant wave. "Get yourself a drink, then come hang with me in the cabana."

I glance over her shoulder at the poolside cabana with white sheer fabric draped over the little roof, swirling in the breeze. Lacy Hamilton and Jenna Sanchez are already reclining on the white mattress with regal superiority.

As the evening wears on, Carlos and I sit side by side on a pool chair, observing the party around us like social anthropologists. After a while he goes to get another beer, and I hear someone behind me.

"Charlotte Reed," a voice says, and I turn in the chair.

It's Toby McAlister, looking very buzzed, his cheeks flushed and his hair tousled like he's already had a closet rendezvous with one of the sophomore girls I noticed flirting with him earlier. I think briefly of the sycamore tree at school that bears the testament of Toby and Alison's short-lived romance. Their own version of paparazzi photos, I suppose. I wonder if it's ever painful for either of them to walk by those initials and be reminded of the past. Then again, maybe not, considering Toby seems to have no problem being here tonight. "Aren't these parties beneath you?" he asks. "PHH's very own celebrity. I heard about you and Tate Collins."

I refrain, barely, from rolling my eyes. If I had a dollar for every person who has mentioned Tate to me in the last few weeks, I wouldn't have to worry about financial aid next year, I swear. "That's over." Maybe if I say it enough, it will finally stop hurting.

"Cool." He shrugs. "Looks like you need a beer," he says, holding out a red cup, sloshing with frothy brown liquid. He's clearly had several.

"I'm not drinking actually," I say. "Designated driver."

"Oh. Very responsible of you." His mouth twists into a grin, revealing a perfect row of teeth. Toby McAlister is obviously good-looking. The problem is that he knows it.

I offer him a terse smile.

"The pool," he says, gesturing to the calm water. "Do you swim?"

"Are you asking if I know how to swim?"

"I'm asking you to swim with me." He hiccups, then takes a swig from the cup he tried to give me only moments earlier. "Come on, Charlotte." He stretches out my name, his brows rising in what I'm sure he thinks is an inviting expression.

"No thanks." I turn back to the lawn and stand up from the chair. "I think I'm going to go, actually."

"No—you can't." He reaches out for me, grabbing hold of my right arm. His fingers dig into my skin, not intentionally I don't think, but because he's using me now to keep his balance. But he's pushing me backward, closer to the edge of the pool.

"Toby!" I say, trying to shove him with my other hand, but we're already stumbling backward, the momentum carrying us both. But just before we fall in, Carlos is at my side, pulling me upright.

"You're such an ass," Carlos says to Toby, who has fallen over into the grass.

"She wouldn't swim with me," he says through a chuckle, splayed out on his back, arms wide, blinking up at the sky. He doesn't seem in any rush to get up.

"I need to go," I tell Carlos and he nods. "Can you find a ride home?"

"I'll just take a taxi. You know me," he adds, batting his dark eyelashes. "I only like to travel in my private limo." He says it with his faux British accent and I crack a smile, mostly to let him know that I'm not mad that he's staying. "Text me when you're home," he orders.

"I will."

The street that Alison lives on is narrow and steep and lined with cars along one side. There are no streetlamps, only the occasional glow from a porch light left on at one of the houses tucked up in the trees.

A dog barks when I walk beside a fence, and I hurry past.

Then, a crunching—like footsteps on gravel—disturbs the eerie calm. My skin shivers, a thread of panic starting to inch its way up to my brain.

"Carlos?" I say aloud.

Something moves, two cars behind me: a shadow receding back into the hedge lining the sidewalk. It's the silhouette of a person.

Someone is there . . . Someone is following me.

For an instant, a sliver of a second, I allow myself to believe it's Tate. That he misses me, that he's come to win me back. But there's no Tesla in sight, and I ruthlessly quash the thought before hope can rise up in place of the panic. I need to leave, now.

I reach my car and fumble for my keys. I slam the car door and glance back in the rearview mirror: one shuddering heartbeat, two, three—still no sign of the shadow.

A thump lands against my car door and I scream, jerking away from the sound.

But it's just Toby McAlister, being dragged by Alex Garza and Len Edwards. Toby's palm slides across my car window as they pull him away, Toby swerving in and out of the street.

I just want to get out of here.

Instead of heading home, I find myself driving west. I can't imagine going back to our tiny house right now, climbing into bed with my thoughts still whirling. I drive north along the PCH, too itchy in my skin to sleep. It's late, and the highway is a winding stretch of open road, the ocean black and gaping to my left, like an abyss yawning open. I reach Malibu quickly and pull into Playa Point beach. The parking lot is empty. It's breezy and cold and moonless, the sky wrapped in a high layer of clouds.

I stand on the shore for almost an hour, staring at the waves as they roll white and foamy across the sand. I remember the night I told Tate how sometimes I wish I could dive into the ocean and let it take me to a faraway land. To a different life.

I strip out of my clothes, a shadow in the dark.

The air is cold against my skin, but I wade out into the deep, letting the frigid water rise up to my thighs and then my waist, until it touches my chest, and then I dive under, letting the ocean take me.

An icy chill passes through me but I don't turn back, I pull myself down, under a series of waves crashing above my head. Bubbles spill from my nostrils and mouth, and when I finally come to the surface, I let out a gasp of air. I spin onto my back and blink up at the flat, featureless sky.

My lips taste like salt—and I think again of Tate.

I dip my head back under again, trying to rid him from my thoughts, wipe him clean from my skin, from every place he has touched me—his fingers branding my flesh. I need the cold, I need it to help me forget. To strip him clean from my memory.

The tide tugs at me, drawing me farther out, to where the pale blue turns to black. I don't fight it.

The night stretches out around me, the minutes and seconds no longer measured. I drift until there is nothing left of me.

When the chill starts to numb my legs and my entire body begins to shiver, I drop my legs beneath me and head back to shore.

He is gone, I tell myself.

SIXTEEN

IT'S ONLY FEBRUARY ELEVENTH, AND everyone is already talking about Valentine's Day. The Student Council has spent the last week cutting out paper hearts and making banners to hang from every doorway and hallway, signifying the approach of one of high school's most highly anticipated holidays—the one where everyone confesses their secret crushes and makes out in the hallways just a little longer before a teacher yanks them apart.

Midway through the day, lockers are already plastered with red and pink paper hearts, secret messages tucked inside. It's a tradition to leave hearts on the locker of your secret crush. Those who get the most hearts by Valentine's Day are the most desired . . . and therefore, of course, the most popular. At the end of the school day, there are still no notes on our locker. I'm relieved, but Carlos looks defeated.

"This will all feel really far away by next Valentine's Day," I tell him, but I think I'm actually trying to convince myself.

That afternoon, I sit for five minutes with my head down on the steering wheel, before texting Holly to ask if I can have the night off from work. She'd asked me to work extra shifts since it's one of our busiest weeks, and I hate leaving her in the lurch, but she replies right away and tells me to go home and she'll see me later in the week. She's been way too easy on me since my breakup. I guess it's one benefit of her hopelessly romantic heart. I go home and take a nap, praying that sleep will help.

When my phone alarm goes off at six p.m. I force myself to get up. I have my internship hours at UCLA tonight, and if I skip, I could lose my position.

"Do you want me to drive you?" Mia actually offers when I walk into the kitchen.

"I'm fine," I say, grabbing a slice of cold homemade pizza that Grandma made yesterday.

The UCLA campus is quiet this time of night, only a few evening classes in session, and I'm able to park close to the science building where Professor Webb's lab is located.

The lights are on inside the lab, but there's no one inside. It will only be me and one UCLA undergrad working tonight— Rebecca, I think, but she's not here yet.

I drop my purse onto a swivel chair and grab one of the white lab coats hung behind the door. Today we are just supposed to babysit a control group of fungal spores that are being tested under an extremely damp environment, to see if they react by releasing fewer than a thousand spores. Likely nothing will happen tonight on my shift, so there will be a lot of watching and waiting.

I sit on one of the stools and pull out my cell phone. I consider calling Carlos, just to kill some time before my lab partner gets here, when I hear the door swing open. I turn off my phone and slide it into my pocket.

"Hey, Rebecca," I say, swiveling toward the door.

But it's not Rebecca.

Standing inside the doorway is Tate. He looks like he hasn't slept—his eyes heavy and dark. But he's every bit as tempting as I remember, his stance confident, his face too perfect for words, even if his gaze holds an edge of pain. Torment buried in his eyes. My pulse leaps, and I have to suppress the urge to run to him.

"Before you say anything," he starts. "Let me explain."

I push up from the stool and cross my arms, reminding myself that I want nothing to do with him. "You don't need to," I say. "This can't work. You and me . . . us . . . we're too different."

"I don't think we are," he says, moving closer, the nearness of him unsettling my entire body. "I messed up—I know I did. And I'm sorry. I never should have let you leave Colorado like that. I never should have pushed you away."

I'm grinding my jaw and I force myself to stop. "But you did let me leave. You kicked me out of your parents' house on Christmas morning. Do you have any idea how that made me feel—how much that hurt me? Are you even capable of understanding? Is your heart so hollow, so numb from whatever ruined you, that you can't even see when you're destroying the people around you?"

"Charlotte." His eyes sweep over me and I glance away, refusing to let his gaze unravel me. "You're all I think about. I feel like I'm going insane not being with you."

I clench my hands into fists, my fingernails biting into my palms, and our eyes lock.

But the door to the lab swings open behind him and Rebecca steps inside. "Oh, hey—" she says, stopping abruptly before she walks right into Tate. "Sorry I'm late," she adds, but only out of reflex, since her gaze is caught on Tate. I catch the moment of recognition in her eyes. She knows he's Tate Collins and it's stopped her dead in her tracks.

"Can we get out of here?" Tate asks, still looking at me. "Just for a minute."

"I can't. I have to work."

"Nah," Rebecca jumps in, skirting around Tate like she's afraid she might accidentally touch him, then drops her backpack on the floor before grabbing a lab coat from the hook. "We're just staring at spore samples all night, nothing groundbreaking. I'll cover for you, Charlotte." She's doing a good job of not looking directly at him. Like everyone else, she knows about my brief romance with the infamous Tate Collins, but she's always been gracious enough not to bring it up. Now, she must sense the tension that writhes in the air between us.

Tate's eyes bore into mine and I shrug out of my white coat, draping it over a chair. I just want to get this over with. "I'll only be gone a minute," I say to Rebecca, but I don't blink away from Tate's gaze.

"No hurry," she says behind me.

I follow Tate into the hall, then out to the shadowy parking lot. He grabs my hand as soon as we're outside, pivoting me around so that my back is pressed up against the cinder block wall. "I can't be without you," he whispers.

I steel myself to look up into his eyes. "You can't be with me either. Not unless you're honest with me," I say, my tone hard and unforgiving. And then I think back to the lonely weeks without him, the ache so sharp it was a physical pain. "Tell me who you are so I can trust you. Tell me what happened to you to make you like this."

I step away from the wall so I'm no longer caged in by his arms. The parking lot is dark, except for the moons of light cast down by the overhead street lamps.

"I've made mistakes in my past, I've hurt people. I can't take that back. But I don't want to make the same mistakes with you. I know you're mad, I get it." He follows me with his gaze but gives me my space. "I just thought if I planned every detail, if I controlled every move, I could make this work . . ."

I burn with shame and anger. "I can't believe I ever agreed to any of this in the first place. It wasn't even a real relationship, it was just another game to you. I was a puppet you wanted to control. And when I stepped out of line—when I came to see you that night in your room in Colorado, you panicked. You couldn't even let me have the one thing I wanted: you."

"I'm screwed up, I know." He steps closer to me—the slowest motion—and I don't flinch away when he reaches toward me, threading his fingers through my hair. "But I need you, Charlotte. I feel like myself when I'm with you. I've even started writing music again—I almost have enough for a new album. I'd forgotten why I used to love it. But being with you . . . It's changed me. I need you in my life. To remind me that *Casablanca* doesn't end right. To eat lime sherbet with you and know you're the only other person who loves it as much as I do. To listen to you talk about your future, to see the world through your eyes. I can be different, just give me a chance to prove it to you."

My skin tingles beneath his touch and my eyes flutter closed, then open again. "A relationship shouldn't feel like this, Tate. You can't keep forcing me away whenever I get too close."

"I know."

"And why now? Why come find me now, after weeks of nothing?"

"Because I couldn't stay away. I've been a wreck since Christmas. I couldn't take it anymore. I had to see you. I had to try." He pauses, just for a moment, searching my face. "Please, Charlotte."

"You need to let me in," I tell him, as if I'm actually considering this. "You need to tell me what you're thinking instead of just disappearing."

"I promise." He drops his hand from my face. "God, Charlotte, I'm so sorry."

I suck in a deep breath, then let it out. "If we're going to do this, then no more control, no more trying to protect me. You have to let me decide what I want. You have to trust me."

"I do trust you," he says, his eyes piercing mine, reminding me of how effortlessly they can split me open and leave me bare. "You mean everything to me. And I need you."

I need him, too. My heart rate kicks up.

Finally, I lean forward, brushing my lips across his. At once, his hands are in my hair pulling me forward, his lips covering mine. He kisses me like he doesn't want to lose me, he kisses me like he won't ever let go again.

"I don't care about everything else. I just want the real you," I say, drawing back just a whisper. Only an hour earlier I thought I'd never see him again, but now, with his lips so close to mine, another thought surfaces, one I can't ignore. One that's been gaining weight long before our trip to Colorado. "I want to be with you. And I want—" The words catch momentarily in my throat, a confession, and then they find form. "I want all of you."

He pulls away, cradling my face in his palms. In his eyes I see that he understands what I mean. That I'm done waiting for him.

"I want you, too," he says, his voice heady and deep.

There is a fever in his touch now, an urgency in his hands along my neck. I feel a flurry of excitement in my belly, followed again by dread. I can't tell Grandma we're back together. Not after what happened.

"Tate . . . can we . . . can we keep this just between us, for now? I know it's not easy, with the paparazzi and all, but . . ."

"Whatever you want," he says. And I wrap my arms around him, smelling the clean scent of him, my lips lingering against his neck. It would be so easy to kiss him again, let him push me back against the wall and feel his hands across my body. I could forget about going back to the lab and lose all sense of time. But instead, I rest my hands against his shoulders and tell him that I need to go.

I start to walk through the door but he pulls me back, kissing me once, long and deep, before releasing me. "I'm not going to lose you again," he says.

"I hope not," I tell him, and I slip back inside.

SEVENTEEN

SUNDAY AFTERNOON, CARLOS AND I are sitting on the bleachers in the gym, watching the dress rehearsal for *A Midsummer Night's Dream*. The opening night of the play is in two weeks and Carlos is writing an article about it for the *Banner*. I'm assigned to take photos.

Normally, I'd be excited to experiment with the school camera equipment, outdated as it is, but it's Sunday—and it's Valentine's Day—and I'd rather be anywhere but here. Actually, I'd rather be one place in particular: with Tate. I haven't seen him since he came into the lab and surprised me three nights ago, but I have a feeling I'll hear from him today.

"The set design is still a little shoddy," Carlos says in a hush.

"I don't think they're finished yet. And you can't print that in your article."

"I think Puck's tights are starting to tear in the crotch."

"Yeah, you can't print that either. And why are you staring at his crotch?" I raise a brow at him.

"The real question is, why aren't *you* staring? You've gotta admit, Jake Cline slays it as Puck."

"And here I thought you were still madly in love with Alan Gregory," I tease.

"I am. I was thinking Jake might make an interesting rebound for you," Carlos says, winking. I look guiltily away. He doesn't know that Tate and I are back together. And I don't plan on telling him. Not yet anyway. He saw how crushed I was after Christmas, and we spent weeks hating on Tate together. I can't imagine how I'd explain taking him back.

"I'm not interested in a rebound," I say.

"But have you really looked at those tights? I mean, come on."

"Carlos!" I turn swiftly on the bench and slap his leg.

"What?" He shrugs innocently. "I'm only trying to help you find a distraction."

I meet his eyes and we both start to laugh, holding our hands over our mouths to keep from interrupting the second act of the play.

I snap a couple photos from our seats, then move closer to the stage to get a better shot of the half-constructed set design. It'll have to be good enough for the article.

"Your phone was vibrating in your bag," Carlos says when I return to my chair. He's scribbling notes on a pad and doesn't look up when I pull out my phone and read the text from Tate: *My house in fifteen?*

I'm at school, I send back.

Another text pops up immediately. *Twenty then?* I smile, but flatten my lips so Carlos won't see.

I'll be there.

He texts me the code to his security gate and I lock my phone, gripping it in my palm.

"Hey," I say to Carlos. "I have to go."

"Where?" He glances up from his notepad.

"To—um, the lab, at UCLA. My professor needs me to fill in."

"On a Sunday afternoon?"

"I know. Sucks. But I need to go."

"But the rehearsal's not over."

"I got the photos I need. I promise they'll do justice to your article," I say, dropping the camera into my bag and hoisting it over my shoulder. "I'll call you later." I wave, already starting to back-step away.

"Okay, lame friend," Carlos says, half teasing. But I sense he really isn't happy I'm ditching him. Especially on Valentine's Day, when we're supposed to be single and miserable together.

I jog out to my car, swing my bag onto the passenger seat, then start the engine. My heart is already starting to race in anticipation.

At Tate's driveway, I punch in the key code and smile to myself as the massive metal gate swings inward, allowing me to drive through. I'd asked him to let me into his life; I guess trusting me with his security code is a good place to start. I park and walk up to the towering front doors. I'm about to knock when I see that one of them is open a crack. I push against it. "Tate?" I call. But there's no answer.

The house is dark, aside from the lights glowing dimly from the walls.

"Tate?" I call again, but still nothing.

I step farther into the house, down the steps into the lofty living room. I press my fingers against the glass overlooking the pool and the back lawn and the glimmer of LA far in the distance.

I don't hear Tate move up behind me until his hands press against my waist, slipping around my hip bones. "Hi," I say, starting to turn around to face him. But he holds me firmly in place, kissing the side of my neck, his lips sliding gently over my skin. The sensation ripples through me like electricity set free from its wires. It crackles and bursts and singes my fingertips where they linger on the cool surface of the glass.

Then one of his hands releases me and he turns me around, holding out a small blue box tied with white ribbon. "Happy Valentine's Day," he says simply.

I take it from him, holding the weight of it in my palm, realizing that this is the first time anyone has ever given me a gift for this particular holiday. "I didn't get you anything," I say, wishing I had thought to bring him something. Even though I have no idea what you buy someone who probably already has everything he needs.

"Yes you did," he says, his voice tender. "You're here—that's all I need."

I raise an eyebrow at him, then begin untying the ribbon from the box. When I open the lid, my gaze snaps back up to him. "It's—"

"Don't say it's too much," he interjects before I can finish.

My fingers slide over the silver bracelet studded with diamonds. I lift it up from the box, my hands trembling slightly, stunned by how shimmery and delicate and beautiful it is. And then I notice the charm attached to the clasp—it's in the shape of a triangle.

"Do you like it?" Tate asks gently. "I thought you should have a triangle that's more permanent than the one you draw on your wrist."

"It's incredible, Tate. I can't believe you did this." It's nicer than anything I've ever owned in my entire life, and even though I don't ask, I can't help but wonder how much it cost him. I'm sure far too much.

He secures the bracelet around my left wrist, directly over top of the triangle I've traced in blue ballpoint pen on my skin. The diamonds sparkle and flicker even in the dim light of the living room, and it feels like more than I deserve.

"If you don't like it, I can have them design something else," Tate offers, still looking unsure, like he's been worried about my response for days now, afraid I would hate it. Which means he probably had it designed before we got back together. He really had been thinking of me while we were apart.

"No," I answer quickly. "It couldn't be more perfect, Tate.

I love it—thank you." I touch it with my other hand, still in shock that he had something custom-made just for me. That he remembered the triangle on my wrist; that he remembered what it means to me.

His eyes slide back to mine, sending waves of heat through my entire body. I reach for him, running my fingers up his jawline, wanting him to know how much this means to me. "I'm serious," I say so he understands. "It's more than I deserve."

"It's hardly enough," he says. "You deserve a lot more."

I smile and tilt forward up onto my toes, pressing my lips against his. His kiss is slow at first, careful, and then I can feel the need in his lips, the heat burning between us.

"Did you mean what you said the other night?" he asks, his breath tickling the soft curve of my ear as his mouth slides up my neck.

My heart stutters and slams against my rib cage, not from fear or hesitation, but adrenaline—a fevered excitement that writhes inside my belly. I told him that I want him—all of him. Now more than ever, after everything we've been through together, I know I'm ready. I want to share this with him—something that will bind us and bring us closer. "Yes."

"You're sure?"

Desire sings through my veins. "I'm sure."

Movement in the glass catches my eye—our reflection. I watch Tate nod slowly. "I'm still going to go slow with you."

I try to respond but then Tate's lips find my throat, kissing me gently and traveling up to my jaw, and all I can do is gasp. I have always craved his touch, but this time it feels different—this time it feels like our bodies throb to the same heartbeat.

His fingers are slow and deliberate as they slide around my hip, then push up the hem of my shirt. Thankfully, I'd guessed I would see him today, and had made sure to wear the pale blue push-up bra I bought at Barney's. The one that makes me feel like someone else—someone desirable and confident and sexy. My skin trembles. I close my eyes as he pulls the shirt upward, over my stomach and then to my neck. I raise my arms, and he lifts the plain green shirt over my head, dropping it to the floor. I'm standing in only my bra. My breathing deepens. His gaze meets mine in the glass, a question in his eyes. I nod wordlessly. His fingers find the button of my shorts, unfastening it deftly, then sliding down the zipper. They fall around my ankles and I carefully step out of them. Tate kicks them away with his bare foot.

I know I should feel exposed—vulnerable—but instead I feel ignited, set on fire by his breath grazing my shoulder. Every fiber of my flesh, every nerve ending is alight.

"Charlotte," he whispers into my ear—a broken murmur—and a tingle races down my neck. Then his palms are around my torso again, sliding up my ribs like a ladder.

I can hardly breathe, barely think. My heartbeat roars in my ears and I'm shaking. Is he going to push me away? Stop us here? My mouth goes dry and I close my eyes, scared of what he might say next.

"Let's go to my room," he finally says, and the relief almost swallows me whole.

Tate's room is huge, the light dimmed by the shades. His bed is neatly made with dark gray pillows and a charcoal bedspread.

He slides his fingers up my cheekbones, carefully, drawing my focus back to him, then pulls me into a kiss. I feel myself sink into his arms, surrendering to his touch, never wanting his hands to be anywhere else except on me.

He pulls away from me only long enough to tear his shirt over his head, revealing his hard, muscled chest, and I barely stop my mouth from dropping open. His hands move around my waist again and I glance up at him, taking in the sharp, angular lines of his impossibly handsome face. His dark eyes glitter as he reaches for me, pushing my hair away from my face. "You're so beautiful, Charlotte," he whispers just before he kisses me.

He turns and sets me delicately onto the edge of the bed, and I bite the corner of my mouth. I reach up and touch his stomach, his abs firm. He tilts my chin upward, brushing his thumb over my lips, and lowers himself to kiss me. I close my eyes, his lips soft and slow at first, like they are remembering what I feel like, what I taste like. "I've missed you," he says again, and I feel the words all through my body. His other hand glides over my bare leg, my thigh, stopping at the line of my underwear. Then his hands travel up to my waist, over the dark fabric, his thumbs pressing into my hip bones. I kiss him deeper, harder, willing him to not let go.

I slide down onto the bed, melting, liquefying, and his body follows. He positions himself above me, kissing my throat. And every second feels like I'm about to come undone, my thoughts scattering, my body trembling beneath his touch.

"Are you okay?" he asks softly when I suck in a deep breath.

"Yes," I whisper.

His hand inches upward, gliding smooth and effortlessly across my body. A slow trickle of desire begins to build.

"You're so soft." He places another kiss against my throat and I tilt my head slightly, widening the space for him to kiss me again. But instead he whispers, "Has any boy ever touched you like this?" His voice is low and calm, deeper than I've ever heard him speak before, and I feel my legs go weak.

"No," I say, my voice thin.

Tate doesn't slow the rhythmic way his hands seem to know every curve of my flesh, moving like liquid, spilling over my skin like heat.

I reach up to feel the hardness of his chest. My fingers travel down to his abs flexing above me, and then I find the edge of his jeans, sagged low on his hips. I circle the metal button with my fingertip, then start to slide it free, but Tate stops me, touching my hand gently.

A smile reaches his slightly parted lips. "Leave those on for now."

I lift my head, starting to protest, but his mouth presses over mine, kissing away the words. His hand skims down my body.

"Is this okay?" Tate's voice vibrates against my flesh and my body pulses around him. I start to murmur *yes* but my body takes over, arching toward him. Blood rushes into my ears, my toes curl, and my palms press against the mattress, gripping the sheets—my lungs gasping for air as I cry out.

I collapse beneath him and his mouth lifts. Slowly, I release my grip on the bed, and Tate's fingers glide back up my thigh. His other hand lingers for a moment against my trembling skin, holding me still so that his lips can kiss me one last time, soft and sweet.

He smiles and rolls over on his back, pulling me with him. I rest my head on his shoulder.

"You all right?" he whispers.

"Mmhmm," I reply, unable to say much more, not yet.

"Good. I'm going to do things different this time," he tells me. "I want to make sure you're ready."

I lift my head to study him. "I am ready," I assure him.

I curl my body around his, and he reaches up a hand to touch my face. With his lips near my ear, he hums a melody against my skin.

"Is that a new song?" I ask.

"It's something I've been working on."

"I like it," I say in an exhale, still feeling heady and like I'm made of air.

"I've been wanting to tell you that I'm going to record a new album." His breath tickles my hair. "I've already written most of the songs, thanks to you. You've inspired me."

I wonder how I—Charlotte Reed, invisible bookworm and colossal nerd—could have inspired him. It's so absurd I almost laugh.

"My manager used to tell me that I needed a muse to write meaningful songs. I didn't really know what that meant, until I met you," he continues, his thumb rubbing my bottom lip. "When I'm with you, the lyrics just appear in my head. I've never experienced it before. The songs are just pouring out of me and I can't wait for you to hear them."

"That's amazing," I say, but my heart is starting to thump erratically, the light-as-air feeling quickly fading away. I try not to think about the articles I read about Tate, how things were before he met me, when he was Tate Collins the pop idol. The girls, the drugs, all the wild things he's alluded to. I let out a breath. "But what will all of this mean for us?"

He slides himself over top of me so we're face-to-face, so he can look me in the eye. "It's going to be a lot of studio time," he admits. "I have to get this album just right. It's a new sound, a new direction for me, and I need it to connect with my fans in a big way." His gaze locks with mine, intense and searching. "But I promise I'll make time to see you as often as I can, Charlotte. You're everything to me. I hope you know that."

I nod, trying to ignore the sense of dread that's lingering deep within me.

"This is going to work between us," he stresses just before he kisses me. "But I have to leave for New York first thing Tuesday."

My lips curve into an uneasy smile and I nod, but my heart is crushed at the idea of him across the country from me when I've just gotten him back. "Don't they have studios here in LA?"

"I'm meeting with a record producer who I think is going to be the perfect fit for my album. He understands what I'm trying to do—something raw and authentic. Less produced. He's usually booked, but my manager got me a meeting, so I can't pass up this chance to work with him."

"How long will you be gone?"

"I don't know. If it all comes together, we could start recording right away," he explains.

"Here?"

"Maybe here. Or maybe in New York. I'm not sure yet." He runs a finger down my temple, his gaze watchful and steady. I can't look away. "But I'll call you. Text you. And I promise to be back soon."

He lowers his head to kiss me and I smile. "I'm sad that you're leaving, but I'm also so excited for you."

"It's only temporary. I can't stand being away from you for too long," he whispers against my lips. "Everything is finally making sense. You. Me. My career. You're exactly what I need, Charlotte."

I kiss him back, winding my arms around his neck. Emotion swirls inside me—happiness, excitement, longing. Just when I finally have Tate, when I nearly have *all* of him, I feel like he's slipping away. But I push the fear away and smile against his lips, enjoying this one moment, right here, right now.

EIGHTEEN

I HAVE BECOME ONE OF *those* girls. Obsessively checking my phone. Peeking at it secretly at my desk. Carrying it in my hand between classes so I can feel the vibration if Tate happens to send me a text. I hate that I'm doing it, but I can't seem to stop. When Mia catches me, I lie and say I'm just anxious to hear from Stanford. Admissions letters will go out any day now, but still, all I can think about is Tate.

He's been in New York for eight days and it feels like a month. So when an e-mail pops up during sixth period, I reach for my phone so quickly that I knock it onto the floor.

The clatter draws too much attention to me, and I have to shove the phone back in my bag and wait until class ends to read it. When the bell rings and I finally get to open the message, it takes me a moment to process what it means. It's an electronic airline ticket to New York City . . . for this weekend.

I stop dead in the middle of the hallway, all sounds muffled around me.

He bought me a ticket to New York City! He wants me to come see him.

I decide that there's no other way. I have to come clean. I can't fly across the country without telling someone. And I need his help. After sending a cryptic text to Carlos, we meet up at the Lone Bean. I guilt-buy him an iced coffee, compliment a shirt he's had forever, and that's when he tells me to spill.

"Something's going on, Charlotte," he says. "I know you."

Finally, after dragging it out, I confess to Carlos everything about Tate: how he apologized at the lab, how he promised things would be different, how we've been dating secretly. And finally, about the ticket to New York.

Carlos actually looks numb, his coffee frozen in his hand, halfway raised to his mouth. "You've been seeing him this whole time?"

"I should have told you, I know, I'm so sorry. But things just got complicated before when everyone found out about us."

"I'm your best friend."

I press my hands over my eyes. "I know. I'm sorry, a million times I'm sorry. But I'm being honest now. And I really need your help."

He looks down at me, rolling his tongue against the inside of his cheek. I've lied to him twice now about Tate—first when I didn't tell him I was dating Tate Collins, and now that I've been seeing him again—and I can see the disappointment in his gaze.

And then I ask him to lie for me. "I told my grandma that you and I are going to a Model UN summit in New York."

"We're not in Model UN club."

"She thinks they were short two people for the trip, so we signed up."

"That sounds so made up."

I know it does. "But my grandma doesn't know that."

"I don't want to lie to your grandma for you, Charlotte."

I can barely meet Carlos's eyes. "She's not going to call you or anything to check, but if she does, just say that you're with me and we're really excited to represent Norway or Iceland or something at the summit."

"*Those* are the countries you want to represent?"

"Pick whichever country you want," I say, laughing.

Carlos's mouth twists. "I'd much rather be Switzerland and stay out of this whole thing."

"Please," I beg. "Just help me do this one thing and I'll owe you majorly."

Carlos sips his iced coffee. "I don't think you should go. You've never been to New York before and—"

"I know you don't like him," I say. "But that's just because you don't know him. He was a jerk in Colorado, yes, but since then he's been amazing. He's really making an effort to change. He texts me every day, tells me how much he misses me, and the fact that he wants me in New York with him is huge. It's just for the weekend, you probably won't even have to do anything. But just in case my grandma calls, I need you to be my alibi."

He grips my shoulders with both hands and stares down at me. "All right, I'll cover for you. But you have to promise me you'll text me so I know you're safe and he hasn't whisked you off to Monaco and made you his bride."

"I will." And I lean across the table to wrap my arms around his tall frame. "You're the best."

"And promise me you'll come back with your V-card," he adds unexpectedly.

I almost choke on my coffee, covering my mouth with my hand and clearing my throat. "Since when do you care about my V-card?" I ask, my voice low.

"Since you seem to be taking a lot of risks for this guy, and I want you to be careful. I don't want you to . . . lose yourself."

I smile and shake my head. He's right, but I won't lose myself. I feel like Tate found me and I've never been less lost. I know exactly where I'm supposed to be. "I can't promise that. But I love you," I say, sipping my coffee. "I'll text you when I land."

He looks like he's about to caution me one more time, but then changes his mind. "Love you, too."

The day is clear and free of smog as the jet rises above LAX, and all of LA seems to glisten.

I can't believe I'm really doing this. I don't even know who I am anymore—this girl who skips school, calls her boss to get out of work, and flies across the country to spend the weekend with a boy who makes her feel reckless and wild and capable of almost anything. The old me never would have been this bold.

But now, sitting in a first-class seat, staring out the tiny oval-shaped window as the sun breaks against the horizon, I'm not afraid anymore. For the first time, I feel like anything is possible.

NINETEEN

NEW YORK CITY IS A glittery mass of lights under the dark sky and a nervous excitement buzzes inside me as the plane touches down.

Hank is standing at the baggage carousel waiting, and he grins when he spots me and carries my suitcase out to a black Escalade. The city feels alive as we make our way through Manhattan, skyscrapers towering overhead, people moving up the sidewalks as a light rain collects on the front windshield. I can't believe I'm really here.

We finally slow to a stop in front of a towering hotel and a uniformed man opens the door for me, holding an umbrella. A bellhop retrieves my suitcase from the back of the SUV and wheels it under the awning out of the rain.

"Your key, milady," Hank says when he meets me at the curb, handing me a plastic key card. Then he turns to the man who's holding the umbrella over my head. "She's in the penthouse."

The streets are glistening in the rain. A reflective sheen that sparkles beneath the line of car headlights.

"Tate will be back at nine and you have dinner reservations at nine-thirty," Hank explains to me.

"Okay."

"I'm glad you're here, Charlotte," he adds. "He missed you. So did I."

"Thanks, Hank," I say, touched, and he walks back to the driver's side door.

The man with the umbrella gestures for me to follow him and we step through the glass doors. I slow to a stop, taking in the arched gold ceiling and the crystal chandeliers. People sit on low-backed sofas and carry cocktails from the lobby bar. It's the most elegant room I've ever seen.

"Miss," the man says, holding the elevator doors open for me.

I catch up to him, stepping inside the mirrored elevator car, and he waves his key card over the panel, then presses the PH button. The elevator begins to glide upward and I hold on to the brass railing, tilting my head up like I could watch each floor pass as we climb higher.

"Your room," he says when the elevator finally stops, waving to the single door across a short hallway. I hold my own key card—the one Hank gave me—over the square panel and the light flicks to green, unlocking the door.

I step through the doorway into a suite that puts the lobby to shame. Chandeliers are suspended elegantly over the living room and dining area. White couches face an already-lit fireplace. Airy curtains hang beside massive, floor-to-ceiling glass doors that lead out to a huge balcony.

"Do you need anything else?" the man asks, setting my suitcase just inside the room. I shake my head and he retreats back into the hall, the doors closing behind him.

I stand for a moment, staring, then I catapult myself onto the king-sized bed, sinking into the sky-blue pillows and fanning my arms wide.

I shriek and then cover my mouth, laughing.

I might never want to leave.

And then I see something to my left, hanging on a hook over a door. It's a dress: a long, sexy black dress. I stand and nearly trip over myself, I'm so excited as I cross the room to read the note pinned to the hanger: *For you.*

I press the note to my lips, grinning.

I am Alice, and this is wonderland.

The girl in the full-length bathroom mirror is a stranger. Watching her I let out a deep breath. The fabric of the dress, so smooth against my skin, clings to the curves of my body. I run my fingers along my hips, feeling the delicate black silk.

I feel beautiful.

It's already nine-fifteen when I walk out to the balcony overlooking New York. Car horns bellow up from below and there is a steady thrumming, like the city has a pulse, a heartbeat that never stops.

When the chill creeps into my bones, I move back inside,

walking around the suite, eventually collapsing back onto the bed. *Where is he? Hank said he should be here by now.* By ten o'clock I feel my eyelids grow heavy but I don't remember drifting into sleep until there is the warmth of someone beside me.

His breath is hot against my neck, and it rouses me from a half dream. Then a hand flattens over my hip bone, sliding down to my thigh. My eyes flutter open.

"I'm sorry I'm late," he whispers beside my ear. "We ran long at the studio." I can feel his lips lingering against the back of my neck. "Are you hungry?"

I nod and turn to face him.

"We missed our reservation," he adds, watching me now, his eyes burning into mine. I want to kiss him, touch him, fold myself up in his arms. So I do. I plant my lips on his and he kisses me back, our mouths intertwined and my heartbeat rising swiftly. He touches my hair and gently tugs it back to look in my eyes. "Let's eat first," he says. And the *first* implies there will be an after, and my heart thuds more rapidly at the idea of his hands on me again. "There's an all-night pizza place only a block away."

"Sounds perfect," I say.

He takes my hands and lifts me from the bed, giving me a lingering once-over. "You, in that dress, are almost too much."

I inch up on my toes to kiss him. "You bought it," I say. "So you only have yourself to blame."

Inside the elevator, Tate slides his hand around my waist as we descend down the floors. I'm about to speak, to ask if he always stays in this hotel when he comes to New York, when his grip suddenly tightens and he presses me into the corner of the elevator. He kisses me again, his tongue soft against my lips, teasing the inside of my mouth, and I sink into his arms. When his kiss moves down to my throat, I say, "Maybe we should skip dinner."

He shakes his head. "You need to eat." And then the elevator doors slide open onto the lobby.

Outside, the city feels just as awake and alive as I imagine it is during the day. Crowds of people move up the sidewalks and I love the anonymity, the feeling of being lost and free in a city where no one seems to recognize Tate. Where we are just two people passing through the drizzling rain.

I am completely overdressed for the modest pizza shop, but no one bats an eye. We order two slices and sit at a small red-and-white-checkered table by the front window.

Tate runs his hand over my leg beneath the table. "You wore the bracelet," he comments, nodding down to where his Valentine's Day gift glimmers on my wrist.

"I love it, I just don't get a chance to wear it that often," I say. "If my grandma saw it . . ." But my voice trails off. I don't want to think about her right now, about the lies I told to be here.

"I'm glad you wore it tonight," he says, smoothing over my thoughts. "It looks incredible on you. *You* look incredible."

I pull in my lower lip, hiding a smile, then take another bite of sundried-tomato pizza. We spend the rest of dinner catching up on each other's week in between doughy, greasy, heavenly bites of the best pizza I've ever tasted. I tell him about the man who called the Bloom Room to order two bouquets—one for his wife, the other for his girlfriend. Both cards the same: *I love you forever.* Tate fills me in on the album's progress—I don't understand the more technical terms, but I can tell from his face that it's going well. And he seems happy.

When we're finished eating, I feel an urgency sparking between us, threatening to ignite us both. The street is bustling with activity and Tate holds me close as we weave around taxicabs. There are no paparazzi waiting for us, no fans screeching his name. We could be anyone. And I really do feel like someone else, like this is our city and we belong here . . . together.

Back in the hotel elevator, Tate doesn't touch me. But his eyes bear down on me, like he's holding himself back. My abdomen tightens and swirls with heat.

When the elevator doors slide open onto the penthouse, Tate grabs me and pulls me through the door after him, wrapping me up in his arms and leading me into the living room. He holds me for a moment, his lips hovering over mine. "I'm incapable of thinking clearly when I'm with you," he says. And my insides flutter, about to burst.

The sliding glass doors overlooking the balcony are still cracked open slightly from when I walked outside earlier, and a crisp breeze rolls in, dampening my suddenly scorching-hot skin.

I hear a familiar chime, the whistling of my phone. I slip

from between Tate's arms. It might be my grandma checking up on me. But when I open it, it's from Carlos. I totally forgot to text him that I landed safely.

You alive? It reads.

I type back quickly. *Yes. City is amazing. Might never come home.*

You better come home. And remember what I said about V-card. Be good. Text me in the morning xo, he replies.

Night. Xo. I can't give him any guarantees that I'll be good, and I can't make any promises that I won't come back to LA a different person.

I'm about to drop my phone back onto the table when I see an unopened e-mail. It's from Stanford. I never checked my phone after I landed, and my heart nearly stops. With trembling fingers, I slide open the message. My eyes scan the words rapidly.

Congratulations! On behalf of the Office of Undergraduate Admission, it is my pleasure to offer you admission to Stanford University.

For a second I can't move. I reread the first paragraph several times before it sets in.

"Everything okay?" Tate asks me from the bedroom doorway.

"I—I'm going to Stanford," I say. I can't believe it.

He crosses the room, his eyes lighting up. "Charlotte. That's amazing."

"I wasn't sure I would get in." I look back down at the phone to make sure I didn't misread it. "My guidance counselor wasn't either. I mean, nobody's sure they will. It's a really tough school. You know that. I'm rambling." I blink up at him: stunned, elated, my mind clattering with a million thoughts all at once.

Tate grins. "I knew you'd get in—I'm so happy for you. We need to celebrate, this is a big deal. I'll call down for champagne—I know the concierge, he won't have an issue serving us. Or we can go out? Whatever you want, this is your night."

I set my phone on the table, focusing back on him. I take a step closer, breathing in the sight of him here, in front of me, and I realize there's no one else I'd rather be with when the news about Stanford came in. I want to share this with him.

I run my hands up his chest and his eyes reignite under my gaze. His fingers go to my chin. "I don't want to go anywhere," I say. His mouth finds mine, and he wraps his arms around my waist and lifts me easily. I shiver in his embrace, my arms going around his neck as he carries me back to the bedroom.

Tate sets me carefully on the edge of the bed and I tilt my head up to look at him. I touch his stomach, his abs hard beneath his T-shirt, and he sucks in a breath. I want to see him. I want to touch his bare skin, and I push my fingers underneath the hem of his shirt. He pauses for a moment, watching me, and then he lifts the shirt over his head, his biceps flexing with the motion.

"I've missed you," he whispers. "So damn much."

My heart is a butterfly, fast and light, beating inside my chest. I have everything I've dreamed of and something I never even *dared* to dream of. I'm not afraid of anything anymore. I know what I want.

Tate.

The night flutters and spins out around us. We strip from our clothes and slide beneath the silky white sheet. His lips make a map along my skin, charting a course where only he has ever been. We kiss, we tangle ourselves together, we go slow. And even though we don't go all the way, it feels like we've branded ourselves together. Each tender kiss, each suspended moment looking into each other's eyes, we discover something beyond desire.

It feels like trust. And I realize I would do anything for him, go anywhere, risk everything, just to be with him.

It's close to midnight when our hands settle, our lips place our last kiss, sleep tugging at us, and I rest my head on his shoulder, his fingers in my hair. I'm tired, sated, overwhelmed. I never thought it could be like this with someone. I always imagined the worst: seeing how easily my mom's heart could be broken, how easily she deluded herself. My sister abandoned with Leo, her dreams forgotten.

But it's not like that with Tate. Here, in his arms in the middle of Manhattan, an acceptance letter in my inbox from Stanford, all of my dreams have come true. Nothing could be better than this one, single moment.

"I love you," I whisper, the words tumbling from my tongue like I have no control over them.

Tate stills for a moment, eyes flicking over mine. In them I catch a flash of emotion, a hint of what almost looks like fear. Then they darken and he rolls onto his back, staring out the window at the ocean of city lights.

I bring my palms to my stomach, feeling suddenly hollow. *Why did I just say that?* Because it's true, I realize—because in this moment, it's the only thing I feel. I am desperately, turned-inside-out in love with him. And nothing else could ever make me feel like I do when I'm with him.

My lips part but I don't know what to say—how to explain.

But then he turns to face me, reaching an arm out and pulling me to him. I rest my head on his chest, listening to the steady thump of his heartbeat, and he kisses my temple but doesn't speak.

The silence feels heavy and unbreakable. He's not going to say it back—because he doesn't feel the same way. He doesn't love me. Maybe he never could. Or maybe he just doesn't know how. I torture myself with every variation, every reason why he couldn't answer me. But eventually, exhaustion wraps its cool fingers around my thoughts and I slip into a sleep so deep that I don't move again until the sound of a police siren outside wakes me so abruptly I sit straight upright.

But Tate is gone.

I climb to my feet and press my lips together, remembering the taste of him against my mouth only a couple hours before.

The black dress is tangled on the floor and I pull it on for lack of a better option, walking in my bare feet out into the living room.

The doors are still open wide and Tate is out on the balcony, leaning against the railing, wearing only his jeans despite the temperature. The air is freezing, and I stop in the doorway, arms wrapped around my waist.

"What's wrong?" I ask.

But he doesn't turn. Maybe he hasn't heard me. I step out onto the balcony, the air cutting across the exposed skin of my arms and legs. I reach him but still he doesn't react, his gaze intent on the darkened city.

"You must be cold," I say.

I want to touch him, but he's like stone. He hasn't even acknowledged me yet. I'm about to ask him to come inside when he finally speaks.

"I was thinking about the last time a girl told me she loved me."

I tilt toward him, leaning my hip against the railing. I shiver. Suddenly, I am cold from more than the breeze.

"Her name was Ella."

I brush my palms up my arms, wishing he would turn and face me, but he's lost out there in the cityscape, looking for something only he can see.

"Did you tell her you loved her back?" I can't help it; I have to know.

He releases a long, slow exhale. "No. It wasn't like that."

"What was it like, then?" I want to know who she was—this girl he's never mentioned until now—and why it seems to hurt him to speak her name. There's a heaviness in the air, a tension, and I can tell this is it, this is important.

His hands clench together in front of him as he leans out over the railing, twenty floors up. "I've made a lot of mistakes," he says, his voice caught in the air and carried away.

"Like what?"

"I was someone else then—a brand, a plastic wind-up rock star, singing when they told me to sing, dancing when they told me to dance. But after my parents went back to Colorado, things just sort of fell apart. I started partying—a lot. Just to escape the pressure. There were nights on tour, after a show, when I wouldn't even sleep." He swallows and looks down at the street far below. "And the fans were everywhere. They would do anything to get backstage—just to be close to me, just to touch me. It was crazy. You can't even imagine what that feels like, that type of fame. You start to feel like you're a god. Like you can get away with anything."

The muscles of his shoulders and arms, bared in the icy night air, are like a fortress I can't touch. And while I shiver, he seems unaffected.

"That's when I met her—Ella St. John." He takes in a breath, then releases it slowly. "She was seventeen when we first met, and she came to nearly every show I did on tour that year. I met her a few times backstage, the bouncers got used to seeing her, so they'd let her come back. We partied in a few different cities and then one night . . ." His mouth flattens, as if he's chewing over the words before he lets them leave his lips. "One night . . . she came back to my tour bus." He stops, gaze still locked in the distance.

"And you slept with her?" I finish for him.

He doesn't nod—he doesn't need to. "The night we were together—the only night," he says, "she told me that she was in love with me. I was so wasted that I thought she was joking. We didn't even know each other."

This is the secret he has kept from me. This is the thing that has weighed on him from the first day we met.

"The next night the tour went to Chicago. She was there, too, backstage after the show. She tried to see me. I remember her face when I came offstage, smiling as she pushed through the crowd. She thought . . . she thought there was something between us. That I would want to see her—that we would, I don't know, be together. But it wasn't like that for me. It was just one night."

"Did you see her again after that?" I ask when he falls quiet.

"A couple more tour stops—she got backstage, tried to talk to me, but I ignored her. I didn't mean to hurt her, but she didn't understand. It's like she thought she was my girlfriend. She even told a couple of my bodyguards that she was. But they knew to keep her away from me by then. She was getting obsessed." I wrap my arms around myself, trying to get warm. Obsessed. Isn't that how I've been feeling? He's all I can think about when we're apart, but this is different. It has to be. Tate's eyes lift, searching for the memory maybe, trying to recall it in the darkness. "I didn't realize what would happen.

If I had known . . ." His voice trails into nothing, swallowed by the silence.

"What happened?"

He shakes his head. "A week after the Seattle show, my manager told me the police found her. She jumped from a bridge . . ." He doesn't finish, but I understand what he means. "She left a note. Said she thought we were in love; that we were supposed to be together."

"She killed herself?" I shiver at the words, the idea that this girl could give up her entire life because of a boy, because of love . . .

"I ended the tour early after that. I stopped performing completely. I walked away from everything, all the parties, the late nights. I couldn't do it anymore. I realized that fame is a responsibility and I took it for granted. If one night could ruin a girl's life—because of me—I didn't want to risk hurting anyone else."

He turns away from the railing, away from me, his entire body a rigid length of muscle, rain sliding over his shoulders.

"Is that why you backed away? That first night at your house, when I told you I'd never kissed anyone?" I move closer to him, touching his arm for the first time. His shoulders flex but he doesn't pull away. "And again in Colorado? That's why you thought you needed control?"

"I didn't think I deserved you. You were perfect—you *are* perfect. I didn't want to destroy you, too. Take away everything you've worked for."

I shake my head even though he can't see me. "I'm stronger than that, Tate."

"Before I met you," he says, his voice low, "I thought I had fucked up my entire life, that there was no going back. But with you . . . with you I keep thinking maybe there's still a chance."

"For what?"

Slowly, he turns to face me, his dark eyes on mine. "To have someone in my life that I don't destroy."

I shake my head, rain falling between us. "What happened to Ella was not your fault," I say, my lips trembling from the cold. "You couldn't have known what she was going to do. You need to forgive yourself for that, otherwise you'll spend the rest of your life afraid it'll happen again." I slide my hands around him so my palms are pressed against his bare back, his heart beating beside my ear. His skin is warm, much warmer than I expected with the cold rain cascading over both of us. "You need to let go of what happened." I feel his chest draw in a breath of air. "You need to trust that you're not going to hurt anyone."

He touches my chin and tilts it up, staring down at me, a storm inside his eyes. He kisses me, slow and fluid, and it feels like all the words he wants to say but can't. "Thank you," he whispers against my lips.

A moment passes, the rain and the city filling the silence. And then I say, "Let's go inside."

He nods, and winds his fingers through mine.

He closes the sliding glass doors behind us and we walk back into the bedroom, dripping water from our feet and fingertips, leaving a trail behind us.

My dress is now wet from the rain, so I unzip the back and let it slip down my legs to the floor. Tate watches me from the other side of the bed. I crawl beneath the sheets and Tate climbs in after, tucking his arms around me. My body is damp and chilled, but Tate's hands roam across my skin, down my spine, then up again, warming me with his touch. I think for a moment that his fingers might inch to other places, reignite the heat inside me to the point of breaking again—finally take us all the way there—but then he whispers against my brow, "Get some sleep."

I peek one last time at the windows overlooking the city, now streaked with rain, before I close my eyes. I want it to be like this forever.

TWENTY

THE MORNING SUN MAKES ELONGATED shapes against the white bedsheet. I wake, blinking, and stare at my outstretched arm. The triangle shape on my wrist has faded. I haven't been tracing it as often. I've been thinking of other things.

Tate is still beside me, lying on top of the comforter while I'm tangled in the sheets. I think he's asleep, but when I turn onto my side to face him, I see his eyes are open, staring out the massive windows.

"Good morning," I say, and my voice sounds slight and sweet.

"Morning." He reaches out for me, pulling me to him, and I slide my hand over his stomach. "You're gorgeous when you sleep," he says. The tension of last night has lifted, but he still seems somber.

"Did you sleep at all?" I ask.

"A little."

I breathe him in and his fingertips trace lines down my arm. "Do you have to work today?" I ask.

"No—I'm all yours."

I smile and press my lips to his bare chest.

"What would you like to do?" Tate asks, brushing his fingers through my hair. "See the city?"

"I would . . ." I respond hesitantly. "But this is nice, too."

His gaze slants deviously and I shift closer, crawling from his chest to kiss him on the lips. His fingertips drift along my rib cage and our kiss turns heated fast, his mouth more insistent, and he slides on top of me. The weight of him is enough to make my breath come fast and uneven. He kisses my throat and then my earlobe, and I shudder as his lips press against mine, sinking deeper, the heat swelling between us.

My body arches into his, my knees drawing upward—looping around him—and my toes curl against his legs. His heart thumps against my chest as he lies fully on top of me, and I know he aches for me, too, his body tired of waiting.

I close my eyes, raking my fingernails up the back of his neck. He moans against my throat, dipping lower as his tongue makes easy circles on my skin. I press my head into the pillow as my body tingles in anticipation.

This is it, I think. This is the moment. No more secrets between us. No more reason to wait.

Tate moves his torso higher, his hips resting against mine. A new coiling ache unwinds in the lowest part of my abdomen, a need like I've never felt before.

"Charlotte," he murmurs, his lips just beneath my chin now. "Is this what you want?"

"Yes." My voice is breathy and quick, without hesitation.

He touches my face, kissing me on the mouth, and I tilt my head back, my hips shifting up to press against his. Urging him closer.

And then something shatters the stillness. A ringing. My cell phone.

I ignore it, kissing Tate again, and eventually the ringing stops. His fingers are at the hem of my underwear. There is almost nothing separating us and my heart trills, wanting to feel all of him against me. But then . . . the ringing starts again.

I tilt my head toward the sound.

It's probably just Carlos, checking up on me. The ringing stops, then begins almost immediately again. Tate shifts his weight, staring down at me.

"I just need to check it," I say, wriggling out from under him. I pull on a robe from the closet and pad out into the open living room. The phone is vibrating on the side table where I left it last night. I pick it up and my stomach sinks. I hit the answer button, clearing my throat and preparing to sound my most casual and composed. "Hey, Grandma," I say, flashing a look back at Tate, now lying on his back on the bed, watching me.

"I know you're not at a UN summit." The voice on the other end is as angry as I've ever heard it. "You're with him."

I'm silent. A knife of fear rises inside me.

"Charlotte, I can't—" She chokes on her words. "Lying to me? I can't believe you, Charlotte . . . after everything . . ."

"Grandma, I . . ." But I'm not sure what to say. How can I explain myself? I want to tell her it's not like she thinks, but I don't want to lie again. "I'm coming home" is all I can muster. My voice so small I think maybe I should repeat it.

She hangs up before I can say anything else.

How did she find out? I open up my text messages and see one from Carlos, two hours old. It's a photo of Tate and me, leaving the pizza place last night. And there's a caption: TATE COLLINS OUT WITH HIS GIRLFRIEND, CHARLOTTE REED, IN NEW YORK LATE ON FRIDAY. And there's another text from Carlos a few minutes after the first. *Photo is everywhere. Ur grandma called me, she saw image on Mia's phone. Not good.*

Once again, the world knows we are together. There is no denying it now.

Tate rides with me to the airport, holding my hand in the backseat while Hank maneuvers the black SUV through the crowded streets of Manhattan.

I've been in New York less than twenty-four hours and now I'm going back to LA.

"We never should have left the room last night," Tate says. "I'm sorry. I've had pretty good luck walking around freely since I've been here, but I should have done more to protect you."

"It's not your fault," I tell him. "And I already told you—I don't need your protection. I shouldn't have lied to my grandma. But I shouldn't have needed to." I stare out the window at the passing city, cloaked in gray as clouds descend over the highest buildings. "I'm eighteen. She needs to learn to let go a little."

Outside the airport, Tate runs his fingers through my hair, kissing me. We both know he can't get out of the car—can't risk being seen and photographed again. If my grandma saw us kissing in another tabloid photo, it would only make things worse.

"When will I see you again?" I ask.

"I should be back in LA in a couple weeks." His face has been unreadable since we left the hotel, a hint of tension in his features. I tell myself it's only because we were forced to stop so close to finally being together.

He gives up a tiny smile now, kissing me once more before I step from the car.

This weekend was almost perfect, almost everything I wanted it to be. And now I will pay the price when I get back home.

I arrive back at LAX in a daze. Maybe I should be, but I'm not prepared for the paparazzi waiting for me. As soon as I descend the staircase toward baggage claim, they are there, hovering like vultures. Had they tailed our movements since last night?

"Charlotte! Charlotte!" they call out. "Where is Tate? How did you meet? Charlotte!"

I ignore them, holding my arm in front of my face. I press forward, trying to find a way out.

"Are you still together? Is it true he's recording a new album? Why did you come back so soon?"

Cameras flash, bursting and popping. My vision swims. I try to glance up while keeping my head down. My eyes scan the periphery for a place to escape. Ahead, I see a ladies' room and run.

Inside, I press my hands against the sink. I breathe in and out. Tate warned me that fame could be hard, that the paparazzi are intense, but I didn't realize how vulnerable I would feel when I was by myself. I realize I'm shaking.

When I look up, I see a familiar face and my breath catches. I'm having déjà vu—I've seen her light eyes and freckles before, someplace just like this. For a second, I can't place it, but then I realize . . . it's Goth girl from the Lone Bean. The one who told me to stay away from Tate. I've barely given her another thought since then. What's she doing here? Why do I keep meeting her in bathrooms?

"You didn't listen to me," she says, staring straight at me. Her black hair dye is beginning to wash out. Just as I'd suspected, I can see a hint of red underneath.

"I'm sorry, I don't even know—" I start, but she cuts me off.

"I told you to stay away," she says before she begins taking swift steps backward. "I told you."

Then she turns and pushes past a woman in the doorway, and is gone.

I look at myself in the mirror, my ponytail a mess from the flight. My green eyes look tired and I realize I look older, somehow—like I know things I hadn't known before. I'm not sure what to think—about the paparazzi waiting outside the door, or the girl with the dyed black hair and her strange warning. I steel myself. Once I make it out of here, I have to face my grandma, too, and somehow that's an even more frightening thought.

Grandma is beyond furious.

I try to avoid seeing her by slipping into the house quietly and sneaking down to my room, but she appears in my bedroom doorway as soon as I drop my suitcase onto the floor. I'm exhausted after evading the paparazzi by cutting through the crowd and boarding a bus—I just want to crawl into bed and hide, but I won't be so lucky.

"I don't even know who you are anymore," she says quietly, her youthful face flushed.

I should apologize, I should admit that I made a mistake and promise never to do it again, but I can't believe what she's saying. My anger is burning away all rationality.

"I'm me, Grandma. Nothing is different."

"Excuse me?" she says, taking a step over the threshold into my room. "Nothing is *different*? Charlotte, you've been lying to me for *months*. The Charlotte I knew wanted to go to Stanford and make something of herself. If I'd told you six months ago you'd be sneaking around and letting some boy fly you all over the country, you'd have laughed in my face."

"I still want to make something of myself," I retort. "Just because I flew to New York for one weekend doesn't mean I'm giving up anything. It's *my* life," I remind her, steeling myself. "And I love him."

It's too much for her. Her eyes widen, her face freezes in place—immobilized in shock. And then she shakes her head, grasping for words. "Don't be stupid, Charlotte. A boy like that only wants one thing from you. I thought you knew that. I thought you were smarter than this. What happens when he moves on to the next poor, naïve young girl? Your broken heart will be smeared all over every gossip page in the country, right there for everyone to see. Every college professor. Every prospective employer. Can you stand there and tell me that's really what you want?"

"He's not like that," I say in a burst of fury. "And this isn't even about me. This is about you. You're so afraid that I'll end up like Mia or Mom, because the truth is, they both ended up just like *you*. You ruined your life because you got pregnant too young. Well, I'm not going to ruin mine—I'm not like you. And Tate's not like Grandpa or my dad or Leo's."

"You do not get to speak to me that way," she snaps back. "And don't you ever lie to me again, not while you're living under my roof." She turns in the doorway and I bite down on all the words crawling up to the surface. I hate her rules, her hypocritical demand for perfection.

I listen for the sound of her bedroom door slamming shut down the hall, then I yell, "And I got into Stanford, if anyone cares."

Leo breaks into a cry behind Mia's doorway but is quickly soothed—Mia must be standing on the other side of her door, listening to everything. Then the house falls still again.

I flop onto my bed, pulling the blankets up over my head. When I was little I used to think I'd disappear if I closed my eyes tight enough. I'd imagine myself someplace new, someplace I'd only ever read about.

Now, just when the world is finally opening up to me, I feel more trapped than ever.

TWENTY-ONE

FIVE DAYS LATER, THINGS HAVE barely changed at home. I haven't made up with Grandma, but then, I haven't seen Tate either—it's not like I could, with him in New York. So we're at a standoff.

I walk quickly through the night air and into the lab at UCLA. Rebecca is already standing at one of the stations, tagging samples. "Hey," she says. "Um, so . . ."

"Thanks for getting started without me." I smile. "That was really nice of you—I know I've been late a lot lately."

"No problem. I didn't realize you were . . ." She pauses, looking for the right word. "Famous."

"Ha!" I can't help but say. "Hardly." I smile at her. "Tate's the famous one. I just got caught in the cross fire."

She nods, and I'm grateful when she doesn't ask any more questions. She's known longer than anyone that I'm back with Tate Collins—she was there the night he showed up at the lab. So in an odd way, she's the only person I haven't lied to. And I barely even know her, beyond our small talk during lab hours. She's not the chatty type, and right now I'm glad for that.

At school on Monday, Carlos had wanted to know everything about New York, about Tate, and then what had happened when I got home and had to face Grandma. But as much as I had appreciated his genuine concern, I hadn't wanted to talk about any of it. Ever since returning from New York, every part of my life has felt constrictive.

I pull on my lab coat, read the notes from the last two undergrads whose shift ended right before ours, then settle onto a stool to help Rebecca tag and label samples. In an hour we will need to transfer two dozen samples into the refrigerated unit. Right now, an hour feels very far away.

As we work, I think about Tate. I think about the night we first met and how afraid I was to let myself feel anything for him—how resistant I was at the thought of a single date. My whole life I've been afraid. I've hardly allowed myself to experience anything. What if I'd grown up in a normal family, I wonder—what then? Would I be here, now, at UCLA, making stupid labels for stupid petri dishes for some stupid project I'm only doing for an application? I stare down at the petri dish in my hand, my fingers trembling slightly. I've never really stopped to think if this is what I want. Any of this. I worked so hard to get into Stanford—all the extracurriculars, the straight As, the perfect essays. Now I'm in, and I thought I'd feel elated, thought the euphoria from my acceptance letter would last. I have everything I ever wanted.

But what if I want something else?

I look over at Rebecca, methodically sorting through glass dishes, and I realize how unlike her I am. She loves the experiments, the endless studies, the order and precision to it all. But maybe it isn't me. Maybe this isn't what I want: this internship, this career path. I'm not sure I want any of it anymore. For the first time, I wonder if this was ever something I wanted for *me,* or if maybe I didn't know who I really was. Maybe I'm just learning that now.

My whole body's shaking; I set down the petri dish and take a step back, shrugging out of my white lab coat. I feel my legs carry me backward. My purse is sitting on a chair and I scoop it up—silently, robotically.

"Charlotte?" Rebecca asks, stopping her work to look up at me.

"I need to go," I say.

"Where? We still have to do the swap in less than forty minutes."

"I can't," I mumble.

"Why not?"

I shake my head at her, tears or maybe laughter pushing up to the surface. "I'm sorry, Rebecca. I hate to leave you short-handed again. But I can't do this anymore."

"Do what?"

"The lab, this internship," I confess to her, feeling heady and also sharply focused. "I really need to go."

And I dart through the lab door, rushing down the hall, desperate suddenly for fresh air. I burst from the science building out into the parking lot and crane my head up, laughing at the sky.

The tarmac is hot at the private airport, heat rising in waves under the late-afternoon sun.

I watch as Tate's plane circles, then descends to land. It's been two weeks since I've seen him, two weeks since I left New York. And I haven't felt like myself since.

As Tate's plane rolls to a stop and the door opens, a rush of excitement overcomes me. He appears in the doorway, a hand over his eyes, wearing a green flannel shirt and dark jeans. When he moves down the steps, I run to him. He scoops me up in his arms, his strong hands wrapped around my thighs, and I bury my face in his neck.

I had considered telling him everything when he returned home—ditching out on the lab, the paparazzi that show up outside school sometimes, the Goth girl I've now seen in not one bathroom, but two—but now, seeing him, I don't want to ruin this moment. None of it feels important.

The only thing that matters is *us*.

"You smell so good," he says against my ear.

"I missed you."

He sets me down on the pavement, his hands still gripping my waist, and Hank moves past us, winking at me as he piles luggage into the Escalade waiting for Tate.

I turn and tug him toward the car, but he stops me before we get inside. "Charlotte. There's something I have to tell you."

The way his tone changes sends a shiver through me. "What is it?"

He glances across the tarmac where another plane glides to a stop on the runway. "I'm going back on tour, to promote the new album. It'll be small to start—just a few pop-up shows—but we're working on a European tour after that."

"What? When?"

"My manager pulled some strings, I'm going to do a surprise gig tonight, opening for December Valentine at the Staples Center."

"Tonight? But . . ." I look away from him, trying not to let my disappointment show. I know he's worked hard for this, and he deserves to be back onstage, especially after the past year. But I didn't think things would happen so quickly. And a small, selfish part of me wants him all to myself—just for a little longer.

"I know it's fast. But they want to create some buzz about the new album release in a few months. And it's just one show—I won't have to leave right away after that."

"So—when?" I ask.

"I leave next week for a show in Sacramento. And then Seattle a few days later." Tate presses me against the side of the car, smoothing my hair back from my face, but it does nothing to soothe the frustration that builds in my chest. "This is because of you, Charlotte. I don't think I could've picked up the pieces of my life without you. Or faced more crowded arenas without you telling me it was time to forgive myself."

I know this is what he wants; I can see it in his eyes. But the irony of it kills me. I've inspired him to leave, when all I want him to do is stay. "How long will you be on tour?"

"A year . . . probably." He pauses, releasing my hair. "This isn't going to be easy. I know you have Stanford next year, and I'll be on the road, but I want to be with you. We'll make it work."

I turn away from him, toward the window. I can't help it, I think about what he told me about his last tour—the partying, the drinking, the girls. *You can't even imagine what that feels like, that type of fame. . . Like you can get away with anything.* His words ring through my mind.

"I don't know, Tate." I'm still facing the window. "A year is a long time." Especially when his life will be so extreme on tour—so many temptations, so many things to pull him back into his old habits. Will I be able to trust him? Could we survive a year long-distance—it seems almost impossible with so many forces working against us.

"It'll be hard," he admits. He touches my arm and turns my chin to face him. His mouth is warm, soft and reassuring as he tries to kiss away my doubt. I run my hands over his scalp, touching him, wanting to remember the way he feels, the way he tastes against my lips, the way his hands move easily across my shoulders and down my arms. He's only just back and now our days are numbered again.

"We'll still see each other," he says. "Just not as often. You'll have school breaks and weekends, and I'll have the jet." But my mind is already whirling forward, picturing the next year of my life without him: alone at Stanford—studying, sleepless—while he travels the world, girls sneaking backstage, wanting him, begging for him.

"What if we could be together?" I ask.

He leans back to study me. "Charlotte . . . what are you talking about?"

The idea had already been taking shape inside my mind, ever since I had stood up and walked out on my internship at the lab. Professor Webb had called and left me messages, but I hadn't called him back. I hadn't known what to say, how to explain that I have been living the wrong life. How to explain that the internship, the lab—it's not what I want. "What if I didn't go to Stanford," I say.

"But you *are* going to Stanford."

"What if I went with you on tour instead?" My voice rises. I don't like the way it sounds, but I don't care.

"You can't give up school for me."

"I wouldn't be giving it up—I can defer it for a year. People do it all the time."

His eyes slide away from me. "I can't let you do that. You've worked too hard to get into Stanford."

"It's my decision," I say, more sharply than I mean to. Are we back to this? Why does everyone in my life think they know what's best for me? "I'm finally making decisions for myself," I add. "I thought you would understand."

"I do, but . . ." His gaze settles on some far-off point across the tarmac, and I feel my frustration hit the breaking point.

"Tate, I love you. I know that's a loaded statement for you, and I understand why. But I want you to know how I feel, and why I know this is the right choice for me. For us." I will him to look at me again, to see how serious I am. "I can't just wait around for you to fit me into your schedule. It's been hard enough doing that these past few weeks and trying to focus on school. Stanford will still be there next year, and I know what I want."

"T," Hank calls from the other side of the car. "It's time."

Tate nods and finally his eyes meet mine, so turbulent it's like we're back on the balcony on a rainy New York night. He opens his mouth, and for a minute I think he's going to say everything I want to hear. "I have to go. I have sound check in a few hours and I need to get ready."

I feel the hard twist of a knot forming in my stomach.

Then he sighs and closes his eyes briefly. Whatever I thought I'd seen is gone by the time he opens them again. "Tonight will be fun," he tells me. "I promise. I'll put you on the list to go backstage. At eight o'clock, go to the steel double doors near the south entrance—they'll let you in."

"And after?" I ask.

"We'll go back to my house. We'll talk. We can figure this out." He's saying everything right, but his eyes still look empty. I feel a chill move through me.

He kisses me on the lips, once and then again, lingering this time, and I watch him duck into the back of the SUV. Tate and Hank give me a ride back to the airport parking lot where my car is waiting. I hop out when we pull up next to my car, trying to ignore the sensation that everything is wrong between us. I watch the Escalade pull out of sight, trying to get myself excited for the concert tonight. My rock star boyfriend is bringing me backstage for his big comeback performance. What could be better? *Nothing*, I tell myself. And then I will my heart to listen.

TWENTY-TWO

THE BEDROOM DOOR CLOSES WITH a click behind me and I tiptoe the length of the hall until I reach the living room. Mia is on the couch, typing on her cell phone. Leo is sitting beside her, playing with a stuffed elephant that rattles every time he shakes it.

"I heard Tate's back in town," Mia says, catching me slinking through the kitchen. The media must already know he's back, and Mia has already read about it on her favorite celebrity gossip sites.

The front doorknob is cool beneath my palm and I squeeze it—my escape.

"Yeah, he is," I confirm. But I don't mention that I just saw him, that I was there when he landed back in LA.

"You're going to see him, aren't you?" Mia asks, as if she could sense my intention just by looking at me. My black skinny jeans, white blouse, and black heels also don't help.

I look back at her. "I have to, Mia," I say, my voice low, my gaze pleading. "Please don't say anything to Grandma."

Her lips thin in obvious disapproval. She feels the same about Tate that Carlos does: that he's hurt me too many times, that it's a mistake to keep taking him back. But she's also my sister, and I think she sees how in love with him I am—she knows the feeling all too well. So she nods quickly. "Okay," she says in a hush. "But you better hurry before—"

She doesn't get a chance to finish her thought, because Grandma appears in the doorway—she must have heard us talking from her bedroom. "Where are you going?" she demands.

My eyes flinch from Mia to her, feeling a pang at her hard gaze. "Out," I say. And then I yank the door open all the way and dash into the dark.

I hear Grandma calling after me, but I push into a run, out to the street and to my car. I know she won't chase after me, but I slam the keys into the ignition and peel away down the street regardless—the adrenaline still pumping through my veins.

My phone rings from my purse on the passenger seat and I fish it out, looking at the screen. It's her. I hit IGNORE.

She's probably going to ground me until graduation for this, but it doesn't matter. After graduation I'm gone anyway. I shove down the sorrow that rises in my throat at how bad our relationship has become. Reaching up, I turn on the radio, hoping the sound will drown out my guilty thoughts.

Traffic is a blur of steady red lights and backed-up cars. I exit the 101, hoping to wind my way through the backstreets, but find I'm only inching slowly closer to the Staples Center. I should have left earlier, should have anticipated this. It's like I've been a step behind all day.

When I finally arrive, a parking attendant waves me into a spot not too far from the front entrance. But the show has already started; I can hear the amplified buzz of music rising out from the stadium, the air vibrating. I run in heels toward the entrance, cursing myself for being so late.

I don't go to the main entrance, where the lights of the Staples sign make everything look smeared in red and blue. Instead, I run along the outer wall to the side of the rounded structure. I'm nervous, I realize; it feels like something big depends on me seeing Tate perform. Like if I miss the show, something terrible will happen.

The steel double doors, just like Tate described, are illuminated by a bright single light against the gray concrete wall. A red-and-white sign reads EXIT. It seems so unofficial.

I knock twice.

Nothing.

I knock again. Still nothing. A car circles through the parking lot, probably looking for an open spot, its headlights fanning across the doors.

I lean into the door and press my ear against the cool metal. I can't hear anything on the other side. Maybe this is the wrong door—the wrong exit.

But then there is a shuddering and the door swings open. I take a half step backward before it collides with my face. An official-looking man with a goatee stands in the open doorway. "Yeah?" he asks distractedly, looking over my head as if expecting someone else. Around his neck hangs several passes of varying colors, credentials that anoint him as the keeper of the backstage.

"I'm on the list," I answer, feeling like I'm in one of those movies where the groupie tries to sneak backstage so she can sleep with the rock star. Except I'm not a groupie, I'm his girlfriend.

"What list?" he asks, scratching the sideburns that threaten to overtake his entire face.

"Tate said to come to this door," I say more confidently than I feel. "I'm Charlotte Reed. My name should be on a list."

His stare is hooded by the dim light over the doors, and the hallway behind him is a shadowed cavern where I can hear the reverberation of the concert echoing down the bare corridor. He reaches into the breast pocket of his flannel shirt and extracts a folded piece of white paper. He pulls it apart and I can just barely see names printed on the other side. There are only half a dozen or so.

"Reed, you said?"

"Charlotte Reed."

He glances at me over the paper. "I recognize you. You're his new chick."

I nod, the fluttering of wings pushing up into my throat again—excitement and anxiety, merging into one.

"Sorry," he says, refolding the paper and slipping it back into his breast pocket. "You're not on the list."

He starts to step back into the hallway, letting the door slide shut, but I stop him. "No." I grab the edge of the door to keep it from closing. "Wait. I know I'm on there."

"Sorry, honey. You're not."

"Will you check again?"

"Don't need to. You're not on it."

"But you recognize me," I say, trying to make him understand. "You know who I am. There's probably just some mistake. I'm supposed to be in there right now, he's expecting me."

"For all I know, he broke up with you earlier tonight and now you're just trying to sneak in to trash his dressing room." He grabs the edge of the door above my hand. "If you're not on the list, you're not getting in here." He yanks the door away from me and my fingers release just before it clanks shut.

"Wait!" I shout. I pound on the door, kick it with the toe of my high heel, but he doesn't come back.

Cursing my choice of shoes, I jog around to the front of the building, where the glass doors emit a blinding glow of white florescent light. There are several people inside dressed in black uniforms, talking casually among themselves, and I approach one of the women standing in front of a poster of Tate's unsmiling face. She barely looks up at me. "Ticket?" she asks, holding out a hand.

"I don't have one," I start. "I'm supposed to be on a list."

"Did you pre-purchase your tickets?" she asks, still not looking at me directly.

"No. I'm on a list," I answer more firmly.

She finally looks up, squints at me. "Sorry, there's no list here."

"Please," I say. "Is there someone I can talk to?"

"Not at this entrance."

"There must be a backstage list, or something—someone you can call?"

She scrunches up her nose, then lets out an exaggerated huff. "Name?" she asks, irritated.

"Charlotte Reed," I respond quickly.

"Wait here." I watch as she meanders—painfully slowly— over to a man standing by the escalators and he lifts his cell phone to his ear. I can't hear what he's saying but he's definitely checking my name. This will be it; finally they'll let me through. After what feels like an hour, he ends the call and the woman walks back over to me. I feel like my skin might tear open along imaginary seams if she doesn't move faster. I can hear Tate from here: onstage, singing, his voice unmistakable, a voice that's whispered words against my ear, now echoing through the Staples Center . . . and I can't get to him.

"You're not on any list, anywhere . . . in any part of the building," she says dramatically, as if trying to make a point.

This isn't happening.

I leave through the front doors, marching back around the building.

I'm almost back to the metal double doors when I see a group of girls—five or six—standing in front of it. The man with sideburns appears again, the hallway behind him casting a florescent glow over the girls' faces. I wait to see them turned away.

But then he lets them through.

They shuffle inside, all long legs and bouncy hair and heels twice as high as mine. The door starts to swing closed behind them but I sprint forward, grabbing it before it slams shut.

I'm about to sneak through when a hand grabs my fingers and pries them away. "I don't think so," the man says, holding me by my wrist and forcing me back from the doorway.

"But those girls," I protest. "You let them in."

"Look, darlin', I can't let you in. It's my job to keep out the crazies."

"I'm not—" Then I swallow, composing myself. "I'm not trying to sneak in. Tate told me to come to this door and I would be on a list. So I don't know what bullshit list you're looking at, but there's no way those chicks are on it and I'm not." My throat tightens against the last words. "So look again."

His face tugs backward a half an inch, surprised by my tone. A little smile quirks across his lips and I actually think he's going to check the list again, or better yet, just let me through. "Persistent little thing, I'll give you that."

"Look, could you at least find Hank? His bodyguard? I'm sure he's here, and he can come vouch for me." Why don't I have Hank's number in my phone? I'm going to make Tate give it to me so nothing like this happens again.

The man's smile flattens. "I don't think so, sweetheart. Don't knock on this door again or I'm calling the police." And he pulls the door closed behind him with such finality that it actually makes me jump.

Shit.

I turn and lean against the door, tilting my head back beneath the halo of light and grating my fingers across my scalp.

A wave of screams erupts suddenly from inside the stadium, and then settles as an acoustic guitar begins to play. I press my hands over my eyes and squeeze. I can't be here, listening to this from outside. It's torture. So I stand and wind my way back toward the parking lot, beneath the beams of light from the streetlamps, past a security guard, past the last few ticketholders hurrying toward the front doors of the stadium.

I can't believe this is happening.

The sky is muted with clouds, hinting of encroaching rain. I pull out my cell phone and send him a text: *I can't get into concert. Not on list.* But I know he won't answer. He's onstage, performing . . . and I'm missing it.

Unfamiliar songs and gorgeous melodies sift out into the night sky. Clear white spotlights shoot upward from the roof, swirling and revolving like fireflies against the clouds, a beacon to the outside world that something big is happening inside the stadium tonight—Tate Collins has returned.

Anger burns behind my eyes, and I listen as Tate plays straight through three songs. I'm missing everything. I'm stuck out here and there's nothing I can do.

TWENTY-THREE

I PUNCH IN THE CODE to the security gate when I pull into Tate's driveway. I still have it saved in my phone from the night he texted it to me.

The rain falls heavily now, splatting across the windshield as my wipers work furiously to push them away. It's an early spring rain, a momentary respite from the normally dry California heat. Tate's house is dark as I pull around the circle drive and kill the engine.

I run up the front pathway in my heels, my hands over my head, and check the door: locked. I ring the doorbell, even though I know Hank will be with Tate at the concert, and there are no butlers or maids or staff to answer the door. I look back at my car. It might be another hour or more until he finally makes it back home. Then I remember the sliding glass door.

I push through the gate at the left side of the house and hurry along the stone path, which is lit with tiny solar lights. I emerge beside the pool—awash in a pearly blue, the surface vibrating with every pelt of rain. I've never been here without Tate, and the darkness feels suddenly foreboding, but I shake off the feeling.

I hurry to the glass doors, touching the metal handle, and the door glides easily open, folding back like an accordion. Inside, I breathe in the dryness of the living room and stand with my back against the glass, dripping water onto the floor. My hands fan across the wall to my right, feeling for a light switch, but find nothing.

My foot slams into the coffee table and I stumble back. "Crap." I touch my right toe, exposed in my black high heels. I'm still not used to wearing these things. I kneel down, gripping the edge of the coffee table for support, and feel a large remote control. As soon as I touch it, all the buttons illuminate, and I notice one larger button marked FIRE. Sure enough, the fireplace directly in front of me sparks to life when I press the button. It's enough light that I can actually make out the features of the living room.

I pull out my cell phone. No missed calls or texts from Tate.

He must still be onstage, or doing post-concert interviews, or signing autographs, or just trying to get out of the stadium without being mobbed. I stand up, moving to the stairs, my heels clipping on the hard stone.

On the second floor at the end of the hall are two wide double doors—the master bedroom. I've only been here with Tate, that one night. I blush at the memory, touching the triangle bracelet he gave me just before he led me here to his room.

There is a faint, recessed light rimming the ceiling that provides enough of a glow to see the entire room. I run a hand across the comforter, the fabric smooth and silky beneath my fingertips. A wide set of sliding doors look out onto a patio. I touch the glass, watching the rain. Waiting.

An hour passes. I sit on the edge of his bed, then flop back on the comforter, listening to the rain pound against the roof. I consider texting Carlos, but I haven't told him yet about my decision to defer Stanford. I can't even imagine his reaction.

Instead, I send another text to Tate, the phone held above me as I type: *Where are you?*

Every few minutes, I sit up and click my phone on again, certain I've missed a call or text. But there's nothing. *Why hasn't he called yet?* Then an idea slips into my brain. I pull up a new web browser on my phone and search for Tate Collins. Social media posts instantly pop up: girls tweeting about being at the concert, grainy Instagram photos of Tate onstage. I cycle through the images, scrolling down. There are shots of him leaving the Staples Center through a throng of girls, unfazed by the downpour as they crowd around a black SUV, Tate climbing inside.

And then the photos change. They're still of Tate, still in jeans and a black shirt, but the background is different. He's at a club, sitting in a booth, lights blazing over his face. And surrounding him . . . are half a dozen girls.

Frantically, I open several more images, all tagged as being posted tonight: Tate downing shots of clear liquid, his platinum watch glinting in the light as he tilts his head back to swallow the shot; Tate with a red-haired girl pressed against his side, whispering into his ear. Tate partying, Tate not here . . . Tate not with me.

What the hell is he doing?

I tighten my grip around the phone and my hands begin to shake, a twinge of pain lancing into the back of my skull.

He's out at some club—right now—partying with other girls. And then the truth starts to settle into my gut: He didn't want me at the concert. It wasn't a mistake that I couldn't get in—that I wasn't on the list—he didn't want me there. He doesn't want me with him now; that's why he didn't come home after the concert. He doesn't want *me*.

I can't stay here. I won't let him find me here in his room, waiting for him like some obsessed girlfriend who can't take a hint. No different than Ella St. John after all. My fingernails dig into my palm, and I climb shakily to my feet, clicking off my phone and shoving it into my pocket. I think back to Tate's face at the airport, his expression when I told him I would defer college—that I wanted to go on tour with him. That I loved him. The blank mask descending over his face, the eyes that could barely meet mine.

My head begins to ache. I let him make a fool out of me. Again. *I'm so stupid. So, so stupid.*

I hurry down the stairs and out the front door, desperate to get away, suddenly certain he's going to bring those girls back here—and that I'll be colossally, unbelievably embarrassed.

277

Well, I won't let him have that satisfaction, at least. My eyes blur even though I try to hold back the tears. My car sways ahead of me, out of focus in the unrelenting rain. I press my palms to the hood when I reach it, bracing myself—for a moment, it's the only thing holding me up.

I swerve around to the driver's side door, wiping tears away with my forearm. I wish I wasn't in heels, I wish I hadn't dressed up for him. In an outfit he bought me that day at Barneys, no less. I hate him for making me give a shit. I hate him for making me fall in love with him. For making me just as much a fool as every other girl in my family. For making me break the promises I made myself, all those years ago.

The tears dull my vision and I reach for the door handle when I hear something behind me. Nothing distinct—the shuffling of feet, a low inhalation. I pause and turn around—my blood frozen in my veins, my mouth caught half open.

Standing a few feet back, just beyond the ring of light spreading out from the porch, is a figure, a dim silhouette. It could almost be imagined: conjured up from the mounting fear that scrabbles down my spine, dancing down every nerve and making the muscles in my body tense. I brush at my eyes again, trying to clear away the tears, to focus through the rain—to separate the figure from the surrounding branches.

And then the outline takes a step forward, and I know it's real.

My heartbeat rises. "Tate?" I ask in an exhale, hating myself for the desperation in my voice, the hope that rises in my heart.

The silhouette takes several more quick steps forward. And

I know in an instant that it's not Tate. The figure is narrower, slighter. It moves closer, crossing the driveway, and finally steps into the muted light from the front porch.

I recognize the face.

It's the girl from the bathrooms. Same short black hair, freckles, and snow-white skin. She's wearing a black hooded sweatshirt and black jeans: dressed to be concealed, hidden in the darkness.

"What are you doing?" I ask, words that seem insufficient.

She doesn't respond.

"You're not supposed to be here," I say again, reaching back behind me for the door handle of my car—but it's locked.

"I followed you," she answers.

A sharp stab of fear edges its way along my thoughts. My eyes flick to my car door; how fast can I get to my keys?

"Don't," she says, sensing what I'm thinking. And I turn my gaze back to her. The rain lightens just barely, and I can see her better in the gloom, the way her eyes stare unblinking.

"Why are you following me?" I ask, stalling as I slowly reach inside my purse.

"I tried to warn you." Her arms are stiff at her sides and her left palm begins to run along the fabric of her black jeans. "But then I saw you at the concert, trying to get backstage." Her eyes never leave mine. "You're not going to stay away from him. I see that now."

"You're wrong," I say, my voice shaking. "Tate and I are done. We're over."

"Liar," she spits, sucking in a breath.

"It's not a lie." My left hand searches for my keys inside my purse, but I can't locate them.

Her eyes narrow. "I've loved him longer than you have. Longer than anyone. I saw his very first concert in LA when I was fourteen. I was in the front row and he touched my hand, looked into my eyes like he was really seeing me. Like no one's ever looked at me before. And I knew he and I were meant for each other. It's just a matter of time; eventually, we'll meet again, and he'll know I'm the one."

I need to get out of here, call the police, find Tate, and warn him. No matter what he's done to me, I can't let him come home to this—another unstable fan. One who might hurt him, instead of herself.

"You can have him," I say. But her face hardens and grows even paler, if that's possible. She takes another step toward me.

"I will." And then adds, "Once you're gone."

My fingers finally coil around my keys, buried at the bottom of my purse. I whip around, jamming the key into the lock, and grab for the door handle. Time moves in fast-forward yet I am in slow motion: I yank open the door but she's too quick, rushing at me, and her hands clamp down against my throat. The door bangs shut again. My lungs constrict, gasping for air. For a second I'm so stunned that my arms are limp at my sides, my vision already starting to smudge out. But then panic crawls up from my stomach and I slam my hands against her face, trying to push her backward. We stumble sideways, to the front of the car, hands around each other, my heels shuffling on the wet pavement.

We're moving too fast, the momentum driving us along the side of my car, sliding across the fender, and then we are stumbling out away from it, across the driveway, into the dark. But we don't make it to the edge of the driveway; the force of her body is too great, and I feel my feet catch beneath me, and then we're both falling.

We thud hard against the ground, the concrete rising up to meet me. Little white spots blur my vision and I realize the back of my head is throbbing, heat spreading over my scalp.

I open my mouth to speak, to tell her to stop, but there is no air to form the words.

I meet her eyes, only inches from mine, coal-black pupils magnified like she's staring straight through me to the other side—hollow but also satisfied. Her hands close even tighter around my throat: pressing, digging, fighting to push the life out of me. And everything begins to slow. I gasp and kick and claw at her, but her face twists into a sagging grin, caught somewhere between laughter and tears.

My nails dig into her cheeks, pulling away skin, but soon I feel the strength start to leave my limbs. And my vision blots with speckles of red.

Everything is slipping away, fading like a vast black curtain billowing over the top of Tate's house and settling down over me.

The sky is beautiful. The clouds receding, drifting away. It's now black and dotted with tiny lights. Stars.

Nothing but the stars. It's all I see. They burn as they fall, raining down and touching my skin, making everything white.

The sky dims. Spots bursting.

The world turns shallow, out of focus.

And then nothing but dark.

My heartbeat is the first thing I feel: hammering every joint, every bone connected by tissue. Knocking my body apart.

I peel my eyelids open, sticky and watery.

The sky shakes above me.

There is a flash of dark hair—the girl, still above me. And then a sudden release of pressure—of her body being lifted from mine, hands leaving my throat. But I can't move. My legs are like anchors. My arms tingle. My head throbs worse than before.

Someone screams: the girl, I think.

Movement, feet against the concrete, hands clawing, scraping.

I realize my eyelids have slipped closed again and I force them open. A face rises into view. I flinch, expecting the girl again—back to finish things. To kill me this time. But it's not her.

It's Tate.

His lips are moving. His eyes are like a bottomless ocean, and I want to sink down into them and never come up again. He's speaking but my mind is unable to parse the words. And then his arms are beneath me, lifting me up, and I feel empty of anything but air, and I let him carry me, my head pressed to his chest.

The black descends once more, only the sound of Tate's heartbeat thumping against my ear chasing me into the darkness.

The steady beeping of a heart monitor rouses me from sleep. Am I in a hospital? When I open my eyes I see Tate. Relief washes over me, until I remember what happened.

"Hey," I say, my voice a sandpapery rasp.

"Hey." He tries to smile, but it's strained. "How do you feel?"

I close my eyes and take stock. The aches are there—my head, my throat, my back where I hit the concrete—but duller, not the agony I remember. I glance at the IV in my hand—yep, hospital. "I've had better days. How long have I been here?"

"A few hours. You have some bruising on your throat and maybe a concussion, so they want to keep you overnight, but they said considering everything, you're really lucky." His mouth twists, like he can hardly say the word. "Your family's up front with Hank, talking to the police. I . . . Do you need anything? A doctor? I should tell them you're awake."

"They'll figure it out," I say. "These monitors have to be good for something." It hurts to see him here, knowing where he's been tonight, at some club with other girls—it's a pain that has nothing to do with the aches in my body, but I don't want him to go. Not quite yet.

He rubs the back of his neck and his eyes fix on mine. But

they are not the eyes I remember—the eyes of someone who can't live without me. They are the eyes of someone who's already gone.

"Charlotte," he begins, "I'm so sorry. I had no idea about that girl—I didn't know I had a stalker, much less that she'd go after you. God, I never meant for any of this to happen. I never would have put myself back in the public eye if I'd thought it would make you a target. You have—"

"I wasn't on the list," I manage to say.

He is silent.

"I watched other girls get in, but I couldn't." I swallow, my voice scratchy and raw. "Do you know how humiliating that was?"

His face tenses and his gaze drops to the floor. "You should rest," he says, instead of acknowledging what happened tonight. How he so callously pushed me back out of his life. "We can talk about this later, when you're healthy again. When your voice . . . when you're feeling better."

I think briefly about telling him to call the doctor after all— surely they can bring enough morphine to numb the pain I know is coming. Instead I study him, the tired eyes and set jaw. "I don't think there is a later for us, is there, Tate?"

"Charlotte, you don't . . . I can't . . ."

I want him to stop there, not to say anything else. But he goes on, and I know I'm right.

"You'll never know how sorry I am for what I did to you tonight. But I can't let you give up college for me. Your dreams, everything you've worked for your whole life. You said you loved me, and I . . . I can't tell you what that means to me. But what happens when you get tired of being on the road—living in a cramped tour bus, spending hours backstage in a greenroom, traveling to so many cities and countries you start to lose count? When every arena looks the same? What happens when the novelty fades and you start to resent me for taking you away from the life you were meant to lead? And who knows how many other crazy fans might be out there. It's safe to say I haven't had the best luck in that department. You think I want to risk what happened to you tonight happening again? I just . . . it can't work, Charlotte. You need to go to Stanford, where you belong. Where you'll be safe." He touches the metal bar on my hospital bed, tightening his knuckles around it.

I should feel some relief, hearing the explanation I didn't get before the concert—he has always worried about keeping me safe, protecting me, even if it means breaking my heart. But instead, I just feel anger—overwhelming rage that once again, his fear of hurting me is driving us apart. "So you're making the decision for me. It doesn't matter what I want, what I need, or what I've told you I can handle. You get to decide, just like always."

His shoulders straighten back, his arm falls to his side. *He's so gorgeous*, I think. Even now, even though every word he says is breaking me apart, I can't help but admire how achingly handsome he is. It makes this hurt even more.

"I wish it could be different," he says, looking away from me now, unable to meet my gaze. "But it's easier if—" He bites down on his lip.

"If we end this," I finish for him, pain dancing across my temples.

He nods. "I can't live with watching you sideline your future for me. And you're right, you deserve more than the occasional weekend visit. There's no middle ground here, Charlotte."

For a moment I can't respond. The tears I've held at bay are biting at my eyes, my lips threatening to quiver. "There's never been middle ground with you. It's always all or nothing." My fingers clench the sheet, holding tight to steady myself. "I think you should go now."

He makes a soft sound—part protest, part sigh. "I'm sorry, Charlotte. For everything."

His fingers slide along the edge of the bed, so close he could touch me, run his hands up my bare arm and kiss me. But he doesn't. He pulls his hand away and turns for the door. He pauses once, his back a rigid line. And I think he's going to turn around, say something else—just one more thing to make everything okay, to make this not hurt so, so much—but instead he steps out into the hall, disappearing from my life.

And I am undone.

TWENTY-FOUR

GRANDMA AND MIA TAKE ME home from the hospital the following day. I ride in the front seat, silent. Everything feels muted: watercolors bleeding across a white page. At home, I brush through the living room and down the hall. Even this house feels foreign to me, the old Charlotte who used to live here someone I no longer recognize.

"You all right?" Mia asks behind me. I hear Grandma across the hall, putting Leo down for his nap.

"No," I say, sinking onto the bed and turning away from her. I can hear her breathing, sense that she's there, but I don't turn back to look at her. Eventually, she moves away, closing the door behind her.

I spend three days in my bed. Mia brings me food, asks me how I am, tries to get me up—but I just don't have the strength. She brings Leo into my room to cheer me up; he grabs my finger and smiles and makes me feel a tiny bit better. Grandma is surprisingly understanding. She hasn't mentioned Tate once.

Carlos comes by every day after school, and just sits with me, not making me talk. He doesn't try to cheer me up like he might normally do. Just sits there.

Slowly, I find my way back to who I used to be. I pull my favorite novels off my bookshelf, reading passages, comforting myself with the words. I open my laptop, paging through photos from old *Banner* assignments, trying to imagine who I was when I took them, figure out if I'm different now. I open my e-mail, go through the assignments my teachers have sent, get a little work done here or there. I'm still behind, but my counselor says that Stanford will understand, that they won't fault me for any grades that slip after a hospital stay. I tell myself that it's good I didn't fill out any deferral paperwork yet—that everything can just get back to normal now. Stanford next year, med school after, the future I so purposefully planned.

I tell myself I should be glad, that it could have been much worse.

That at least I didn't ruin my life.

On Thursday night, Mia comes again to my door, knocking softly to see if I'm awake. She sits on the end of my bed and touches my hair, pulling it away from my shoulders. I can feel the tears welling up in my eyes; I squeeze them shut, trying to hold it back.

"Does your head still hurt?"

"No. It's not that," I say.

"I know," she says gently. "He broke your heart, didn't he?"

I nod and cover my eyes with my hands, a whimper shuddering from my lips.

"They're not all bad," she says, touching my shoulder. But I laugh: a short, painful laugh.

"I'm sorry, Mia," I say, looking up at her, this girl I used to idolize when we were kids.

"For what?"

"I haven't been a good sister. Not since Leo. I think . . . I didn't understand . . ." I remember all the ways I judged her. I didn't want to help her, even when I could have.

"We've each made our own mistakes," she says. And the forgiveness in her eyes almost makes me break down all over again.

I look down at my hand, at our mother's ring. It used to remind me not to be like her, but I fell in love just as hard as she always did.

"I don't think I need this anymore," I say, sliding it from my ring finger.

Without looking at me, she slides it onto her own. It fits perfectly—maybe even better than it fit me. Her skin is darker, closer to the shade of our mother's, and it looks just how I remember.

Flashes of our mom dance through my mind, the ring always on her finger. She was so beautiful. But she was so lost. Destined to love men who couldn't, or wouldn't, love her in return.

I am more like her than I ever realized.

After Mia leaves, I stand and walk down the hall, finding Grandma in her bedroom sitting at the edge of her bed. In her lap is an old photo album, one I've only ever seen a few times.

"Can I talk to you?" I say, moving slowly through the doorway.

"Of course."

I sit next to her, watching her fingers trail over a photo of her and my mom when Mom was just a baby. Grandma was so young then, just a teenager. She looks a lot like me.

"I should have listened to you." Somehow, impossibly, I'm crying again, the tears never ending.

"No." She shakes her head and reaches over to hold my hand. "I should have listened. I thought I was protecting you, but I was pushing you away."

"I don't understand," I say.

She smiles and raises one eyebrow. "You deserve love as much as anyone, Charlotte. You deserve the best kind of love—the kind that will last forever. Maybe this wasn't it . . . with Tate, but I know you'll find it someday. I just want you to be happy, that's all I've ever wanted."

My mind surges back to Tate, the memory of his face hovering over me, his eyes like the darkest part of the sea, just before he lifted me up from the pavement. I thought he loved me—even if he didn't know how to say it—but like Grandma, that love was bound up in his own fears, in his need to protect me, to control everything.

"There's something I have to tell you," I say, looking into her blue-green eyes. "Something I've decided to do . . ."

She squints to focus on me.

"I want to defer college for a year. I thought I was doing it so I could be with Tate, but I'm doing it for myself. I need to take a year off; I need to figure out what I want to do with my life. I know it seems scary to wait a year, but I promise it's not. I'm not giving up my scholarships, I swear. It'll all be there waiting for me. I just want to be sure I'm ready."

"What will you do?" she asks, her smile dropping a little.

"I'm not sure . . . I haven't really figured that out yet. Maybe I'll get another job, maybe I'll use the money I've saved to travel somewhere—finally get out of California for more than just a day. But I want the time to decide, to figure out who I am and what I want." It's strange to be so honest with her—to admit to something like this. But it feels like I could tell her anything in this moment.

I wait for her to respond. She's silent for a moment, and then she squeezes my hand, her eyes glimmering. "I used to dream of going to Europe . . . before I was pregnant with your mom. But I never had the chance."

"This is *my* chance," I tell her.

The bed squeaks beneath us as she shifts to look at me. "Okay," she says.

"Okay?"

"Take a year—do all the things I couldn't do."

"Are you serious?"

She nods and pulls me into a hug. I feel the tears dampening my shirt before I even realize she's crying. "Thank you," I say, and I mean it. I've never been more grateful for anything in my life.

TWENTY-FIVE

Six months later

IT'S LATE SEPTEMBER AND I find myself back in LA. It's Mia's birthday, and at my grandma's urging, I flew home for the party. The roar and heat of the city is both familiar and overwhelming.

After graduation last June, I left. I used the money I had saved from working at the Bloom Room and I bought a one-way plane ticket to Europe. It's been three months since I've been home—three months that have flown by.

Now Carlos is stretched out across my bed in my room at Grandma's, twisting one of my hair ties around his fingers. "I can't believe you've been hoofing it around Europe all on your own," he says, watching me as I pull open my suitcase and make a pile of dirty clothes I need to wash while I'm here.

"It wasn't as daring as you make it sound," I assure him. "I was on a bus most of the time, usually with other tourist groups."

"Yeah, but you stayed in hostels and probably ate baguettes with cheese straight out of a paper bag."

"I did," I say, tone serious. "You know me. Such a rebel." We both laugh.

"And you're going back so soon?" he asks.

I nod and look up from my laundry. "I found a part-time job at a little flower shop, and an adorable, cheap room to rent in Vernazza. It's right on the coast. It's so beautiful, Carlos. You should come visit me."

Carlos sighs. "I'll try. How long will you be there?"

"Only through the winter, maybe a little longer. Then I'll be back home to work for Holly and save up more money, and start at Stanford next fall," I say, looking up at him. "But I definitely want to do a little more traveling to photograph as much as I can."

It started out like it would for anyone else traveling: just a way to document what I saw, so I could remember everything when I came back. But it's become more than that. Seeing the world through the camera has made me look at things differently.

"So you're living in Italy now and you're a photographer?" Carlos raises one eyebrow at me. "Every time I think I've figured out who the real you is, I'm totally wrong."

I collapse onto the bed next to him. "You and me both." Despite our words, nothing has changed in our friendship. It feels good to be with someone I know so well after being away. I snuggle in next to him.

Carlos touches my wrist, lifting my hand into the air. "No more triangle?"

I run my fingers over the place on my skin where I used to draw the symbol. Now my skin is clear and tan, not even a remnant of ink left behind. I used to do it almost religiously, drawing it over and over, thinking the triangle would protect me. "I guess I don't need it anymore."

"Guess not." He squeezes my hand, then sets it back on the bed before he hops up.

Carlos grabs his book bag, sliding into his loafers. "When is Mia's big party?"

"Today at four." I had decorated the house all morning, blowing up balloons and pinning streamers across the doorways while Grandma baked the cake. Mia and Grandma seem different—happier. Mia's gone back to school part-time and Grandma is actually dating someone, a guy named Paul. I'll get to meet him tonight at Mia's party. Everything's changed . . . not just me.

"I'll be back later for the festivities," Carlos says, then lets himself out. I pull on my boots and leave a few minutes later. There's someone I need to see, too.

When I enter the store, Holly practically runs to the front doors to wrap her arms around me. "Tell me everything," she says. We sit at the counter and I tell her about riding the train from Spain into southern France; about the retired couple I met who had been traveling through Europe for over a year and let me ride with them through Genoa and down into Italy. I tell her about the aqua water and the towns that cling to the white cliffs that rise up from the sea. I tell her about getting the museum pass in France, and the miles and miles of gorgeous art, how inspiring it all was, how I've been keeping a sketchbook as I go and photographing everything. She's thrilled to hear about my flower shop job halfway across the world. Yet when I'm done, she leans forward and asks, "What about Tate?"

I haven't heard his name spoken out loud in so long that it sends goose bumps down my arms. Traveling through Europe has been a nice distraction, and it's helped me resist Googling his name to see how the tour is going, see how he looks, see if he's back to his old ways: hot girls, late nights, too much of everything. The last time I saw him was in the hospital room. But I've thought about him more often than I'd like to admit. "I haven't seen him," I say.

"But you miss him?"

I nod. "I can't help it."

"He was your first love, those are always the toughest to get over. And you've sure gone out of your way to get as far away from him as you can."

"I didn't leave LA to escape him," I say.

"It may not have been your only reason for leaving, but if it wasn't for him, you might never have realized that you needed to experience the world." I know she's right, but it's still hard to admit that anything good came from Tate and I being together. It feels more like he tore me down the center, my heart spilling onto the floor.

"Keep sending me postcards," Holly says when she hugs me good-bye at the front of the store. "My refrigerator is covered with them."

She kisses me on the forehead before I go. Tears well in both of our eyes as we wave good-bye.

I drive down all the old streets. I can't help but remember the rides with Tate along the same roads, and all the places we went to together. I lived here my entire life, yet everything reminds me of those brief few months with him. I wish I could forget.

But I can't. I don't think I ever will.

TWENTY-SIX

AFTER ONLY FIVE DAYS AT home, I'm escaping the city once again. The first leg is to New York, and then I'll go on to Rome from there. I shuffle down the aisle of the plane and find my seat: the window seat in the second-to-last row. I'm relieved to be leaving. I'm not ready to be back in LA, to face the real world and the rest of my life just yet. Being here for five days was hard enough.

People are still shoving their luggage into the overhead bins and trying to locate their seats when a flight attendant weaves her way down the aisle. I buckle my seat belt, and when I glance back up, the flight attendant has stopped beside my row. She leans over the man in a suit sitting in the aisle seat. "Charlotte Reed?" she asks. In her hand is a folded piece of paper.

"Yes?" I say

"You've been upgraded."

"Excuse me?"

"To first class, you've been bumped up to first class. Would you like to follow me?"

I don't move—for a moment, my mind goes blank.

"Must be your lucky day," the man in the suit says, smiling at me. But I just blink across the empty middle seat at him.

"Are you sure?" I ask, gazing up at the flight attendant.

"You're the only Charlotte Reed we have on the plane, so pretty sure."

"Don't argue with the woman," the man says good-heartedly, raising a bushy eyebrow. "Take your upgrade before they give it to someone else." He stands up and takes a step back, making room for me to exit the row. I grab my neck pillow and my bag filled with books for the flight, and follow the flight attendant to the front of the plane.

As we near first class, I keep waiting for her to turn around, to realize her mistake and usher me back to my cramped seat. But when we pass through the blue curtain dividing the first-class cabin from the rest of the seats, nerves begin to rise up inside me, remembering the last time I sat in first class. I don't want to think it, but I can't help it: *Did Tate do this?*

But when the woman stops and gestures to my seat, I see that the row is empty. No Tate. I exhale an audible sigh of relief and settle in beside the window. She returns a moment later with a bottle of chilled water and a cool, damp towel that smells like cucumbers. I tilt my head back, closing my eyes.

Faintly, I hear two flight attendants talking at the front of the plane, and I open my eyes to look at them. Their faces are close together, saying something I can't hear, and then their gazes lift, both smiling.

Someone steps onto the plane, a last-minute passenger.

My fingers tighten around the armrests, bracing against the metal as *he* comes into view.

Tate.

My stomach constricts, watching him walk down the short aisle and stop in front of me.

He found me. He *did* do this. After all these months, we're now face-to-face again. Casually, he slides down into the seat beside me. He's wearing a dark sweatshirt with the hood pulled up over his head—as if it were enough to keep his identity hidden. The air is instantly engulfed with his scent, subtle and cool and almost undistinguishable if you didn't know it was him—if you didn't know what Tate Collins smells like. But I do.

The same flight attendant who led me up to first class approaches our aisle and asks if Tate would like anything, but he waves her away. He stares straight ahead, not even looking at me, like we are two strangers who just happen to be on the same flight, in the same row. And just when I open my mouth, about to ask what the hell he's doing, he cuts me off.

"I missed you," he says, turning finally to look at me. The shock of his eyes, dark and pained, is almost too much—I had forgotten the way it makes me feel, like my insides are unspooling.

I can't look at him, so I turn away, can't see his gaze like a blade driving into me. Outside, people in reflective red vests direct our plane toward the runway.

"Charlotte," he says, and I can tell he wants me to turn around, but I refuse. "I can't stop thinking about you. I tried to go on tour—I thought it was what I wanted—but it felt wrong without you. All the songs were for you, and you weren't there to hear them." I hear him take in a shallow breath. "When I found out you were in LA, I had to see you."

I look back at him, my heart racing at being so close to him again, his body only inches from mine. The memories are still too vivid and my body aches with the memory of him.

"Don't go back to Italy," he says. "Stay here, stay in LA." His hair looks grown-out beneath his hooded sweatshirt, dark and messy, a new image for his tour, I imagine. He looks good, really good, but I tamp the thought away.

"Why would I do that? Don't you think you've had enough chances?" The tension crawls up my throat, making my voice sound brittle and cracked.

"It'll be different this time. We can make it work."

I finally swivel around, looking him dead in the eye. "Funny, I'm pretty sure you've said those words before. But I'm not the same girl I used to be. You hurt me, Tate—you screwed up. You pulled away when you realized I was falling for you, when I was willing to give up everything for you—you just abandoned me. Worse, you claimed it was for my own good. You kept thinking you were protecting me, when really you were just protecting yourself."

"That's not it." He shakes his head and leans forward, his hands flexing against his knees. "I didn't want you to give up your life for me. I was trying to do the right thing for you."

"I was following my heart. I wanted to be with you, of course I did. But I also wanted it for me. Being with you was maybe the first thing I ever did that was just to make *me* happy." It hurts to say it out loud, to know how desperate I used to be for him. "But you didn't trust me to know what I wanted. You thought only you could make my decisions."

The flight attendant passes by us again and I lower my voice. "You broke my heart, Tate. And there's nothing you can do to fix that."

Without thinking, I unclip my seat belt, reach down for my bag, and stand up. "You can't buy me back into your life with a first-class seat—it doesn't work like that in the real world."

I step in front of him to reach the aisle, trying not to let any part of my body graze any part of his. But even without touching, only fractions of an inch apart, my skin ignites at the memory of his hands on me, his lips sliding across my neck while my heartbeat pulsed beneath his touch. He left scars all across my skin, invisible marks I can't scrub away no matter how I've tried.

I pause in the aisle. A few of the other passengers glance up at me. "And don't follow me anymore," I hiss down at him.

But he doesn't even look up.

When I shuffle into my original seat, the guy in the suit looks over at me and frowns. "Didn't like the first-class treatment?"

"Overrated," I answer.

I'm not the same girl I used to be, I think again. And it's true. I'm not. I am stronger because he broke my heart. I'm stronger without him. And I won't let him to do it to me again.

TWENTY-SEVEN

I SIT CROSS-LEGGED ATOP THE old rock wall overlooking the harbor, watching the sea gulls circle the boats below. It's hot today, the salty air clinging to my skin, and I twist my hair into a bun to keep it from sticking to my neck.

The hourly train has just arrived in Vernazza; I can hear the sounds of tourists streaming down toward the bay, stopping to buy mint gelato and cups of strong espresso before they are drawn to the water's edge. Kids screech and laugh as they swim out into the impossibly aqua sea, and people sun themselves across the rocks, their skin a coppery gold. There is a soft breeze as the tide rolls in, and I turn my camera around to snap a photo of the pastel houses crowded along the cliff's edge.

Tonight, I will post the photos to my newly started blog, *Girl Beside the Sea*. I don't have many followers yet—I started with just Carlos, Mia, and Holly—but I'm slowly starting to find an audience. There's something satisfying about knowing people actually want to see my photographs and drawings.

I was inspired by my new boss, Lucca, who owns *Il nome della rosa*, a flower shop a block up from the ocean. He has his own blog where he writes about the medicinal qualities of the flowers he sells, and how certain types of pollen can afflict you with *Delirio di amore*: Delirium of Love. Although, my Italian still isn't very good, and Lucca speaks very little English, so I could be wrong about the pollen thing. I'm also not entirely sure if what he's paying me to work is fair, but I can make rent on my room and afford a few meals out a week at the amazing restaurants in town, so I don't really care.

I've found an easy rhythm here, a routine that comforts me, and it replaces the stinging memory of Tate with something that doesn't hurt. Most evenings, when the harbor is empty and quiet again, I wade out into the ocean and dip my head all the way under—letting myself be drawn out by the current—trying to drown all thoughts of him. It's finally working, however slowly.

I lift my camera and snap a photo of a little girl wearing a pink-and-yellow swimsuit as she chases a dog out into the water, hands splashing as the waves lap up against her legs. The dog barks at her, tail wagging.

"*Mi scusi*," a voice says behind me.

I set down my camera and turn, smiling. Tourists often ask me questions about the town, sensing that I might speak English. But when I look up at the person standing beside me, everything swerves briefly out of focus.

"Before you say anything—" Tate says, his eyes slipping to

mine, and his T-shirt pressed tightly against his skin. "I want you to know that what you said on the plane was right—I'm sorry, Charlotte. Especially because it took me this long to figure that out."

I stand up from the stone wall, the smile fading from my lips. I can't believe he's actually here. He seems so out of place among the tourists and the tiny houses and the sand and sea. This has been my home, my secret place, and to see him standing here among it all is a shock to my system.

"I wanted to make sure I did everything right with you, that I was careful . . . but in the end, I hurt you anyway," he continues.

A black-and-white bird lands on the wall next to me. I glance at it, and then away to the sea, dazed.

"The truth is," Tate says, and suddenly I can't look at anything but him, "I'm in love with you, Charlotte."

My lips drift open. Despite myself, despite everything, I'm stunned. He's never said those words to me before. And I always thought it was because he never really loved me—never *could* love me. But maybe I was wrong.

"I've been in love with you since the beginning, maybe since that first night you agreed to go on a date with me. And I know that it might be too late—I've screwed everything up—but I'm *still* in love with you. I tried to be without you, I tried to forget, but I can't get you out of my head. And now I know that I don't want to."

An orange kite whips across the sky above us, its tails

fluttering in the wind. I lift a hand, shielding my eyes from the sun, and Tate takes a step closer.

"I hurt you . . . I know I hurt you, and I'm so sorry. You're the only thing in my life that makes sense. Even the music, the thing I used to think I wanted above all else—it's meaningless without you. And . . . I want to start over. No more rules, no more control. No more pushing you away when I get scared, or making decisions that should be yours. I want to do this right this time, finally." He pauses again. "Can we start over?"

It's taken him so long to get it, to realize he made it impossible for us to be together before. And maybe I should hate him for that. But I can't. Instead, I realize that I've been waiting to hear him say it. I've needed to hear him admit that he hurt me, that he's sorry, that he's loved me all along. Tears skim down my cheeks, warm and salty like the air.

He takes another step toward me, and the closeness of him ignites every nerve—every fiber of my body—making my skin quiver and ache to feel his touch again. He extends his arm, staring into my eyes.

"Hello," he says with his palm open like he wants to shake my hand. A first introduction. "I just happened to be traveling along the Italian coast, when I noticed the most incredible girl I've ever seen sitting beside the ocean, taking photographs. And I was wondering if I could take you out on a date—nothing fancy, of course. I hope you're not that kind of girl." His dark eyes are so familiar, glinting in the afternoon light.

I stare down at his hand, suspended in the void between us.

I want so desperately to touch him, to slide my fingers along his, to say something that will make him mine again—but for some reason I can't. I don't. I'm too afraid.

After a moment, he clears his throat. "Okay." And he drops his arm, glancing away from me. "I'm sorry I came here . . . I won't try to find you again. I love you, Charlotte. I hope you have a happy life—the life you deserve. Because you deserve a good one."

He turns away—his shoulders slumped, every line in his body defeated—and moves back up the stone street toward the center of town.

A distant memory surfaces, itching up to the front of my thoughts. A few years ago, Carlos and I had a ten-dollar palm reader tell us our fortunes on Venice Beach. She said that my fate line was divided, that I would have two paths and I would need to choose which life I wanted. At the time, I thought it was stupid, something only my mother would have believed in. But maybe she was right. Maybe the choice comes down to this: a life with Tate or a life without him.

And for all the pain and heartache . . . I still love him.

I run—my heart suddenly exploding with fear that I'm about to lose him again. I grab his arm as soon as he's within reach and I feel his muscles tense beneath my touch. The world spins, tilts off axis—everything shuddering in slow motion—and he turns back to face me.

I can't lose him again.

His fingers find my face, clearing away the tears that stream across my skin. He lets out a slow exhale, and his eyes light up once more. I lift onto my toes and press my lips to his and he kisses me back, pulling me deeper against him. And it's all the kisses we've missed: the lost months, the nights I lay awake in my rented room, windows open to let in the ocean air, thinking of him. His fingers tangle in my hair, his mouth drawing me closer, and he kisses me like he won't ever let me go—not for a thousand years, not for anything. And I don't want him to. There are no boundaries now, no edicts, no limitations—only a beginning.

This moment is our first kiss. Our first *I love you*. Our first forever.

ACKNOWLEDGMENTS

ELIZABETH CRAFT

Wow. Many people made this book happen, most of who deserve more credit for it than I do. Thank you first to my pal Les Morgenstein at Alloy for saying yes. Also huge thanks to the rest of the Alloy team: Josh Bank, Lanie Davis, Elaine Damasco, Romy Golan, Joelle Hobeika, Sara Shandler, and, most of all, Annie Stone, editor extraordinaire.

I'm beyond grateful to the team at HarlequinTEEN who got behind this book in such a big way—especially Natashya Wilson and Margo Lipschultz. Being part of the Harlequin family is the fulfillment of a nearly lifelong dream.

Thanks to my agent, Christy Fletcher—I swear I'll write the next one eventually.

As always, I'm lucky to have endlessly supportive friends and family. Special shout-out to Adam Fierro, Sarah Fain, Gretchen Rubin, and Mindy Wilson, who read the initial pages and said they made her heart pound.

Shea Olsen, *Flower* wouldn't exist without you. Thank you, thank you, thank you.

SHEA OLSEN

It takes a village. And in writing this book, it took more like a small metropolis. First, thank you to Elizabeth Craft for being the brainchild behind *Flower*; without your initial idea, the seed of this story never could have taken root.

To the rock stars at Alloy for being a true force of nature. Annie Stone, you are made of sugar and sunny days, brilliant edit notes and genius plot fixes. Without you, this book would be a pile of goo on the twenty-ninth floor of Manhattan. And to all the other staggering minds at Alloy, I thank you: Josh Bank, Sara Shandler, Lanie Davis, Joelle Hobeika, Romy Golan. You guys leave me speechless . . . in all the best ways.

To Margo Lipschultz, for seeing the beating heart in this story and giving it a major jolt. You are lightning disguised as an editor. And your skills astound me! To Natashya Wilson and everyone at HarlequinTEEN, thank you for believing, for your passion, and for your commitment through this long trek. To my agent and fairy godmother, Jess Regel, for being magical and sparkly.

Thank you to my husband for being the best partner in life a girl could ask for. To my parents, for raising me in a home overrun with books and imagination and art. You impress me every day. To Andee and Andra and Mel—you know why.